THEIR VIRGIN CONCUBINE

Masters of Ménage, Book 3

Shayla Black and Lexi Blake

THEIR VIRGIN CONCUBINE, Masters of Ménage, Book 3
Shayla Black and Lexi Blake

Published by Shayla Black and Lexi Blake
Copyright 2012 Black Oak Books
Edited by Chloe Vale and Shayla Black
ISBN: 978-1-937608-09-5

This is a work of fiction. Names, places, characters and incidents are the product of the author's imagination and are fictitious. Any resemblance to actual persons, living or dead, events or establishments is solely coincidental.

THEIR VIRGIN CONCUBINE, Masters of Ménage, Book 3

Shayla Black and Lexi Blake

Bonus material and excerpts at the conclusion of this book.

Chapter One

Kadir al Mussad watched the gorgeous blonde with the swaying, tight ass walk by and wondered if there was something wrong with his dick. She was lovely and obviously available. No ring on that finger. Wearing a gray skirt that barely covered her essentials and red stilettos, she was definitely dressed to attract a man. As she passed, she turned slightly, her eyes widening as she took in his thousand dollar custom-made suit and handcrafted Italian loafers. He could see the hot blonde silently itemizing him, doing her best to estimate his wealth down to the last dollar.

And she would fall short by a few billion.

"Hi." She carried a few folders, but not where they'd hide her breasts. At least a D cup and, from the placement of those large globes high on her chest, he would bet she'd purchased them herself. Like the rest of the blonde, they were magnificently constructed and hard as a rock.

His dick practically yawned. "Hello. I'm looking for Mr. Townsend."

Her painted mouth curled up in a sex-kitten smile. "He recently changed his last name to James."

Good for Dex. A little warmth flooded Kade's system at the thought of his friend finally finding his true place beside his two biological brothers, along with their shared wife, Hannah. "Excellent. Then where is Mr. James this morning?"

Dex was the head of security. He would be the one to talk to about the little problem Kade was having. He needed information on one of Black Oak Oil's employees. Little things like where her office was and whether or not she had all her teeth. All the things his eldest brother, Talib, hadn't seen fit to mention when he'd ordered Kade and their middle brother, Rafe, to fetch this girl and bring her home to Bezakistan. The sheikh could be a bossy asshole at times.

God, if Talib didn't settle on a wife soon, Kade was going to lose his bloody mind—and a lot more. Of course, the problem was that once Talib settled on a wife, Kade and Rafe would have to settle for her, too. One wife for all brothers. God bless Bezakistan.

He had to hope this candidate looked better than the mousy pictures included in Talib's dossier. It wasn't that she was ugly, merely plain and deeply somber. And the photos were grainy, a driver's license picture and a little black and white image that looked like it had come from a school yearbook. Neither had been promising. And her background was so bland he'd forgotten most of it already. Grew up in a small town. Apple of her parents' eyes. Graduated from college with a degree in economics. Yep. He'd gone to sleep just after reading that tidbit.

"He's in a meeting, but you can wait in his office." Her eyes softened, an obviously practiced move. "Or you could buy me a cup of coffee."

Nothing. Not even a stir. His cock was still completely flaccid, despite her less than subtle come-on. Damn it, he was barely thirty. His dick should be standing up and shouting "let's party!" Kade would rather take a nap. He sighed. Maybe his dick's lack of responsiveness didn't matter since he'd likely soon be chained to some boring, dull-as-dishwater intellectual because that was Talib's type.

Maybe he should try to convince his cock to take the blonde up on her offer.

Before he could, a flurry of chaos walked by, her brown hair caught at the back of her head in a messy bun. She quickly rushed down the hall, barely containing a haphazard stack of files in her arms that stuck out this way and that, the edges poking at all sorts of odd angles. She was talking on a cell phone tucked between her ear and her shoulder, her face animated. She plowed right into the blonde, who dropped the two little folders she'd been carrying. The stack in the brunette's arms exploded, paper filling the air like a ticker-tape parade.

"Goddamn it," the blonde cursed. "Fucking researchers."

"I am so sorry, Amanda." The brunette spoke in a soft Texas twang as she dropped to the ground on her hands and knees, phone tumbling across the office carpet as she began wrangling the wild herd of papers. "I was talking and I wasn't looking where I was going. I'm really sorry."

"Here, let me help you," a deep voice said. Rafiq, his brother, always the gentleman, hurried up the hall and got to one knee.

"Thank you," the blonde purred. Then she realized Rafe was talking to the little brunette and frowned down at her. "There's a reason everyone around here calls you Pandora."

Pandora. Goddess of Chaos. The messy bun on the back of the brunette's head looked like it would unravel at any moment, unleashing a cascade of brown curls lit with strands of honey blonde and warm red. She turned her face up, and Kade nearly cheered.

His dick was back in top form now, standing tall and eager. *Oh, yeah.*

There was nothing at all artificial about Pandora. She was soft and feminine, with bee-stung lips and blue eyes that were nearly hidden behind a pair of big glasses that might have been fashionable in the eighties. She wore a shapeless blouse, but as she moved, she popped a button, and he caught sight of creamy white cleavage flushed with a hint of pink. Clearly, she was flustered and embarrassed.

"They don't call me Pandora because I unleashed evil on

7

the world or anything," she explained. "I'm just clumsy. I apologize to you, too, sir. So sorry."

Then Pandora bit her lip in a way that made him wonder how she would suck a cock, provided that she'd ever sucked a cock before. Her air of innocence had him wondering. He could teach her how to suck a cock. His cock. His brother Rafe's cock. She looked back at him.

She was far more polite than the blonde, who impatiently tapped her stiletto, palm outstretched, as she waited for Pandora to organize and return her folders. Clearly, Amanda wasn't going to lower herself to help. So the sweet brunette picked up the blonde's folders and carefully placed the documents inside before handing them up to the other woman. Kade watched her every move. Poised on all fours, Pandora's ass stuck up in the air. Even encased in an ugly khaki skirt, there was no hiding those curves. That ass was made to take a cock, her hips perfect for holding on to as a man drove inside and made her howl with pleasure.

There was a vicious swat to his knees, and he looked into Rafe's impatient eyes. "Are you going to help or not?"

Kade heard the unspoken end to that sentence. *Or are you going to stand there and stare at her ass?*

He wanted to stare at her ass. A single grunt from his older brother made him sigh and drop to the floor. Folders were scattered everywhere, paperwork spread out around her like a multi-colored quilt of chaos. Pandora, indeed. She'd shaken up his day. He wondered if she could also rock his world.

"What about that coffee?" Amanda asked him, her voice dropping to a seductive murmur.

He didn't bother to look up at the blonde. "I'm not thirsty right now. I'll just wait for Dex."

She tsked, huffed, and stomped off. He smiled.

"So, once we've cleaned up this little mess, would you like to get a drink?" Kade asked Pandora in his smoothest voice.

His brother's head came up, his mouth dropping open.

Rafe's expression silently said "idiot."

Why were Rafe's panties in a wad? Could he not see the bounty in front of them? Now that Kade was close, he could smell her shampoo. Citrus, orangey and tangy. Delightful. He took a deep breath. What the hell would her pussy smell like? He would just rub his nose all over and keep that spicy, feminine scent with him all fucking day long. Damn, it felt good to be horny.

"Are you all right?"

He opened his eyes and stopped sniffing the female. *Fuck.* The good news was she didn't seem to know what he was doing. The bad news? His brother was looking at him like he was the world's biggest moron. Oh, well. Rafe often had that look on his face. Kade tried not to take it personally. "I am very well, thank you."

"He's a bit slow, if you know what I mean," Rafe said with a sharp bite to his words.

Pandora's eyes widened with sympathy. "Oh. Really? Okay. I'll just show you where everything goes. It's so nice of you to help me."

Rafe sat back on his heels, a brilliant smile crossing his face as he held back laughter. Kade wanted to punch the asshole in the face, but it was so good to see his brother smile again that he let his violent impulses go. Still, he had to repair the damage wrought by Rafe's insult. He didn't want pretty Pandora to think he was slow. Except in bed, where he would go very slowly and savor every inch of her.

He caught her hand in his. Soft skin, warm, slightly calloused on the side of one finger where she'd hold a pencil. He flipped her hand over, his thumb tracing the blue lines of her veins before covering it with his other hand. He wanted her to feel surrounded by him, a little taste of what he and Rafe could give her. "My brother is teasing you, *habibti*. I have two degrees from Oxford University. He thinks I am slow because he has three."

9

That pretty pale skin flushed right up again. He liked that he would be able to tell so much just by looking at her. He would know when she was lying, when she was happy, when she was aroused. He was used to jaded women, but his little Pandora was far from that.

"Sorry. I guess I'm a little naïve. I only have the one degree, and it's from Hale University in West Texas. Go Bullfrogs!" She gave a charming little laugh and seemed unable to stop speaking. "Dumb mascot. Really. You do not want to be in that costume in August in Abilene. Hot. And cramped. It's the only mascot uniform that forces you to hop. They told me it was because they wanted realism, but I think they just wanted to torture me. Terrible way to try to find your school spirit. Though it built strong quadriceps. That's the thigh muscle. Wait. You know that because of Oxford and stuff. I'm going to stop talking now."

"Hello!" A muffled feminine voice called out from the proximity of the floor.

Pandora pulled her hand out of his with a grimace and started shuffling through papers, looking for something. "I dropped my phone. Dang!"

Then she went right back to her hands and knees, frantically searching. Now Kade wasn't the only one looking at her ass. Rafe was practically drooling, his eyes travelling from the graceful curve of her spine to the round cheeks of her backside. Rafe's gaze cut over to his with an interested gleam.

Kade raised his eyebrows and pointed at his watch. It was early, but if they took her to lunch, maybe they could be in bed by twelve thirty. Their condo wasn't far. Feed her a little. Maybe a nice bottle of wine. Then, before long, they'd hopefully sweet talk the glorious little bundle of chaos into getting in between them.

Rafe frowned and held up his folder, the one that contained the name of the woman they had come here to see. Piper Glen. The supposed savior of Bezakistan. Hopefully not some cold-ass intellectual.

Fucking Pandora would have to wait.

Rafe nodded regretfully and mouthed, "Dinner?"

Yeah. If they weren't on a plane home with their future wife in tow. He longed for the old days when no one thought a sheikh should be faithful to one woman. They could have married whoever and kept little Pandora as a treat on the side. But no. Now he had paparazzi and tabloid rags and Sunday news shows commenting about where he put his dick.

Which still hadn't gone down.

He sighed and started cleaning up again.

"Mindy? Are you still there?" Pandora scrambled to put the phone against her ear. "Did you get the check? Good. Buy your books and don't forget to save some. I can't send anything else until next payday. I love you. No. I don't want to hear about him. Unless he's dead. Then I do. Darn it. No, I don't wish him ill. Thank you. You're a good sister." She shut her phone, a ridiculously old contraption that Kade was surprised still worked. "Sorry about all this. I was talking to my sister and I got distracted."

She pushed the last of the papers into a haphazard pile that would likely make Rafe crazy. His brother was fastidious, but Rafe simply smiled as he handed her the perfectly placed pile he'd gathered.

"We all get distracted at times," Rafe said, the smooth words coming out like he'd never ogled her ass. He bowed politely. "I wish you a good afternoon."

She smiled, pushing her glasses back up. That smile was fatal. Kade just stared because she lit up the fucking room. "Thank you so much. Good afternoon to you, too."

She turned and walked away, her flats shuffling as she tried to balance the papers and her phone.

"Oh, we have got to have that, my brother." Rafe stood beside him, his head angled to one side as he watched her walk away.

Kade silently thanked the heavens because Rafe had been as out of sorts as he'd felt the last few months. "Yes, we do. Let's find Dex and get this over with so we can take Pandora out for happy hour. Then we'll make her even happier. We should find out her name before we fuck her."

An arm slapped around his shoulders suddenly, and Dexter James shoved his six foot five inch, two hundred twenty pounds of pure muscle between Kade and his brother. "Her name is Piper, and I'll kill you both if you lay a hand on her."

"Piper?" *That* was Piper Glen? That gloriously messy little fuck bunny was the drab girl in the pictures that Tal wanted to marry?

Two ideas struck Kade as Dex started to lead them to his office. First, his oldest brother's taste had come up in the world. And second, he better knock out Dex now because he planned to get a lot more than his hands on that sweet woman.

* * * *

Piper Glen managed to make it to her teeny-tiny office without another catastrophe. Except now, she couldn't open the door.

"Allow me." Gina Jacobson twisted the handle with a smile and eased the door open. "Here's your kingdom."

An eight-by-eight cubby hole was hardly a kingdom, especially with its glorious view of a dumpster in the alley behind the building and its location as far from the elevators as possible. The little room had been given to the lowly researcher. Anyone else would have run. Piper merely sighed as she put her files down, grumbling a bit.

"What happened now, hon? Did that guy from the mailroom plow into you? I swear, I can take him. I have two toddlers. One skinny twenty-year-old is no match for me."

Piper slumped down, the last couple of minutes washing over her like a bad horror film. "Nope. It was just me. Pandora struck again."

The employees of Black Oak Oil had christened her Pandora, unleasher of evil on the world, because she'd caused a complete building-wide blackout on her first day. It wasn't her fault that dumb fuse had blown because her coffeemaker was from the sixties. Some days, she was like one big pitfall waiting to happen.

But she was smart and a darn good researcher.

Gina groaned in sympathy and leaned her hip on the side of Piper's desk. "Tell me all about it, hon."

The older woman was a gossip, but a sweet-natured one, unlike Amanda who was a raging... something Piper knew she shouldn't even think because her mom would turn over in her grave. "I was talking to my sister and ran smack into Amanda."

Gina waved that off. "Oh, hon, that's inevitable. And I bet you bounced right off those fake tits of hers. I've often thought that she should rent those boobs out as a bouncy house for bored babies."

Piper looked down at her own chest. They were probably as big as Amanda's, but hers were real so they sagged a little. Even at twenty-five. And her clothes wouldn't fit right. She sighed. It didn't matter. She wasn't here looking for love. She was done with that. Johnny Tyler, affectionately known to his friends as Cooder, had proven that men were just dogs with a bone. If she couldn't keep someone like Johnny happy, she probably never would find a decent man. And that was fine. She was going to have a career. See the world. Her female parts had been put into hibernation long ago.

Except they had hummed back to life the minute Hottie Number One had laid a hand on her. Her heart rate had tripled and her skin had sizzled with life. Too bad her mouth hadn't stopped working. She talked way too much when she was nervous. "Hey, do we have a couple of new guys around? Tall, maybe Middle Eastern but talk with British accents?" Hottie Number Two had been just as beautiful as his brother. She was

13

sure they were related.

Gina's eyes widened. "Are you talking about Rafe and Kade al Mussad? Yep. You are. Every woman who meets them gets that glazed look in her eyes. They're here a lot. I'm surprised you haven't met them before." Her voice dropped to a gossipy whisper. "They're filthy rich. They represent all the business interests for Bezakistan. Aren't you working on their green project?"

Yep. And all the paperwork was in a giant heap that she would have to painstakingly reorganize. She could do it tonight. It wasn't like she had anything else to do. This job was her gateway to bigger and better things. "Yes. I'm getting all the numbers ready for the guy on the other end. Tal."

Gina stared at her. "You just sighed when you said his name."

"I did not." Except she kind of had. Tal was her counterpart in Bezakistan. Black Oak Oil was working with the government of Bezakistan to start a green energy project, and Piper was in charge of putting together all the research. She'd been e-mailing and talking on the phone to Tal for several months. "He's just nice."

"Tal, huh? In Bezakistan? I don't think I've heard of him. What I do know is that the sheikh, Talib, is just as gorgeous as his brothers. Have you met this man you've been talking to? You might want to take a look because I've heard they grow them hot over there."

Piper shook her head. Not Tal. Tal was sedate and very polite. His voice was soothing and intelligent. She couldn't imagine him looking like the two movie-star gorgeous men she'd just met, and she kind of liked it that way. "I seriously doubt it. He's really...smart." And organized and creative. And she didn't even know how old he was. Probably older. And married. With lots of kids. But she could dream a little.

Gina hopped off the desk. "I don't need a smart man. Give me a dumb hot guy any day of the week. My Matthew couldn't find his head in his ass, but his chest is a work of art. Are you coming to lunch with us?"

Piper forced a sunny smile on her face. "Can't. I have so much work."

Gina shrugged and walked out, the door closing behind her.

Piper's stomach growled, and she wished she hadn't left her bagged lunch on the train. It hadn't been much. A peanut butter and jelly sandwich and a few baby carrots, but it would have been better than nothing.

She thought about her tiny studio apartment. She'd sent the last of her money to Mindy to pay for her school. There wouldn't be more for another week when her modest check from Black Oak came in. She took mental stock of her fridge. The next week didn't look good.

She glanced at the calendar, her stomach taking a dive. Well, at least she wasn't hungry anymore. Tomorrow was supposed to have been her first wedding anniversary, if she'd managed to get down the aisle. She could still feel the white satin on her skin as she tried on her wedding gown. She'd looked at herself in the mirror and, just for a moment, she'd been a princess.

Tears filled her eyes. Turned out, her prince preferred strippers to nice girls he'd met at church. She'd been left at the altar with a note and the judgmental stares of everyone in her small town. And she'd still had her sister to put through school since Mindy's scholarship had mysteriously dried up the minute Piper was no longer connected to the mayor's family.

Piper took a deep breath. She couldn't go back there. She was here now. Granted, she had a job that paid next to nothing and an office she could barely move in, but this was her kingdom. It wouldn't be forever; it would grow. Until then, she would make it work.

With a deep breath, she put aside thoughts of shattered romances and beautiful men with sun-kissed skin. Piper reached for the stack of papers in front of her. She had a job to do.

Chapter Two

Rafe fidgeted. The plush chair he sat in was comfortable, but his brain wasn't on the supple leather and masculine elegance of Dex's office. His knee bounced—a sure giveaway that he was deeply impatient. Kade gave him a wry smile, reminding Rafe why he refused to play poker with his clever younger brother. He didn't have Kade's poker face. Dex would likely see right through him, but hell, he wanted to go find Piper and take her away.

That's what his ancestors would have done. His own mother had been the latest in a long line of beautiful captive brides, each selected, abducted, and blissfully married after a whirlwind courtship designed to sweep her up and make her fall madly in love forever. Rafe wasn't unaware that they had a big task in front of them. Oh, they could romance Piper. They might even be able to get the innocent little thing into bed. But finding the right path to ensnare her heart would be more difficult. That was, of course, if Talib still wished to proceed after hearing whatever Dex James had to say and meeting Piper himself. The way he felt about her now, Rafe would be hard pressed not to kick in his older brother's teeth if he didn't.

"Are you two insane? She's not your type." Dex closed the door behind him with a resounding thud.

Rafe was curious. "Why would you say that, friend?"

Dex raked a hand through his hair and frowned, as though putting off the moment when he had to speak. "She's a very sweet girl."

Kade's lips flattened to a hard line. "And you think we do not like sweet girls?"

"You might like them, but you should damn well stay away from them, especially Piper." Dex didn't hesitate now, clearly in full-on big brother mode. "That girl is one of the nicest women I've ever met. She's smart and funny, and okay, a complete klutz, but on her it's endearing. She's Hannah's friend. They came from the same small town. When she was looking for work, she called Hannah, and we gave her a job. I would have given her a better one, but she insisted on this research position even though it's entry level. She wants to be involved with this project and learn everything from the ground up."

Because she had a core of integrity. Rafe had already discerned that. He had been following her up the hallway before she'd accidentally run into the very plastic Amanda. He'd stopped to get a drink from the water fountain when she'd walked by, all curves and hips. In an instant, his thirst had changed.

Rafe had prowled up the hall after her, plotting to offer his help with carrying her folders, but then he'd heard her talking to her sister on the phone. She'd paid for the girl's school. Of course, he'd only heard a part of the conversation, but from what he gathered, she would not allow her sister to work more than a few hours a week while attending university because she'd had to do it herself and did not wish the girl to struggle. Family was important to this woman, and Rafe both understood and respected that. In fact, he found that quality deeply attractive.

Rafe had taken the opportunity to carefully inventory the woman's appearance. Cheap clothes, shoddy shoes she must have purchased at a thrift store, a cell phone that had seen better days. The soft beauty obviously sent her sister every spare cent. Learning that she was Piper, the focus of Talib's current interest, only made his curiosity peak more.

The reports Talib had sent said nothing of her sinfully sexy innocence. Instead, they had been filled with all the information the sheikh would find important, an amalgamation of numbers and dates that formed the sum of Piper Glen's life to this point. Tal hadn't mentioned how sweet she was, likely because he wouldn't particularly care. He had noted her very high IQ. Nowhere in the report did he mention how she'd sacrificed for her sister. There had been one or two lines about her family, but nothing that got to the heart of the woman.

What sort of game was Talib playing? He feared it was working since Kade was already mentally putting a ring on her finger and placing her between the three of them in bed. Rafe wanted to know more about Piper before he allowed himself to become attached. But time was running short. He couldn't take the months he would have liked to get to know her. They had one objective—get her back to Bezakistan where they could see if she would make a suitable bride—then seduce her accordingly.

If she was everything she appeared to be, Rafe would enjoy having such a woman. He could become necessary to her. He could care for her, seeing to her every need until she turned to him like a flower to the sun. He could show her his world and make himself a place in hers.

Dex sighed. "Look, I know the drill, guys. Hell, Slade and I practically invented the drill. You find a hot little piece of ass, get her in between the two of you, make her scream down the roof, then take her to dinner and give her a nice parting gift. I get it. But Piper is off limits because A, I like her and she deserves better than to be a notch on your bedpost, and B, if she ends up crying to my wife that you two used her, and Hannah finds out I could have protected her, my wife will have my balls. She's pregnant again. Do you know what a hormonal woman can do to a set of balls? I know we talk about testicles like they're the be-all, end-all of strength, but those fuckers are fragile. If you want some action, talk to Amanda. You saw her, right? Blonde. Big boobs and sharp tongue. She'll be up for your games, but Piper won't know what game you're playing, much less how to play."

Amanda? Rafe slid his brother a long glance. Clearly, Kade wasn't interested in that shit either. Dex so conveniently forgot his own history, which included seducing the lovely young Hannah before he and his brothers married her. They both let Dex go on and on about the horrors of uncommitted sex and how much they could scar Piper's gentle psyche and heart or whatever, simply because he thought Rafe and Kade would never settle down.

Rafe held up a hand. "You are wrong in this, friend. We are not simply looking for a woman for the night."

Dex stopped and stared. "What do you mean?"

Kade sat back, one leg casually perched over his knee. He looked like the negligent playboy he was, but Rafe knew his younger brother was quite serious now. "It means we *must* choose. Tal is nearly thirty-five, so our time is almost up. Gavin explained this to you?"

Gavin was the CEO of Black Oak Oil and the James brother with the closest ties to Bezakistan. He was also Dex's eldest brother. Along with their middle brother, Slade, they shared Hannah.

"Sort of," Dex said. "Talib has six months to pick a wife, right?"

It was so much more complicated, but that summed it up neatly, so Rafe nodded. "Yes. We toyed with the idea of revising the constitution to more accurately reflect the modern world, but we've run into trouble with that."

Kade jumped in. "If we start playing with the constitution, we've been told we open it up to all sorts of revisions, including those from some of the more religious factions in our country who would prefer a government that was less Westernized and more like our neighbors."

"And we know very well that several lawmakers would like to strike down the royal family's marriage customs to weaken us," Rafe added.

Dex's eyes narrowed slightly. "You share a wife so you don't have to split up the country, correct?"

"Exactly," Rafe confirmed. "It's a tradition that began long ago in our mountain regions as a way to keep a family's wealth intact without cutting off the younger siblings and is still largely practiced by our population today. Primogeniture was the Western world's tradition, but it forced younger sons into poverty, religion, or war. We did not wish that on our children. The same holds true today, though many do not see it. They view our tradition of bride sharing as barbaric, but it keeps the family centered on a common purpose."

Dex grinned. "Well, you're not going to get any argument from me, buddy. Lightning would strike real damn fast, and my balls would be toast for sure."

"I'm glad you agree. The trouble is that our brother has proven rather picky." Rafe was being generous. Talib had been a nightmare. Not that he and Kade hadn't voiced some objections themselves.

Collectively, they'd looked into twenty women over the past two years. All twenty had been rejected. Talib didn't want another royal because he didn't want the headache of dealing with two royal families, or some princess with a trained smile in the ballroom but a haughty demeanor in the bedroom. He didn't want a fame monger or a curiosity seeker, either. Bezakistan, with its unique customs and culture, was always a source of interest and mystery, after all. Talib wanted someone intelligent. She had to be educable about media affairs, have a lovely smile, be reasonably photogenic, and be kind. She had to like children, puppies, and rainbows, yada yada yada. None had passed Talib's tests.

Which was just as well since Rafe had hated every one of those twenty cold women. They had been lacking in heart and a little hard in the soul. Kade would not have hesitated to take one or two of them to bed, but he'd made it clear that he had no interest in marrying any of them. Now the deadline for the three of them to find a bride and wed her breathed hotly down their necks. If they didn't select one soon, the throne would pass to their cousin, Khalil.

No one who liked their chic yet charming country as it was wanted that.

"We're actually here because Talib has found a possible candidate." Kade's sly smile told Rafe they were on the same page. Dex wanted to give them a lecture? They would give him a surprise.

Dex's eyes rolled slightly. "Seriously, you're looking for a wife, but you're taking a little detour to salivate over my researcher? Not cool, guys."

Rafe put the folder with Piper's information on the desk, his palm remaining on it. It contained the original report and Tal's observations about the girl, along with a few snippets of instant messaging conversations they'd shared. Rafe had already memorized them and had been intrigued, but meeting the girl had increased his understanding and enthusiasm a hundredfold. "You are right, of course. That would be very ungentlemanly of us."

"And obviously your wife's friend is far too sweet for nasty men like us." Kade grinned.

"Dude, I'm glad you understand what I'm saying." Dex held up his hands. "I'm not trying to disrespect you. I really do know what it means to be in your place, having a certain…itch and liking it scratched frequently. Slade and I had to hunker down and try to survive big brother until Hannah softened him up. But Piper isn't a good-time girl. She's the kind of girl you marry. Can't you find someone else?"

Rafe's lips turned up as Dex fell neatly into their trap. "I would not wish Piper heartache. Now, this is the name of the woman Talib wishes us to investigate as a potential bride. He thinks she's quite intelligent and possesses many of the qualities we seek. If you could tell us all you know about her before we approach her, perhaps fill in any gaps in our report, we would be so grateful."

Dex pulled the folder toward him. "Sure thing. Any woman you choose will be one lucky lady. Your country is beautiful and that palace is something else." He opened the folder, caught sight of Piper's name, and sighed. "You're a son of a bitch."

Rafe couldn't help but smile. "So, you'll set up lunch for us?"

He growled a little. "You two better take fucking good care of her. No, damn good care. No fucking her. Not until this thing is settled." He picked up the phone and started talking.

Kade slid Rafe a slow smile.

Yes, they would take damn good care of her, indeed. Eventually, he suspected, they'd take fucking good care of her, as well.

* * * *

Piper looked around the restaurant, hoping no one noticed her thrift store clothes. She felt deeply out of place, and yet she couldn't help but stare. It was beautiful, completely unlike anywhere she'd been before, but then there was only one place in her hometown that would qualify as a restaurant. Patty's Pie Hole didn't look like this.

Gosh, she hoped she didn't break anything and could figure out which fork to use.

"What looks good to you, *habibti*?"

His voice was like rich chocolate. Rafiq. He'd introduced

himself that way, but quickly asked her to call him Rafe. He'd been the one to hold open the door for her and to help her out of the car. He probably knew she was likely to take a header right on the street.

"What does that mean?" He'd called her that twice. She wasn't sure if he just kept forgetting her name. Black Oak Oil didn't hand out security badges with employees' names.

"*Habibti?*"

Piper nodded, trying not to let her eyes widen as she took in the prices on the menu. She could buy a cow for what they charged for a steak. Mr. James had explained that she was being treated, but she wasn't used to being treated this well. "Yes, sir. I don't know what that means."

Kadir, or Kade as he liked to be called, elegantly slid his napkin over his lap. "It's the Arabic equivalent of sweetheart."

She hid a smile. At least men were the same across the world. She'd been around men all her life who called every woman, from eight to eighty, sweetheart or darlin'. They were either trying to be charming or were wretchedly bad at remembering names. But it was still somewhat endearing. "Oh, that's nice. So, what exactly can I help you with, Mr. al Mussad? I assumed you were getting all the research notes and projections from Tal."

"Tal?" Kade asked.

Rafe didn't miss a beat. "Yes, Tal. You know the man who's doing the field research in Bezakistan for the Clean Energy Project, brother."

Kade leaned forward. "Seriously? Tal? Is he shitting us?"

Rafe sent his brother a deeply quelling look before turning back to her, and Piper frowned. It was as if the two were having a secret conversation through a series of raised eyebrows and short hand gestures.

"I have received the information from Tal," Rafe assured. "But I wanted your opinion. Gavin James thinks highly of you. You did your undergraduate work in economics?"

She smiled. If there was one thing she was proud of, it was her degree. It had taken her five years because she'd had to work full time while she went to school, but she'd graduated with honors. "Yes, I have an undergraduate degree in economics. I've started my graduate work with a specialization in the economic viability of renewable energy sources."

"Very impressive. So you believe this project of Black Oak's will be viable?"

She was intensely excited at the prospect. Bezakistan could be a huge economic and scientific experiment. "I think given your country's unique position in the world's fuel market and how open your economy is, you have the opportunity to make enormous strides. Brazil has gone to an almost completely biofuel model for their transportation systems. Imagine what you could do with a combination of biofuel, wind energy, and solar power. You could change the world. You could bring power to countries that can't afford it."

Bezakistan was the perfect testing ground. The country was rich with oil, but they also had millions of acres of deserts, perfect for solar power and wind harvesting. Their infrastructure was one of the soundest in the world, and almost everything was controlled by one man: Sheikh al Mussad. And, as Dex James had explained when he called to arrange this luncheon, she was sitting with his brothers.

God, she hoped she didn't make an idiot of herself.

"But is it a financially viable model?" Kade probed.

This was the hard sell. She and Tal had been working on this proposal for months. She was interested from a humanitarian and ecological standpoint. But she knew money moved the world. Good thing she would merely be gathering all the data. Tal would present it to his sheikh. "Not in the first five minutes, but I think the patents alone on some of this technology could make up for the money you put into it over time."

At least they were looking at her like she had a brain in her

24

head. Rafe sat back, his arm going over the back of the booth, hovering above her shoulders. Gosh, he was attractive. His pitch black hair was perfectly cut and intelligent dark eyes looked out from a face that could be on the cover of a magazine. Kade was equally appealing. Piper had to remind herself not to drool.

"I am more than willing to listen to your information on this subject," Rafe said, gesturing for a waiter. "Would you like something to drink while we do? Wine, perhaps?"

And be a slavering pile of goo by the time dessert rolled around? Nope. She'd proven long ago that she couldn't handle liquor. She was nervous as hell, but it would be worse to fall asleep on the gorgeous gods of men who held her career in their hands. "No, thank you. I'll just have some iced tea."

"Of course," Rafe said, though he looked almost disappointed. "Three iced teas and a plate of the oysters, please. We should be ready to order lunch in a moment."

The waiter scurried off.

Kade set his menu aside. "How do you feel about travel, Piper?"

"I've never been outside of Texas. I read a lot about the world. I have a list of places I would love to see, but I just haven't had the opportunity yet."

"Why, may I ask?" Rafe leaned closer and scooted in a bit, giving her his undivided attention. "You're young. Many young people, even in my country, get out and see the world. I have heard many Americans like to backpack across Europe."

Kade sniffed a little. "I don't know why. I stayed at a hostel once. My fathers were very angry with the way I was spending money, so I attempted to conserve. I see now why so many horror films have been made about them. Backpacking is apparently a very smelly experience."

She laughed. She could just imagine the very urbane Kadir al Mussad surveying her father's ranch. "I still would have loved it. I'm from West Texas. Trust me, once you've stood downwind of a herd of cattle, you can handle a little humanity. I planned a big trip to celebrate my graduation from high school. Not Europe, but I was going to drive up the West Coast from San Diego to Vancouver. I bought a little convertible and put all kinds of money away from summer jobs. I was going with a couple of friends."

"What happened?"

Oh, so many things. Her heart clenched as it always did when she thought about those months. "Life happened. My father died suddenly. My mom had passed away a few years before that after a battle with cancer. I had to stay with my sister. I thought it would just be for the summer. I had a scholarship to the University of Texas in Austin. I assumed I would find a foreman for our ranch and a guardian for my sister and still head out in the fall." She was about to get misty. Why was she getting so personal? She always talked too much. These men had invited her to lunch for business, not to hear her life story. "I'm sorry. We were talking about patents."

Piper noticed that Rafe wasn't the only one who'd moved closer. The booth was elegant and fashioned into a semi-circle. Piper sat between them, and neither man seemed to have a need for personal space. They were beginning to crowd her. Kade's long, muscular leg brushed her own, sending an odd wave of heat through her. The heat wave swelled when Rafe smiled.

"No, *habibti*. Continue," he bid. "Why did you not go to the college of your choice?"

Rafe was so close she could feel the heat of his body, smell the musky cologne he wore. She stared at the strong column of his throat, the firm line of his jaw, the sensual shape of his lips. Piper tore her gaze away.

"Uhm, I couldn't leave my sister. Once I found out the ranch was deep in debt, I had to sell it, along with our home. No one wanted to take Melinda in. She was fourteen and a little wild. You have to understand that the town I lived in was very small and conservative. A week after my father's funeral, some of the women of the community stopped by to tell me they

26

thought Mindy should be placed in the foster system."

"You had no family left?" Rafe asked, his voice deep with sympathy.

She forced a smile, but knew it looked bitter. "Oh, we had family, just none interested in us. My mother's parents were millionaires. When she didn't marry the man they'd chosen, they cut her off. My grandparents wouldn't even help pay for my dad's funeral, so I had to find a way to bury him properly. They've never met me or Mindy. They said they had no use for mongrels."

And she'd once again said way too much. Why did she just talk when she got nervous? It was like an illness. Once she started going, Piper Glen would tell anyone anything.

A strong hand covered hers, encasing her in warmth—and a heat that sizzled up her arm. She blinked up with a silent gasp to find Rafe regarding her. "It is good for you that they are not in your life."

"Yeah." *Though a check would have been nice.* "It's good. And Mindy and I came through just fine. I worked at a clothing store during the day and took night school classes…and here we are. Mindy's in her sophomore year of college. She settled down. We're good."

The waiter placed the iced tea in front of her, but suddenly she didn't have a hand because Kade took hold of her other. Guys from Bezakistan were really touchy-feely. Piper went with the flow. She'd heard people from other cultures didn't have the same boundaries as Americans.

Kade's hand squeezed hers lightly. "You were left on your own at eighteen years old to raise your sister. That must have been very difficult."

"It wasn't like I had to change her diapers or anything. Though getting her back and forth from color guard was a nightmare. Seriously, those color guard moms are like a cult. If I had to sell one more box of candy or make another homecoming corsage, I was going to blow my head off."

"That would be a shame since it's such a pretty head." Slowly, Rafe released her hand and reached for one of the ridiculously well-presented oysters. "Here you are, Piper."

They looked awesome. And the minute she put a hand on one of those things it would inevitably slide the wrong way, fall out of its nice little shell, slip across the floor, and some very important person would break a leg. "No, thank you."

"You do not like them?" Again Rafe's gorgeous face turned down, and she felt a bit like she'd insulted him. No, upset him. "Dex told us you liked seafood. It was why we chose this place. I'll have the waiter take this away. We can find a restaurant that is more pleasing to you."

They both started to stand, as though perfectly ready to leave.

"No! I love seafood. I adore oysters. I'm just really clumsy with them, and the waiter didn't offer me like a bib or anything." Because yeah, that would be classy in a five-star place like this.

Kade laughed, the masculine sound running a shiver up her spine. "You're worried you will make a mess?"

"Worried? No. How about absolutely certain. There's a reason they call me Pandora. I tend to make a mess wherever I go." Her reputation hadn't bought her a ton of friends at Black Oak. Women like Amanda seemed to genuinely hate her.

Rafe slid back into the booth and settled closer. He squeezed a lemon over the oyster and picked it up once more. "Pandora was the most beautiful woman in the world, you know. She was a gift from Zeus to Prometheus's brother."

Piper knew the story. "She was a trick. Zeus's gifts always came with a price."

His lips curved in a satisfied smile. "Oh, *habibti*, the discussions we could have. You are right, but I think this was one trick that worked for the world. Without Pandora, the gifted one, there would have been no women."

Kade shuddered. "That would be truly horrible."

28

"She opened a box she wasn't supposed to and unleashed suffering on mankind," Piper argued.

"You view this story in the wrong way. By unleashing suffering, she also unleashed joy. Men before Pandora did not know love or happiness or true comfort because they cannot exist without their opposites to define them. Pandora made mankind." Rafe brushed a stray piece of hair from her face. "You are afraid of many things, *habibti*. Do not be afraid to try. Do not be afraid to fail. Be afraid to simply exist never knowing either the high of success or the low of failure."

He held the oyster up, offering to control the shell.

His words, those beautiful words coming from deep inside him, coated her ears with that rich chocolate voice that filled her like a sensual spell. She shouldn't take him up on the offer. He was practically her boss. No, more important even, since he could influence the presentation of all her research. But she was twenty-five years old and suddenly she realized just how much fear had ruled her world. Fear of losing her sister. Fear of failing. Fear of being hurt.

She looked him in the eyes, a spark flaring inside her as he placed the shell to her lips and tilted the oyster in. Soft, with a lovely acidic flavor from the lemon. The oyster slid down her throat, a decadent experience.

Rafe looked down at her, pleasure oozing from his pores. "It was good?"

She nodded, feeling a flush creep up her cheeks.

Kade's hand slid around the back of the booth. "What else have you been afraid to try?"

The answer to that would probably have shocked them. Sex. She hadn't tried sex, but now it crept across her mind, luring, tempting her. Rafe would treat her well. Kade must surely know how to woo a woman between the sheets. She suspected either of them would make her first experience wonderful. She shivered, picturing losing herself in a downy bed, wrapped in those strong, sun-kissed arms.

As her cheeks turned hotter, Piper reached for her iced tea and began gulping. With those thoughts, she feared she'd just opened her own Pandora's box and that she might not be able to close the lid again.

Chapter Three

Unable to sleep, Talib al Mussad looked out his office window in the palace, onto his garden, still shrouded by night. He wondered what his brothers were doing. Bloody hell, who was he fooling? He wondered what Piper was doing. He was a thirty-four-year-old, powerful-as-sin multi-billionaire, and he was practically mooning about a little bit of fluff. Except that Piper wasn't just a bit of fluff. The woman had proven herself to be blisteringly smart, and she shared many of his interests—the environment, history, economic concerns, bad B movies…but would any of that translate into being an effective queen? What if she buckled under the limelight, the expectations, the appearances? What had seemed so rational days ago now sounded mad.

Piper had no real polish and no concept of what it took to run a country. Being a queen was about more than having a brain, a heart, and a compassionate spirit. Though those qualities certainly helped, surviving being royal today had become largely about media relations, the ability to be graceful under pressure. By all accounts, Piper currently struggled to walk down a hall without tripping—and that was before donning designer heels and walking to an explosion of flashbulbs with all eyes on her, as everyone would expect of their wife.

If he and his brothers wed her, it was inevitable that Piper would struggle to fit in. The possibility troubled him, and Tal wondered if she would come to hate him for making her their captive bride. But her knowledge and passion for the Clean Energy Project would be a much-needed boon for Bezakistan's future. Having a Western wife would help further separate his country from some of his neighbors and be an asset in global relations. So if Rafe and Kade approved, none of his concerns could derail his course. Her feelings could matter even less. She could be taught everything she needed to know. Bezakistan desperately needed a queen, and he couldn't get Piper out of his head.

But even if she handled being a queen, how would she feel once she realized she could be a target of violence as well? Dark voices started to whisper in Talib's head. He'd already cost one woman her life. How could he even think about risking another?

"Tal?"

He turned slightly and caught sight of his cousin, Alea. She was dressed informally, but the troubled frown on her youthful face matched her personality. No amount of trying to convince her to finish university had helped. During her first year, she'd been abducted and rescued from a nightmare of sexual slavery by two of Tal's old friends, Cole and Burke Lennox. Since then, nothing Tal had done, no amount of therapy—psychological or retail—seemed to cure the darkness that had settled into her soul. Of course, he couldn't exactly cast stones himself.

Six years ago, he'd been taken and tortured in an attempted political ploy. And he'd learned the hard way that a sheikh bled and prayed just like any other man. Yes, he'd been rescued, thanks to Cole Lennox, but nothing had been able to banish his darkness, either.

"You are not sleeping," he chided.

"Neither are you."

"Touché. What is it, dear?" he asked gently.

At least she didn't flinch when he approached her now. It had taken six months before she stopped screaming every time any male came near.

"It's Khalil. I don't trust him."

Alea no longer trusted anyone, but in this case, Tal agreed. "What has he done now?"

"I overheard him giving an interview about your lack of a bride

As if Khalil's little mouse of a wife would be the strong pillar of a queen Bezakistan required. "I have six months to marry. I assure you I will do my duty to my country, then my part in this archaic ritual will be done. Bezakistan will be safe."

"He's also harping about and how you're going to send the country into deep debt with this new green energy project."

Little bastard. Tal sighed. "He's trying to build his case with the people, as pitiful as it is. For now, Khalil has very few options. I will, of course, assure the country that the green project is the best course of action. After all, I have facts and figures on my side."

And his potential bride would be instrumental in that. Piper had all sorts of interesting ideas on financing the project. She thought out of the box. Her creativity and drive to make things happen were two of her most appealing qualities.

If only she was a bit more attractive. But it was perhaps best that she was not. He had no intention of falling for his bride. She was a means to an end, and he would pay her well. Love would be dangerous, and Piper was too smart to expect romantic gestures. Theirs would be a marriage of minds. If she wanted anything more, she would have to look to his brothers.

"Who is this Piper woman?" Alea asked, peering at the file on his desk between them.

Damn. So much for keeping her a secret until he and his

33

brothers reached a final conclusion. "She's a woman I'm vetting as a potential wife."

Alea flipped the folder open and scanned, her mouth turning down. "An American?"

"Yes. She is from Texas."

Alea gave an amused huff of a laugh. "Good, cousin. Perhaps she will come with her six-shooters and teach you a thing or two." She sobered. "Do you like her?"

"I like her very much actually." He often found himself smiling at their conversations. Her soft, Southern voice alone was adorable.

But would that be enough upon which to base a marriage? Tal worried a bit that she hadn't seen his face, nor he hers, really. All he had of her after a rushed investigation was a grainy driver's license photo that was nearly five years old and a high school yearbook photo. Piper was young; he knew that. But after several months of conversation, Tal was convinced that she was mature beyond her years. Intellectual interests mattered to her. She had a solid moral character and a very big heart. She would make an excellent mother someday. All admirable qualities, of course, but nothing to truly tempt his heart and make her someone his enemies could use to weaken him.

That made her perfect.

"I'm glad, Tal. I hope Rafe and Kade don't shoot you down. They were right about that ambassador's daughter, though. She was completely selfish. She would have been a terrible mother. And the Swedish girl had the most obnoxious laugh. The press would have crucified her. The Miss America contestant was polished and would have played well with the press, but she lacked heart." She shrugged. "You've had a tough bride hunt."

Indeed, something had been wrong with every candidate, and Rafe and Kade hadn't been shy about saying so. They'd had valid points, but if they could not collectively settle on a single bride soon, their country would be in ruins. He prayed that his brothers could look past Piper's sensible façade and see the wisdom of his unusual choice.

His computer trilled, a satellite call coming in. He steeled himself. He was about to find out if his idea of bringing a smart, economically intelligent Western woman into his family would fly. He hit the button to answer the call, not bothering to shoo Alea away. She wouldn't spread gossip. In fact, Alea would be instrumental in preparing any prospective bride he brought to Bezakistan for the ceremonies.

His brothers' faces came into view, and Tal skipped the greeting. "Did you talk to Dex? Did he give you the information you needed?"

He'd sent them to Dex, hoping that if the James brothers got behind the match, it would make securing Piper's agreement simpler. Getting her out of the country would prove less difficult if her employer colluded with them. And Dex would be able to talk more personally about Piper, in a way Rafe and Kade would be sympathetic to. If they took the time to ask a trusted friend about her, perhaps they'd be curious enough to meet her with an open mind. Tal didn't need Dex's information. He knew everything of merit about Piper, right down to how often she bought groceries. Which wasn't often enough. Piper was hurting for money, and Tal consoled himself with the fact that, if his brothers approved of her and they changed her life, at least he could remove all financial burden from her.

Rafe nodded. "He did. In fact, we met her for ourselves, and Dex confirmed everything we observed. We took her to lunch and discovered that she is a very kind and intelligent woman. When can we move forward?"

Tal sat back in his seat. "You don't intend to fight me on this?"

Kade leaned into the picture with a grin, his hand sporting a thumbs up gesture. "Not at all. Let's move. The sooner the better. I want to get to the concubine portion of this wedding."

Tal felt a frown slide across his face. The "concubine" portion of the wedding ritual was a very vulgar way of describing the traditional handfasting period. He and his brothers would pledge their willingness to wed at a banquet. Then, to determine their compatibility, they would all share a life—and a bed—for thirty days. During that time, none of the grooms could end the arrangement, but the bride could if she was displeased with them in any way, including sexually. If she didn't cry off during that thirty days, they would be, by Bezakistani law, married.

But Piper Glen wouldn't sever the handfasting because she was a reasonable woman. She would understand a sound bargain when it was struck. And he couldn't afford to let her walk away with Khalil lurking in the shadows, waging a PR campaign battle for Bezakistani hearts and minds.

"You approve of her, then?" Tal had thought he would have to fight them. On Rafe, he'd intended to use logic. Piper was a professional economist whose life work happened to be in the energy field. Bezakistan's whole economy was based off energy. She made sense, and his middle brother was too smart not to see that.

And then there was Kade. He'd had a plan for his youngest brother, who seemed to think they would marry a supermodel with the sex drive of a porn star. He'd intended to trade fists with Kade until he finally gave in. But if his youngest brother already approved without the fisticuffs, Piper must be at least marginally attractive.

"We do. Obviously we have not discussed marriage with her. She seems to think you're some lowly researcher." Rafe's eyes narrowed. "I'm actually somewhat worried that if we tell her what we truly seek, she will turn us down. She has no interest in fame. Nor, I suspect, will wealth sway her."

That was Tal's assessment as well. "But she's quite passionate about this project. I believe the better proposal is to promise her that she can help head the project as our wife."

"Perhaps. She would at least listen, then." Rafe's mouth turned down. "But I think she is more romantic than you believe. Tal, I'm quite convinced that she is a virgin."

He heard Alea shuffle out. *Damn.* He wished she hadn't overheard his brother debating Piper's purity. It, no doubt, upset her. But Bezakistan was Alea's country, too, and she would suffer along with everyone else if it fell to Khalil's incompetent hands.

"So she's been smart enough to exercise her good character and save herself for a long-term relationship. I see no problem with that."

Rafe hesitated, then shook his head. "Under all that intelligence, she is still a woman with a woman's sensibilities. She might be hoping for the fairy tale."

Kade's face came back into view. "She'll agree to this because we will bring her pleasure. A whole lot of it. She is innocent, and we can show her a whole new world, both in bed and out of it. Piper has never even been out of her country. Between all the new sights and exotic locations, along with the ecstasy we'll show her, she will be ours. So, when can we get this sucker done?"

Rafe's eyes rolled. "He's horny."

"You're truly sexually interested in Piper?" Talib asked.

She seemed sweet, and he deeply enjoyed their talks. Since he rarely found an intellectual equal as enthusiastic about the subjects he adored, he was looking forward to bringing her to the palace so they could spend hours talking about economics and politics. But he was a bit worried about the bedroom portion of their marriage. Had he missed something? The photos he had of her showed a somewhat mousy woman with a decently attractive face, but nothing to truly stir a man's blood. Over the past two months, he'd come to feel an affection for her on an intellectual level, which had become a warm sort of friendship. He wasn't sure he liked the idea of Kade, the playboy, treating her like one of his brainless fuck bunnies.

"Absolutely, I'm interested. She's got a geek chic thing that's hot. Her breasts alone are worth salivating over. And that mouth..." Tal raised a disapproving brow at his younger brother, and Kade cleared his throat, then continued. "But I agree with Rafe. We have to play this fairly cool with Piper. If you put this all out in a cold, factual way, like a business deal, she'll run."

Piper wasn't like the other women he'd semi-courted. They'd been interested in power and privilege. They'd been worldly women. Piper wasn't. She could very well be scared off by the enormity of taking her place at his side to run a country. And by the fact that she would be marrying three virtual strangers.

He couldn't let that stop him. His country was at stake. Time was running out. If he didn't handfast soon, Khalil could challenge him in court and argue that there wouldn't be enough time for their potential wife to know her mind. Typically Bezakistani princes knew their prospective bride for at least a year before deciding to enter into a union. He could barely offer her the obligatory month of handfasting. Nor did he have time to woo her. He needed her in bed with all three of them and bound to them as soon as possible. Then he could woo her. Well, his brothers could.

And if he managed to impregnate her, all the better for him and his country.

His stomach turned a bit. When had he become such a cold fucker? He knew the answer to that. He knew the timing down to the minute, when those rebels had killed his guards, taken him into custody, and proceeded to spend days torturing him until his soul fled. Only duty to his country and family remained.

Piper Glen was just another duty he had to perform.

"We're going to have to be sneaky bastards if this is going to work," Kade added. "But that's all right. Bezakistani men have been capturing their concubines for generations. It should be in our DNA."

Indeed. Tal sighed. "If we're all in agreement, then I will set the plan in motion. You two make sure she is prepared to depart when I advise you to move in. One way or another, we're binding her to us next week."

He ended the call and shut off the webcam, but didn't close the computer. He intended to enjoy one last conversation with Piper before she discovered what a bastard he was.

* * * *

Piper happily ate her leftovers while she looked over her latest financial projections for the Clean Energy Project. She'd felt a little dumb asking for a doggie bag at such a swanky restaurant, but she likely wouldn't see Rafe or Kade again, and it was way better to look silly than to be hungry. She would know. She'd been both, and she came down firmly on the side of food in her belly.

She hummed a little as she stared at the endless list of numbers that added up to one happy fact: She could make her green energy theories work if she could find a company big enough and a country willing to try it.

Her computer chimed, letting her know an internet call was coming in. She sat back, surprised. Tal. Most often, he sent instant messages. They'd only spoken over the phone a few times. This must be important. She hit the button to open her line.

"Hello?"

"Hello, Piper. How are you this evening? It is night in Dallas, no?"

She loved his voice. Deep and musical. "It's just past eight. Isn't it the middle of the night in Bezakistan?"

"Yes. I don't sleep much. I like how quiet it is this time of the morning. It's still dark outside. It feels a bit like I am the only person in the world. Except for you."

She laughed a little. "Well, I assure you I'm not the only person here. I can hear Mrs. Lindman next door yelling at her husband about the laundry. Oh, and someone is having a party above me. The cops will be here soon. It's just another Friday night at the Holloway Manor Apartments."

"The police will come?" He sounded horrified.

"Yeah, they're kind of regulars around here. It gets a little wild sometimes. The good news is, it's close to the train stop."

"You had to take the train home from work? You did not have an escort?"

She laughed. Things must be very different there. "I take the train home every day, Tal."

"I was given to understand you went to lunch with the al Mussad brothers so they could listen to your proposal."

She sighed, her heart fluttering a bit. They'd discussed the proposal a bit, but mostly she'd let them feed her and stared while they talked about how beautiful their country was. Piper winced. Tal was probably calling to tell her how little she'd done to help their cause. "Yes. Well, I don't know how interested they were in numbers."

"They took you to lunch but did not escort you home? And you live in a dangerous neighborhood?" His growl sounded more than a bit frustrated. "I apologize for my countrymen, Piper. I assumed they were gentlemen."

"Oh, they were wonderful. Truly." She'd had the best time with them. She just hadn't exactly been as focused on business as she should have been. "I had to go back to work. I had so much to do."

Tal was silent for a moment, and she could almost feel his displeasure over the line. She wondered what the cultural standards were for business lunches in Bezakistan. Perhaps they were more stringent than here? Either way, Rafe and Kade were royal. She was surprised they'd made time to hear about her project at all. She'd never expected them to escort her anywhere.

"Really. They were very polite," she assured.

"I would hope so." He took a long breath. "I have already heard that they were very impressed with you, Piper. They're interested in taking the project to the government board."

"Oh, wow. Really? That's *great* news!"

The government board was a select group of Bezakistani intellectuals and politicians, headed by Sheikh al Mussad himself. The man was known to be very intelligent and very private. She'd read his numerous papers on the business of energy. The man had an absolutely fascinating mind. And she'd had lunch with his brothers. She was far from her little hick town now.

The good news was, all she had to do was put together the numbers in a logical presentation. Tal would present it to the sheikh. There were risks involved, yes, but if al Mussad and the rest of the government board were listening, this should be a slam dunk.

"So what do you need from me? I just finished my latest round of projections, and they're really good. I'll e-mail them to you in a minute. Anything else I can send?"

There was a slight pause before Tal's voice came across the line, low and more intimate than before. "You. Come here and bring those projections to me."

Was he crazy? "Uhm, I think you need a geography refresher, Tal. Dallas. Bezakistan. It's thousands of miles apart, not a walk down the hall."

He chuckled a little. "Piper, come to my country. I've been asked to extend an official invitation. The al Mussad family would be thrilled if you would stay at the palace and grace us with your intelligent counsel."

She sat for a minute, his words sinking in. They wanted her to get on a plane and fly halfway across the world to meet with a billionaire sheikh in a fabulous palace? Her shoes were secondhand. She'd never been on a plane. She couldn't just go to a different country. She needed gateway travel first. Like

Manhattan. Nope. Too big. Chicago. Yes, that was more her speed. When she knew she could handle the Windy City, she would think about the Big Apple.

But she couldn't go to Bezakistan. Could she?

"I have *so* much to do here. How about a video conference? I'll be available whenever you want."

"They prefer to do business with a hand they can shake. I've already discussed this with Gavin James. He has agreed to transfer you here for the time being."

"*Transferred*? As in out of the country?" The idea was so foreign, she didn't know how to make heads or tails of it. "For how long?"

He hesitated. "At least a month, but I suspect it may be longer."

"But...I have an apartment here."

"You will have a place to live in Bezakistan. The al Mussad family allowed me some input, and I promise your residence will be to your liking. It is very near mine, so we will have plenty of time to discuss the project. I have made all of the arrangements. You need only say yes."

Her head was racing a million miles an hour. Tal made it sound so simple, but... "I have a lease. Then there's my furniture and belongings. I can't just leave it all."

"For your trouble, the al Mussad family will purchase you a lovely residence upon your return. For now, your things will be put into storage."

Piper gasped. "I can't accept that. It's too much."

"Indeed not. If this project is the success they believe it will be, a new residence is merely a small token of their appreciation. So now that the trivialities are settled, I'm supposed to inform you that a team will come tomorrow morning to help you pack what you need and make any other preparations necessary so this transition is as easy as possible."

"B-But...I don't even have a passport." Her mind raced with the enormity of the decision in front of her, though it sounded very much like there wasn't a decision at all. The al Mussads had already decided, and Gavin James had concurred.

And that, it seemed, was that.

"Fear not. Everything will be taken care of. It will be for the best." His voice softened a bit. "This is your project, Piper. Your voice gives it the best chance possible to succeed. I know this is moving quite quickly, but your presence here will be good for Black Oak and Bezakistan. The country needs you now."

"Tal, you know everything about the project as well as I do."

"Indeed not." His voice turned gentle. "I know how unsettling change can be, Piper, but if you do not come, you will always wonder what would have happened. Please. Help us change."

Tears pricked her eyes. Change. It terrified her, yet she needed it so badly. She'd come to Dallas for a job, hoping to shake her life up. For so long she'd done what was acceptable, expected. She'd been forced to give up much of her youth in order to ensure her sister's safety and home life. She'd worked two jobs and gone to school, and all she had to show for it was an apartment she was sure had played host to several murders. She'd accomplished much…but lived little.

Bezakistan. It could be more than numbers on a page. What would they think of a little hick from small-town Texas?

Piper sat up. They would think she was smart and competent because she would show them. She was more than a bad pair of used shoes. She had built this project—and it could change the whole world if someone was willing to take a chance on it. If she expected Bezakistan to do that, she had to be willing to take a chance herself.

"All right." There was a breathless joy in her voice. "I'll come."

"Excellent. I look forward to greeting you, Piper. This is good. You will see. Now get some sleep, little one. You have much preparation and a long journey ahead of you. Tell those al Mussad boys that if they do not care for you properly, they will answer to me."

The connection broke, and Piper rolled her eyes. Yeah, she wouldn't be seeing Rafe and Kade again. Even if she did, a pair of princes would never care what a lowly researcher or two thought.

She walked to the window, wonder pinging inside her. Wow. Very soon, she would be starting a new adventure, discovering a new place. Piper grinned, determined to conquer it.

Chapter Four

Piper stared up at the jet and hoped she didn't live up to her nickname. She could only imagine what her own unique brand of chaos could do at forty thousand feet.

"You are nervous, *habibti*?" Rafe put a hand on her elbow, helping her up the stairs.

"I've been known to cause electronics to crash." She really hoped the enormous plane was immune to her superpowers of destruction. "I thought we were flying in a private jet. I was expecting something smaller."

"This is private. It's a Boeing 747-430, but you'll find we have extensively redecorated."

"This huge thing is going to take three people across the world? I don't even want to think about the carbon footprint that's leaving." She was going to have to have a little talk with the sheikh when she met him. Politely, of course. But if he was about to become the world's leading producer of green energy, he needed to start flying commercial.

"Don't think about that. And do not judge before you've seen it. It is a very long flight. Fourteen hours. That is why we're leaving so late. I want you to rest so you are ready to meet our brother." Rafe gave her a reassuring smile with just the hint of even white teeth. Everything about the prince was polished, from his smile to his manners. He was smooth as silk, and Piper couldn't help but wonder what his wife or girlfriend was like. Probably a model.

"What? Who is a model?" Rafe asked, stepping up to the top of the stairs.

She'd said that out loud? Piper grimaced. She'd spent way too much of the last couple of years alone in a library or going over data in lonely rooms. She was used to talking to herself. *Come up with something clever to deflect the situation. Quick!* "I was wondering if your girlfriend is a model."

A brilliant smile broke over his face and he laughed. It was so nice to see the usually somber man chuckle that she forgave him for laughing at her. "I do not have a girlfriend, Piper. I date very little, in fact. The customs of my country are a bit unusual. I think many women would run if I told them what I would require from a serious relationship."

"What do you mean?" She'd heard a whole lot about Bezakistani customs over the past two days, but nothing about dating or marriage. Piper found herself deeply interested.

He shook his head. "No, *habibti*. You will not tempt me into one of your long discussions. I promised my brother you would sleep."

She frowned, but admitted privately that she *was* tired. The last several days had been amazing, filled with anticipation and a flurry of work. Two hours after she told Tal she didn't have a passport, Rafe and Kade had delivered one to her. How was that possible, especially when she knew darn well that every government office had been closed at the time? She had no idea how and hoped it wasn't forged. After assuring her the passport was indeed valid, the al Mussad brothers had taken one look at her ratty apartment and its street corner hopping with illegal activity, and insisted she come with them to their condo immediately.

They were really bossy and didn't like it when she said no. Oh, they didn't argue with her or get angry. They simply manipulated the situation until she'd found herself settling into the guest bedroom at their very posh condo with endless views of the city at two in morning, wondering when she'd lost control of the situation.

And their bossiness hadn't stopped there. She wobbled on her new heels as she hunched through the doorway of the private jet. The three and a half inch Pradas with a square heel and a silver buckle were easily the sturdiest of her new shoes. But they were shoes she hadn't bought herself. Rafe had insisted the shoes were necessary to her new position in Bezakistan. He'd told her he was simply making sure she followed his country's customs.

She'd tried to call him on it. No country customarily wore Manolo Blahniks and Louboutin stilettos. She'd looked up the price of those shoes on the internet. If this was Bezakistani custom, then the whole country would be bankrupt very soon.

And still, she was wearing them. She didn't want to offend her hosts...and she liked the appreciative gleam in their eyes when she donned the sexy shoes.

"Piper." Kade's warm voice washed over her as he stood. "Welcome. We're so happy you've allowed us to escort you to our country."

She wanted to frown at him, but he was so gorgeous and a bit earnest. She couldn't bring herself to chastise him much. "Allowed? Somehow I don't think you would have taken no for an answer."

A little smile creased his perfect face. "Well, we are determined and persuasive. You know, the men in my country are legendary for stealing their brides. It is said in Bezakistan that a man who cannot steal his bride is a man who does not deserve a wife."

She glanced back at Rafe. "Is this one of the customs you were referring to earlier?"

He nodded. "Indeed. But even as we steal our brides, we take great pride in bringing her pleasure, in protecting and cherishing that which we fought hard to take."

He phrased it like he meant more than one groom for a bride. Okay, so English wasn't his first language. But when he talked like that, she went all gooshy inside and lost the ability to breathe. What would it be like to be Rafe's captive bride, bound to him by his will and the pleasure he gave her?

Piper shivered, then forced herself to stop staring. If they caught her, she'd only be embarrassed. But she'd never get used to being surrounded by such exotic, masculine beauty. It would be smarter to remember she had a job to do when she got to Bezakistan. Then it would just be her and Tal and a whole bunch of number crunching.

And her life would be exactly the way it was now. Same routine, just a different living space. She was a bit shocked to realize that she'd miss Rafe and Kade.

It wouldn't matter. She needed to put them out of her head. When they got to Bezakistan, Rafe and Kade would go their way and she would go hers.

As she tottered deeper into the body of the plane, she focused again on her surroundings, still adjusting to her new contact lenses. And her jaw dropped.

The plane looked like something a movie star would own. She'd expected rows of narrow seats that had to be placed in an upright position for landing. This looked like a decadent living room. The walls were done in a sultry amber that caught the harsh overhead lights and softened them. There was a curved velvet couch in soft chocolate tones. When she sat, she'd bet it would be like sinking into a slice of heaven. A long table sat toward the front of the plane draped in white linens, all staged for the fine china she'd bet was securely stowed until after takeoff. Even an ornate chandelier hung overhead.

"Wow. This is not what I expected."

"When we reach a good altitude, the staff will bring out our dinner." Kade sat down, patting the seat next to him. "I've prepared a feast for you."

Rafe snorted. She kind of loved it when he made the inelegant sound. It reminded her he wasn't perfect.

She turned back to Kade. "*You* prepared the feast?"

He shrugged, a graceful movement of strong shoulders. "I told the chef what to cook."

That was enough for her. Kade couldn't know what the last couple of meals had meant to her. The difference between a homemade ham sandwich and a perfectly seared filet was infinite. "I appreciate it."

His face lit up and he reached for her hand, pulling her down to sit with him. "It is my greatest pleasure. Now, tell me about your day. Did the movers finish?"

Rafe sat on her other side, both men far too close, but she felt so comfortable in the soft velvet, surrounded by their heat and the musky spice of their exotic scents. They seemed to like having her between them. Everywhere they went, they managed to maneuver her into the middle.

Piper smiled wryly at Kade's question. The movers had been ruthlessly precise—and a little judgmental. "I don't think they appreciated my design style. One of them asked if I wanted to throw it all away and just start over."

Actually, they'd been completely horrified at her secondhand floral-print couch. She'd picked it up at a garage sale, telling herself that the extra stains were really just flourishes.

Kade froze, then jerked his phone from his pocket. "They were not paid to embarrass you." He stood and walked toward the back of the plane, speaking in quick, angry-sounding Arabic.

Piper blinked. "What's he doing?"

Rafe's face had gone dark, his lips turning down. "He is taking care of the problem, *habibti*." He settled back as a modestly dressed woman walked out of the back of the plane and set a tray with a bottle of wine and three glasses on the table.

"Your Highness, we will be taking off in twenty minutes. Please let me or the staff know if there is anything we can do for you or your guest."

"Thank you," Rafe replied while his brother continued to speak into the phone in what she thought of as hyper-drive Arabic, able to slay a man in a hundred syllables a minute.

"Enjoy your wine." Rafe passed her a glass of the golden fluid. It had become very obvious to Piper over the last few days that the al Mussad brothers weren't practicing Muslims. When she'd asked, she'd been surprised to discover that unlike the countries around them, Bezakistan wasn't very religious. It was open to all forms of faith and enjoyed a strictly held constitution that prized secular government. But not everyone wanted it to stay that way.

She took the wine to soothe her nerves. Flying for the first time made her more than a bit apprehensive. A few feet away, Kade continued his tirade.

"Why is he so mad?"

Rafe's head cocked slightly. "Surely you must know that he will not allow anyone to upset you, *habibti*."

The more he spoke that word, the more it felt like an intimacy. She'd thought it was simply an offhanded endearment, but the way it rolled off his tongue felt so personal. "They didn't."

A lie, but she wasn't going to let them know how much it hurt to have someone look down on her.

"Yes, they did. And it is not allowed."

It must be nice to throw edicts around and expect them to be followed. "It wasn't a big deal. I shouldn't have complained. It's stupid, I know. No one's opinion should matter but mine, but it hurts when someone looks down on what I worked really hard for. I know that couch isn't worth much, but we had to sell our ranch after my dad died and we were so far in debt that everything had to go. I managed to keep our clothes and some of Mindy's things, but I agreed to auction off everything else. We went from a three bedroom house with acres and acres of land to a studio apartment with nothing but a suitcase each."

"Your childhood things were sold?" He sounded horrified and more than a bit angry.

She soothed herself with a long drink. "I don't miss most of it. Just one thing, really. I had a copy of *Charlotte's Web*, but it was signed and it was a first edition, so the bank sold it." She'd read that book a hundred times. Even long past childhood, she would turn to it, the story of a little runt pig who didn't belong calling to her. She'd never fit in her small town. She hadn't found her place in the city, either. She often wondered if there was anywhere she would belong.

Rafe's warm hand cupped her cheek. "I wish I had been there to help you, *habibti.*"

Oddly, Piper wished he had, too. She'd been so alone. She was still alone for the most part, but she had a few friends. And now she had this adventure. Mindy was safe, and that was worth the world to her. "It was a hard time, but I made it through."

"You were very young to be responsible for a teenage girl."

She sighed, the weight still so close to her shoulders. Back then, she'd felt more like Prometheus than Pandora. "It was so much worse because my town was small and closed minded. They watched my every move like circling vultures just waiting for me to step out of line so they could take my sister from me. Then I ended up dating Johnny Tyler, the mayor's son. Mr. Tyler asked me to tutor Johnny in economic affairs. Then his dad decided I would be a political asset, so Johnny asked me to marry him."

Rafe sat back, seeming to grind his teeth together. "It is good to have a smart wife. Many men would find you an asset to their careers."

"I didn't want to be an asset. I wanted to be loved. And Johnny did, too. Except he wanted to be loved by a stripper named Starlight. I rather suspect that wasn't her real name."

Rafe didn't find her joke funny. He simply stared down at her, his dark eyes so intense that she thought she might drown. Wow, he was so beautiful. He and his brother were far more attractive than Hollywood heartthrobs. And they both had larger-than-life presences that made her sigh wistfully. *If only…*

He curled a soft touch around her chin, tilting her face up so she had nowhere to go. "He was a fool to allow you to escape. When the right men come along, they will not be so foolish. These men will never let you go. They will be clever. They will catch you and tie you to them so tightly that you will never wish to leave."

She might be waiting for that man forever. *Wait. Had he said men—plural?*

Piper didn't get to ask her question because he shocked her by leaning forward and brushing his lips against hers once, then again, his mouth warm, gentle, coaxing. Her breath caught, and her skin started to hum. The world tilted on its axis, and she kind of liked where she landed.

"We're about to take off. She should put on her seatbelt." Kade's voice broke the moment. He stood over them, his face full of thunder, but it seemed directed exclusively at Rafe.

God, she'd just been caught kissing his brother. And she'd wanted more—far more. The minute Rafe kissed her, Piper had felt something deep inside her open. This really was an adventure. There really was a whole world out there, and she'd been tiptoeing through her postage stamp-sized patch of it like a scared little mouse.

But she didn't have to be that girl forever. She wasn't in some tiny Texas town anymore, and she wasn't dependent on the good thoughts of others to keep her family together. Her sister was grown and happy. No one could judge her now. She was free. Was she going to spend her freedom hiding, or was she going to finally experience life?

Kade sat down beside her, his hand grazing her thigh. Piper

shivered under his touch until he buckled her belt and gently tightened it. What was wrong with her, that she would kiss one brother and respond to another minutes later?

Kade frowned. "My brother is a terrible kisser. I apologize for his very selfish behavior toward you."

"How would you know?" She couldn't help but tease him and try to lighten the mood.

He smirked. "Because many women have said I am much better."

And then they were off, arguing in rat-a-tat-tat gunfire Arabic. She really needed to learn the language because, even though they were arguing, the words had a cadence, an exciting musicality.

The plane started moving, smooth as glass. She picked up the wine. Maybe it was time to live a little. Maybe it was time to put aside all her fears about doing what was right and just do what felt good.

The plane shook suddenly. The hostess picked up the wine bottle, leaving the glass in Piper's hands. The beautiful woman smiled at her, ignoring the two fighting brothers. "Enjoy your flight. It is an honor to serve you on your first trip to our country."

Piper smiled back, warmed by the woman's words. If everyone was so friendly, she was going to love it. She held the glass out. "I'm worried I'll spill."

"Don't worry. If you spill, they will just buy a new plane."

The beautiful woman winked as she moved away, but not before Kade grabbed a glass. The plane taxied down the runway, and Piper was ready for takeoff.

* * * *

Two hours and two glasses of wine later, Piper was certain what her next move should be in the big adventure she was determined to make of her life. She just wasn't sure who to do it with. She looked across the aisle. The brothers were both gorgeous, both kind. Both unbearably sexy.

And after this flight, she would likely see very little of them. She would join her friend Tal and disappear into a world of numbers and PowerPoint presentations and arguments about implementation. Piper looked forward to the work. It was important to Black Oak, Bezakistan, and the world. But she hoped to have time to actually see the country, maybe even go on a date or two. But as her co-worker, even if Tal wasn't married, he would be off limits.

Truthfully, her relationships hadn't worked out. She'd barely dated in high school, and when she'd gotten engaged, Johnny seemed to lose all interest in her. He'd barely kissed her, much less touched her more intimately. The sad fact was that Rafe and his probing kiss had been the most erotic experience of her life.

But she didn't have to stay virginal. Rafe and Kade were obviously quite experienced and used to casual sex. They would give her a good time, never hurt her. And, if her instincts were right, they weren't exactly disinterested. There had been many seemingly random touches when one or the other—or both— got way too close to be normal.

But could she just ask for what she wanted? She seriously doubted either man would really come on to her. The kiss aside, they had been very gentlemanly. After their scrumptious meal, she had twelve hours left with them. But how could she choose which brother and how could she look at one after she'd had sex with the other?

The hostess, Jasmine, picked up the now-empty tray that had once held a piece of honey cake. Piper had eaten everything, deeply enjoying both the full stomach and the Mediterranean flavors.

Rafe and Kade were speaking to each other in Arabic again. They had gotten some kind of call from the palace and, for a time, they passed the phone back and forth. Now, it seemed, they were simply conferring with one another.

"Where is the restroom?" she asked the hostess.

"Follow me. I will show you the way. And when you are ready for sleep, the bedroom is just past the bathroom."

"There's a bedroom?"

Jasmine frowned. "But of course. The sheikh's room has been set aside for your use. His brothers will share the smaller one."

Piper gasped. She would have to fix that since she didn't need very much space and had even less need for opulence.

Mind made up, she opened the door to the bathroom. Naturally, it wasn't some tiny space that better resembled an upright coffin with a toilet, like airplane lavatories she'd seen on TV. Of course not. The al Mussad brothers wouldn't perform their bodily functions in anything less than a palace. The bathroom was spacious and elegant and offered a lovely shower made entirely of Carrera marble that she was pretty sure could hold a whole football team. A long vanity with double sinks lined the other wall.

Shaking her head at the magnificence of it all, she washed up, glancing out the little window. The night was dark , but the moon shone like an enormous pearl, its incandescence illuminating the world. She put her head against the double paned window. She couldn't go back to where she used to be. Really, she didn't want to. She simply wasn't sure which choice moved her forward.

She was changing, becoming someone she liked very much—a woman who seized adventure by getting on a plane and changing her life at the spur of the moment. Now, she wanted to be someone who knew what it meant to be loved.

Piper groaned. It wouldn't be love with whichever of the al Mussad brothers she chose as her first lover; she knew that. But they could share affection and pleasure. She'd had so little of either in her life. Why not?

She sighed, wondering just what she'd say.

Hey, guys, I'm a virgin. Didn't do it for religious reasons or because my hymen is terribly important to me. Just kind of got busy. I didn't put it into my day planner, so whoops. Who wants to help me get rid of my V card?

Yep. That was sexy. Not.

Johnny's words came back to her like an old voicemail she kept forgetting to erase. *You're just not hot, Piper. You'll make someone a good wife someday, but I just don't want to fuck you. I should want to fuck my wife, right? You need to find someone with lower standards.*

If that jerk hadn't wanted to sleep with her, was she seriously fooling herself that either of the two ungodly gorgeous men out there would want to? Maybe they were just being playful. And polite. She didn't understand their customs. Maybe their behavior was the norm in Bezakistan.

With a sigh, Piper exited the bathroom. Her curiosity got the best of her, and she peeked in the bedroom. She stopped in her tracks. *That* was a bedroom?

An enormous bed dominated the spacious room. Lush and gorgeously draped with silk and satin in shades of taupe, cream, and soft blue, this place was something straight out of a romantic movie. That bed wasn't meant for a peaceful night's slumber. It was meant for feats of athleticism. And maybe with more than two people.

She shook her head. Sex had definitely overtaken her brain.

Piper stepped out of her shoes, reveling in the plush carpet beneath her feet. Someone had laid a pretty white negligee across the champagne-colored duvet. The garment was her size. A silky eye mask sat on the nightstand, along with a small bag of her toiletries. Tooth brush, toothpaste, a moisturizer that hadn't been bought at the drugstore on clearance. She touched the beautifully constructed bottle. Designer. No doubt, the product was the top of the line.

The al Mussads knew how to take care of their charge. They would know how to take care of a woman, too. She just had to choose one and enjoy.

"Do you like it? Kade picked it out for you. He might not care about your office attire, but he certainly likes selecting lingerie." Rafe stood in the doorway, leaning his strong body against the portal. He'd loosened his tie and a bit of sun-kissed throat peeked through. His midnight black hair was slightly messy, making him look less like a prince and more like an everyday man. Almost approachable, even. She longed to touch his hair to see if it was as soft and lush as it looked. Rafe kept his hair ruthlessly short and under control, so she appreciated this look at the moment. Kade's was longer, brushing his earlobes, but always looked soft.

She was alone with Rafe. He had kissed her first. Maybe…

Her heart rate tripled as she met his stare. "It's beautiful. In fact, everything you've bought for me is. I don't know how I'll ever repay you."

He stepped forward, invading her space. "Do not concern yourself with repayment. Would you wish to insult me? I enjoy giving you nice things."

"Thank you," she said softly. "I want you to know I appreciate them."

"I am glad." Rafe smiled faintly. "Piper, Kade and I would like to talk to you."

She didn't want to talk just now. He stood so close. The last thing she wanted was another kindly lecture on what to expect in Bezakistan. And though she loved the fact that Rafe could talk about books and culture with her, she didn't want an intellectual discussion. She rose up on her toes, her lips meeting his for a long moment. Gosh, his lips were sinfully soft.

"Piper?" He pulled back slightly, his expression somewhere between concerned and confused.

She moved forward, her body softening against his. Without the heels, she felt so tiny against his tall, muscular frame. She had to stay on her toes to position her lips beneath his. "Rafe, I want you."

"Oh, Piper..." A shudder went through his body. "Those are such sweet words, *habibti*."

No, *he* was sweet. She nuzzled his neck, loving the way he smelled so spicy, exotic, and masculine. His skin was warm, and she wondered what it would be like to sleep against him, his body cradling hers. A deep longing went through her. One night. It was all she would have with him, but she would know how it felt to be held and wanted.

She caressed her way down to his waist, trying to pull his crisp white dress shirt from the waistband of his designer trousers so she could touch more skin.

"Piper," his voice was soft, but firm. "Wait, *habibti*. You must stop."

She kissed his jaw, trying to reach his lips. He stepped back, his hands warding her off rather than pulling her in.

Shock slapped her suddenly. She was making an idiot of herself.

Piper took an awkward step back, tripping over her own feet and landing on her backside. Humiliation swept through her, stinging her veins. She felt a hot flush race up her face.

"*Habibti*, let me help you." Rafe reached down to assist her, a graceful god taking pity on the mortal.

Piper shook her head, scooting further away, unwilling to look at him. "I'm fine. I'm really sorry. That was wrong of me."

It had been stupid. So dumb. Tears threatened. Of course he didn't want her. Johnny had told her that she wasn't sexy. She simply hadn't listened. Instead, she'd wanted. Craved. Taken his sweet kiss earlier to mean something more. She needed to be realistic. Wealthy, smart, royal... A man like Rafe would only look at her with charity in his eyes.

She needed to get him out of here, or better yet, she needed to go. She didn't belong in this room.

"What happened?" Kade walked in and bent to her, completing the perfect picture of horror. "Piper, what's wrong? Are you hurt?"

She put her hands up, holding the men at bay, still refusing to meet their gazes. "I'm fine. I'm just going to grab my things and find a smaller room to bed down."

She would do that. Grab *her* things, rather than all the gorgeous trappings the brothers had bought for her. The romantic bed and lacy nightie had danced through her head, creating the mirage that she was beautiful and Rafe might want her. But she wasn't beautiful. Sexy high heels didn't make her a sexy girl, just a walking disaster waiting to happen. When she got to her new place, she would find the Bezakistani equivalent of a mall and buy some sensible shoes. Flats. Shoes that didn't make her believe she'd become some femme fatale.

"This is your room. I made it ready for you. And I didn't just tell the servants what to do. I picked everything out. You do not like it?" Still on one knee, Kade held out his hand to her.

"It's beautiful." She hauled herself up, pulling up on the bed, but the silky duvet slid and just as she got to her knees, she slid right back down and into Kade's waiting arms. Darn it.

"I'm fine," she snapped. "You can put me down."

Kade didn't. He stood, rising to his feet without the aid of anything to balance him and never once tipping her over. He simply stood, cradling her in his arms. "I think not, Pandora. I think I might carry you around, lest you destroy the plane."

He teased her with a sexy little grin, but it didn't matter. Perhaps they found her amusing, charming in a quirky, offbeat way. Somehow that made her humiliation worse. Tears pooled in her eyes. "Please put me down."

"Damn it, Kade, you should not have said that to her." Rafe rolled his eyes at his brother.

Kade's arms tightened around her as he sank to the bed. "I meant nothing bad. What the hell happened? Why are you crying, Piper? If Rafe said something unkind, I can beat him."

"I should like to see you try," Rafe grumbled.

Maybe when they started arguing again, she could slip out and find a place to hide. "It's fine. I'm just tired."

"Piper kissed me." Rafe's words became soft, his shoulders relaxing as he looked down at her. "I was trying to explain the situation when she fell."

Kade's face went blank, and he set her down next to him on the bed. "That is twice you have kissed Rafe."

Shame swept over her. "I'm sorry. I know I didn't have any right to do it. I apologize and hope it doesn't make you think less of me. I'm not usually aggressive." They might just ship her right back to the States the minute they landed. She wondered if she still had a job at Black Oak Oil. Once Gavin heard how she'd behaved with his friends, not even her relationship with Hannah would save her.

"Do you not want to kiss me? Is it only Rafe you want?" Kade's handsome face twisted with worry as he asked the question.

"What?" She sat up straight, her eyes widening with confusion.

Rafe sat beside her, his weight making the bed dip. She had to scoot or she would have fallen into him. "Piper, I was looking for the words to tell you that I could not kiss you again without Kade. We had a horrible argument about it earlier. He threatened retribution if I took you by myself. He is very good at revenge." His hand came out, tracing a line down her arm. Everywhere he touched caused a shiver of sensuality. "I was not rejecting you, *habibti*. Never that. I simply intended to invite my brother to join us."

Her breath caught. *Both* of them? That was insane. She'd barely been kissed before and now she was going to lose her virginity to two gorgeous men? That just didn't happen. Unless they were making fun of her. Yeah, that definitely did happen. And it stung.

"Very funny, guys." She struggled to her feet. "I'll just go to the other bedroom. Good night."

When she got to Bezakistan, she could hang out with Tal and crunch her numbers. No more trying to break out of her shell and be a new woman. Lesson learned—painfully.

"You're not going anywhere." Kade gripped her arm and pulled her back to the bed, his face darkening. "Piper, I must know. If you have no interest in me, then tell me now. This cannot work if you do not allow me to try and win you over."

"What can't work?" She was brutally confused, especially when some unnamed emotion seemed to pass between the brothers.

Rafe sighed, his whole body rigid, as he rose and paced the floor. "You must understand the way relationships work in our family. It is traditional in wealthy Bezakistani families that brothers share."

Share? "A house? I can see where that makes financial sense."

Kade's lips curved up in the sexiest grin. "Yes. We share a house. But more."

Though his smile suggested otherwise, he couldn't possibly mean what she suspected. "You share cars?"

Rafe's nose wrinkled up. "I would never let him near any of my cars. He is a slob."

Kade shrugged. "I don't want your cars. You have old man taste."

"My Bentley is top of the line," Rafe argued.

"Boring." Kade made snoring sounds.

If she didn't stop them they would argue over who had the best car. "Are you telling me that you share girlfriends?"

They both directed their gazes to her once more, eyes sharp and focused, like two gorgeous predators who'd just been offered a tasty meal.

"Yes, *habibti*. And we are looking for a woman to share. We have not found one who satisfies us."

Piper huffed, her brain making connections. Lord, she could be so naïve. "So when Britney in Accounting said you took her out for a double dip, she wasn't talking about an ice cream cone."

They both flushed.

"She was a lovely girl, but a mere fling," Rafe said quickly with a dismissive wave.

"I have no idea who you're talking about," Kade said over his brother.

She doubted that. "Red hair, double D breasts?"

He shook his head. "I can only think of you."

Yep, he was the charmer. "Right. So…what exactly are you two saying? I don't understand how all this works."

Kade sighed and moved closer. "Piper, I've had a lot of women. I tried to bring them pleasure, but I was never tempted to develop our time together into anything more than a pleasurable romp. You're different."

She shook her head, refusing to go there with him. "I might be naïve, but I'm not dumb. You're a billionaire. You're royalty. I'm from a West Texas town that often smells like the backside of a horse. You don't have to promise me anything. I'm interested in physical relations, too."

That was as delicately as she could put it.

"You want to fuck?" Kade asked. He didn't seem to have a delicate bone in his body.

She flushed. She'd rarely heard that word uttered before she'd come to Dallas. "I find you both attractive."

"I do not know about fucking, *habibti*." Rafe's hands went to his dress shirt, pulling off his tie and unbuttoning his cuffs before he pulled the garment off. "But we can play a bit. We can please you. And we can certainly sleep beside you."

Kade's head came down on her shoulder. "Please, Piper. If you don't, I must sleep on the couch. I lost at cards with Rafe last night, so he gets the other bedroom. Think about my poor back. I'm practically an old man."

He was barely thirty. And she was struggling to take her eyes off Rafe's bare chest. They grew men awfully muscular in Bezakistan. Rafe's torso was more than worthy of Hollywood idol status. Every inch of the man was cut and defined. Broad shoulders tapered to a tight chest and lean waist. His skin was bronzed and perfect.

"Kiss her, Kade. She enjoys kissing."

Before she could take another breath, Kade tucked a finger under her chin, turned her head toward him, and he took her lips. Rafe's kiss had been soft, intimate, and toe-curling, but Kade's blasted her instantly with wicked sensuality. He went deep, seductive, alternately teasing and dominating.

For Piper, kissing had always been awkward. She'd never known what to do with herself. She'd tried moving this way or that, but always felt a bit inept. Not with either of these men. Even now, Kadir didn't give her a chance to feel graceless. He took control. His hands sank into her hair and overwhelmed her. She didn't fight the feeling, sinking into the lovely abyss with a sigh.

His tongue traced the seam of her lips, demanding entrance. She acquiesced, wanting to please him. She'd never really liked the feeling before, but Kade was far past anything she'd experienced. His tongue slid along hers, a decadent treat. She relaxed in his arms, drugged by the heady sensation.

"Touch him, *habibti*." Rafe moved in behind her on the bed, pressing his front to her back. His arms slid along hers, lighting up her skin where they touched. "He has been waiting for your touch. I know this because I have been waiting, too."

Kade kissed her cheek, his face cuddled against hers. "Touch me. I want to feel your hands everywhere."

It was like she'd suddenly been given the keys to the playground after being locked out all her life. Kade pulled his shirt off, proving he was every bit as glorious as his brother. He grabbed her hand and brought it to his chest before kissing her again.

Their mouths mated as she let her fingers explore the hard ridges of his torso. Two hands cupped her hips. Rafe. He wasn't waiting for a turn, and she suddenly realized there would be nothing civilized about this. Her single previous experience had been an almost intellectually-driven decision by Piper and the boy she'd dated in high school to make out because that was what teenagers did. It had been a disaster of gangly arms and legs, and they'd very politely decided to not take it any further.

She couldn't even think now. This had nothing to do with her intellect and everything to do with her body and, yes, her heart. She was crazy about these men. Rafe was smart and kind, and she loved talking to him. Kade was sweetly sexy while staunchly protective, always looking for any possible source of distress. She could see that now. That explained why he'd been so upset about the movers. He didn't like to see a woman hurt.

No, she couldn't keep them. They belonged with someone glamorous who would fit in their world. But she could have tonight.

Kade released her, and Rafe immediately moved in, turning her head toward him and taking her mouth in a voluptuous kiss. His tongue surged inside, playing against hers. A delicious thrill went through her as an ache started low, in between her legs. She sighed. This was longing, this deep desire that made her female parts swell and throb.

"You don't need this many clothes." Kade's hands worked the buttons of the blouse Rafe had insisted accentuated her hourglass figure. In seconds, the blouse drifted off her body, the feel of cotton replaced by strong warm hands on her flesh.

Before she knew what was happening, her bra dropped away as well.

Cool air caressed her skin briefly, and the enormity of this night crashed over her. She was half naked in a bed with two men. Two *gorgeous* men. She wasn't in their league, not even close. She probably needed to stop this and exercise some sanity.

As she opened her mouth to talk, Kade leaned over and licked her nipple. Instead of spouting reason, the only sound out of her mouth was a breathy gasp. Fire shot through her veins, sizzling her very skin as she looked down at his jet black hair and his mouth on her breast. He bit the nipple, a playful little nip, before his tongue soothed the tiny erotic pain. Piper had never once imagined that her breasts were so deeply connected to her other female parts, but every tug of his mouth sent a rush of heat to her womb.

"He likes breasts." Rafe's voice was a warm seduction in her ear. His hands slid to the fastening on her skirt, flicking it open. The sound of her zipper sliding down made her shiver. "I like them, too, but this is what I wish to see."

Rafe pulled her skirt down her hips and teased a bit of exposed skin along the edge of her underwear. Then Kade sucked her nipple into his mouth, and all thoughts of taking the sensible road and ending this fled. She had to experience their touch, craved the feeling of their hands and lips on her. So she let her fingers sink into Kade's hair and brought him closer to her skin.

As she did, Rafe's long fingers inched under the elastic of her panties, toward the heart of her femininity. "I want to see this. I must see you now."

"You want to see *that* part?" Piper felt herself flushing. "Rafe...can't we turn off the lights first?" That would make this so much easier.

Kade's head came up, his eyes hot, but he wore a wicked little smile on his face. "No one will turn off the lights, *habibti*. And tell me what part of your body Rafe is touching. I want to hear you."

She nearly forgot to breathe. Rafe's fingers skimmed over flesh no other man had felt, and suddenly she had to wonder why she'd waited so long. It felt really good. She was swollen and wet. Oh god, she was wet. She wiggled a little, trying to escape his digits, coming ever closer.

Kade's eyes went hard and he put his hands on her hips, holding her in place. "Stop struggling. What's wrong? Is he hurting you?"

"That is not what it feels like," Rafe said, slowly sliding his

65

fingers over her nub. What was it called? Clitoris. Yep. He was stimulating her clitoris. It wasn't like she'd never touched herself before, but when he did it, the sensations were way stronger than any she'd ever created. Piper knew she'd never been this wet. It probably wasn't normal.

Still preventing her escape, Kade gripped her, his lips hovering over her mouth. Rafe crowded her, too, his body heat like a furnace blast. They completely surrounded her.

"Tell me what's wrong?" Kade demanded.

She closed her eyes, so embarrassed she wanted to shrivel up and die. "I'm too moist. You know, down...there. I should go clean up."

She felt their chuckles. Kade's palm cradled her breast again. Rafe's lips brushed up her spine.

"You are worried about being too wet?" Rafe pinched her clitoris. "You think I would not like your pussy all wet and glistening for me? *Habibti*, I want you as wet as I can make you."

She felt a little dumb, but even as she said the words, her hips moved in a silent attempt to convince him to touch her with more force. "I don't know if that's sanitary."

"Little virgin. You *are* a virgin, right, Piper?" Kade crooned, then drew her nipple into his mouth.

She flushed from an overwhelming mix of embarrassment and arousal. Despite her insecurity, need swamped her with a dizzying wave. She moaned. "Yes."

"We thought so. This is lesson number one, *habibti*." Kade's hand slid down to join Rafe's. Two sets of fingers played down there, slipping through the petals of her sex. She gasped as one long, masculine finger worked its way into her channel. Then Kade drew his hand out. "There is nothing polite or sanitary about making love." He sucked his finger, slick with her juices, into his mouth. "Hmm, you taste like heaven."

"See, he likes how you taste. I know I will like it, too. Lie down and spread your legs for me. Let me get my mouth on you," Rafe insisted. "Let us show you how good we can make you feel. You've waited for so long, and you deserve something sweet. Let us please you."

She might be a virgin, but she wasn't stupid.

Piper fell back on the big bed. Rafe left her laying in her underwear, a cotton pair with rainbows on them. Crap, she really should have rethought her choice of undergarments.

"This will not do." Rafe pulled them off and tossed them aside with a shake of his head. "*Habibti,*' if I could open the windows at forty thousand feet and shove these out without depressurizing the plane, I would." He looked at Kade. "Did you not buy her suitable undergarments?"

Kade shook his head. "Just the lingerie. I see no need for her to own panties."

Piper came out of her sensual haze when she realized she was completely naked, and they were still fully dressed from the waist down. She crossed her arms over her chest self-consciously.

"You will not cover your breasts, Piper." Kade's voice came out on a low growl. "I want to look at you."

Rafe was a bit softer. "You're so beautiful, *habibti.* Let us see you in all your glory. You will find that Kadir is an impossible baby when he does not get his way. Do you really want him to pout or would you rather we give you the pleasure I promised?"

She had a choice. She could scamper off the bed and find that crappy pair of underwear or she could be the Piper she wanted to become. Brave. Fearless. Ready to take on any challenge. She'd used her responsibility as a shield for years. What she'd really been was afraid. She saw that now. She'd hidden behind shyness, and what did she have to show for it? A fiancé who'd walked away after barely kissing her. Of course getting her heart broken scared her. Already, Rafe and Kade had the power to tear her up emotionally.

But at least she would have felt *something.*

She forced her hands to her sides and was rewarded with a sunny smile from Kade. He cuddled close to her, his lips covering hers in a sweet little kiss. "Thank you, *habibti*. I want nothing between us. Now, ask Rafe for what you want. We need to hear you say the words."

Piper frowned. "You know what I want."

She was *so* not saying it.

Kade shrugged. "I am a very dense man. Ask my brothers."

He was a conniving man; that's what he was. But his brother was nodding, backing him up, even as he moved between her legs. The ache flared up as Rafe touched her sex again, his fingers playing in the hair there. "He is not smart. You will discover this for yourself. He will make the worst…partner of all of us."

"That I would not agree with." Kade sounded almost insulted.

Rafe put his nose right between her legs, right in her girl parts, and took a long whiff. Holy all-the-bad-things-she-shouldn't-say. "Give him what he wants, Piper. I find I am hungry. Then, darling girl, we must discuss grooming. When we reach Bezakistan, I must turn this charming forest into a desert. It is a cultural thing, of course."

She had no idea what he was talking about. He was playing with her labia, gently tugging one side and then the other into his mouth. It was maddening. She wanted, oh god, she wanted his tongue inside her. And she wasn't going to get it until she asked for it because they were horrible, mean, nasty men with amazing hands and mouths. Kade's fingers played with her nipples as he sent her another sinful grin.

"Please kiss me down under…there." There she'd said it.

Rafe's head came up. "Down under there? It almost sounds as though you want me to kiss you in Australia. That is a much longer flight."

She growled in frustration, a little feminine sound she'd never made before. *Jerks.* "I want you to kiss my… pink part."

Rafe nodded. "You have many of those. Kade, kiss her lips. She seems to want that."

Kade chuckled against her lips. "You must do better, *habibti*. The word is pussy. Tell him to eat your pussy. He is hungry to shove his tongue inside and eat you like a ripe fruit. You will come, Piper, all over his mouth, and he will feel ten feet tall. Say it."

She cringed a little. It wasn't a word a nice girl from West Texas said. But maybe nice girls didn't get to come. "Would you please eat... Oh, good lord, just eat my pussy, please."

Rafe smiled smugly. "With great pleasure."

She nearly screamed when his tongue shoved inside her. Pure pleasure flooded her system. Nothing had ever felt so intimate, so right, as having Rafiq al Mussad putting his mouth on her pussy. And Kade was right. With this experience, she had moved past blushing euphemisms like girl parts and, ugh, her flower. It was her pussy, and Rafe tongued hers, forcing her desire higher and higher. Every muscle in her body tensed, and breathing took a backseat to simply feeling. Her nipples beaded harder, and her clit throbbed. She fisted the lovely duvet and arched her back with a cry.

"Come for us, Piper. Have you ever come before?" Kade asked, his hand caressing her breasts.

She'd played a bit, little bursts of quick pleasure, but *nothing* like the tidal wave Rafe was building inside her.

"Never," she panted.

"I must be a part of this." Kade moved down her body. Rafe cupped her backside, pulling her up so he had full access to her pussy. He moved his head slightly, never letting up on the slide of his tongue in and out of her pussy, but allowing his brother to slip a hand over her clitoris. "We will be the first men to give this to you, Piper. You must not ever forget that. No matter how powerful the man in whose bed you sleep, we were the first to make you come."

He pinched her clit in perfect time to his brother's tongue

penetrating her, and Piper came apart. Pleasure reverberated through her, shaking her like an earthquake. No way to fight it, and why would she want to? She simply let it take her and throw her into the whims of ecstasy. The orgasm sizzled like a flash fire through her system, burning away the mouse she'd been before and leaving a woman in her place.

Panting, she lay back against the bed, her heart pounding in her chest. Her eyes fluttered closed as a sweet lethargy drugged her system.

"You liked that?" Kade asked, and she opened her eyes to see him smile down on her.

She nodded, certain that she would like the next part even more. She put her hands on Kade's strong shoulders, then looked at Rafe with pleading eyes. "Make love to me. Both of you. I want you so much."

A cloud passed over Rafe's face. "Piper, we want you, too."

He crawled to her other side. She could feel their erections straining in their pants. They really needed to get far more naked if she was going to get rid of her pesky hymen.

"Piper, we have to talk," Kade said gently.

Their hands were on her, but they weren't acting like lusty men who couldn't wait to take their woman. They were now keeping a healthy, almost embarrassing distance.

"You're a virgin." He nuzzled her cheek, but she didn't feel any sexual intent in his touch, just a sweet affection.

Because she wasn't some sexy thing who made a man crazy with lust. In the last few minutes, she'd thought maybe… But oh, god, they were just being nice, just killing time on a long flight. She'd come on to Rafe, and they'd felt sorry for the silly little virgin. They were amusing themselves at her expense.

"I think we should get to know each other better." Rafe's logic hit her system like an iceberg splitting the Titanic open and laying waste to everything inside. His tongue had been inside her body. How much more did he need to know? It was an excuse. He didn't want her. Or he didn't want the responsibility of taking her virginity. It was an old-fashioned idea and, for a moment, she wanted to argue with them, to tell them she could handle it.

"Let us hold you for a while." Kade wrapped a hand around her waist. "We will keep you close while we sleep. When we get home, we will sit and talk."

Right. They would talk about what a nice girl she was and how someday, some faceless, nameless, but really smart guy was going to see her for the beautiful woman she was, blah, blah, blah. This had meant so little to them, they hadn't even bothered to get naked. No, they'd stripped her to the bone and kept their pants on because they didn't want any more intimacy with her.

All the lush sensuality and wonder she'd felt just moments before turned to ash. "Get out."

Rafe's head came up. "Piper, everything will be fine, *habibti*. Rest. We will take care of you."

She was deeply aware that before they'd shown her how beautiful this could be, she would have acquiesced and taken what they offered. She would have enjoyed being cuddled between them like some fragile doll they were too afraid would break. Or some gift they meant to give to someone else because they didn't want it themselves. But she wasn't the same woman she'd been even a few hours ago. And she wasn't going to lie here, humiliated and vulnerable, so they could feel good about consoling the idiotic virgin. "I asked you to leave, Mr. al Mussad. Are you going to honor my wishes or are you going to stay here against my will?"

"Please don't do this. You do not understand." Rafe blanched as though he'd just realized she meant what she said. "*Habibti*, your virginity is important. It is precious."

She pushed her way up and grabbed the shimmering gown placed across the bed. If she didn't, they would argue and cajole until she gave in and hated herself all the more. She clutched the silky fabric to her breasts. "Fine. It's a precious flower. Excellent. I'm completely intact. You've done well. Now go away."

Kade frowned, rising to his feet and circling the bed. He would be the dangerous one. He would charm and cajole. She had to stand her ground against him. "I'm not going anywhere, Piper. You act as if we are rejecting you. We've done nothing of the sort."

She didn't want to argue semantics with them. She wasn't stupid. They could put it in a million flowery words and it amounted to the same thing: She was good enough to play with, but not tempting or pretty enough to make love to. She was deeply sure she would eventually discover that their rejection was a "cultural" thing. Well, she was heartily sick of hearing about their culture and all the ways she needed to change.

"I asked you to leave, Kadir. If you don't, I will. And I can assure you that when I get a chance to talk to the sheikh, I will certainly mention how his brothers treated me."

"I assure you my brother will be thrilled I managed to leave you intact," Kade snarled at her, getting into her space with a challenging stare. "He sure as fuck better be. I'm on edge right now, Piper. Denying myself is not something I suffer often or well. It would be best if you did not push me."

Everything that was female in her rose to his masculine challenge. She wouldn't have been surprised if he'd started beating his chest. "I think you don't have much trouble denying yourself, Kade, not when it comes to me. Just go away and find some other fool."

Kade's eyes flared, but his brother put a restraining hand on his chest.

"Stop. This can only end one of two ways, and both of them would be very bad for us. You must calm down. You cannot fight or fuck your way out of this. She needs time."

Rafe's very calm voice set her on edge. Piper kind of wanted the fight. At least if they fought with her, she could pretend that she roused the same emotions in them that they created in her. "I don't need time. I understand now. Just…leave."

She refused to go. Oh, that had been the original plan, but what they'd done was just mean. They'd manipulated her for some reason she couldn't understand. Maybe it had been a fun game to see just how far she would go. Maybe she would find herself on a plane right back to the States tomorrow because she'd proven to be immoral and not worthy of admission into their precious country. It didn't matter. Whatever was going to happen would simply happen. There wasn't a lot she could do about it now. Since they'd stripped her of every bit of her control, she wanted to stand her ground now and make them retreat.

Kade turned and stormed out, slamming the door behind him. Rafe picked up his shirt and shook his head.

"This is not how I would have ended the evening, *habibti*. Please reconsider. I can call Kade back. Let us hold you. This is all we can offer you now."

She wished he would just leave. "Please go. I'm tired. I need a shower."

His eyes narrowed slightly, and she saw plainly that he was forcing himself to walk away. "I will leave for the night, Piper. But do not think for a second that this discussion is over. It has just begun, and the minute the plane sets down, we will be in my country and playing by my rules. I might seem like the softest of my brothers, but never forget that I am a prince. Royalty has taught me to be ruthless, and I get what I want. Sleep well."

The door closed behind him, and he left Piper alone. With shaking hands, she walked to the shower. As much as she washed, she couldn't rid herself of the feel of their hands on her. When she finally slept, she dreamed that she was between them, wrapped in their love.

Chapter Five

The wheels of the plane touched down, jarring Kade from his deeply unrestful sleep. He sat up and wondered why he'd even tried to sleep in the uncomfortable as hell chair.

"We're here, sir. The limo is waiting to take you to the palace. The luggage will follow shortly. His Highness has been in touch with the pilot to make sure the flight went smoothly. He's expecting you all within the hour." The very competent hostess handed him a thermos of coffee.

He needed it. His head hurt and his back was going to need a serious adjustment. "Thank you. Is Ms. Glen awake?"

It was a stupid question. She wouldn't have stayed in bed during landing, but he couldn't exactly ask if Ms. Glen was still pissed as hell that he and Rafe couldn't fuck her last night.

The hostess smiled serenely. "She has already had breakfast and is looking lovely and fresh and ready to meet the sheikh."

The hostess walked away, and Kade sat back as the plane began the long roll down the runway. This airport was private. He didn't have to worry about paparazzi here. But once away from here, that would change quickly.

Rafe walked out looking a bit like Kade felt. His eyes were tired and there was a slope to his shoulders that let Kade know his brother hadn't slept well, either. "Piper isn't any happier this morning than she was last night. It is a good thing we 'forgot' to bring the suitcase of clothes she'd packed or I fear she would be right back in her dowdy wardrobe out of sheer spite."

It had been Kade's idea to leave behind the trunk of her old clothes. He'd made sure there were no mementos or special objects in the case. Just her old clothes that would help her cling to her old life. "All of this could have been avoided if our brother wasn't such a prick."

Rafe's phone rang. He grimaced. "Speak of the devil." He took his phone and hooked it into the conference room's sound system. Rafe clicked the answer button right before he shut the door so Piper wouldn't hear the conversation. She might just demand to be taken home if she did. "We've landed, Talib."

"Excellent." His brother's deep voice flowed out of the speakers.

Half the time Talib was his hero. The other half, he was everything Kade himself could never be. Self-sacrificing. Stalwart. True. He was the very image of the last sheikh, a man who had brought their country enormous wealth and who had fought off invaders almost all his life. "How is our little Piper doing? She is well?"

"She is pissed off," Kade shot back. For all that he loved his brother, he was still mad about not giving Piper what she needed last night. What fucking century were they in that the sheikh had to take her virginity?

He could almost see his brother's brow arching as his voice became coated with ice. "Piper is angry with the accommodations? They were not to her liking?"

Rafe sighed, sending Kade a glare. "Piper was overwhelmed with the plane. She was sweet and gracious with everyone we met. Once she settles in, she will represent the palace with true grace. Piper was upset because she does not understand our customs, and you will not allow me to properly explain them."

"How so?" A deep chuckle burst forth. "Ah, did you and Kade play a bit more than you should have? That explains Kadir's surliness. I've begun planning our handfasting banquet. It is only a few days away. You'll have your turn then. I must say, I'm a bit surprised you're this eager to bed Piper. She hardly seems your type. I rather thought I would have to fight you over wedding her."

Kade looked at Rafe, who had a little shit-eating grin on his face. He held up a hand when Kade was just about to question Tal's eyesight.

"We all know how short we are on time, brother. I understand your reasons for wanting Piper. She is intelligent and understands the chief business of our country. While she is very smart, she is also innocent of our very worldly ways. She will likely be content to live in peace and quiet. The women we previously discussed were all used to the glamorous life."

Ah. Now Kade understood. Tal was selecting their bride based on very strict criteria, and if there was one thing Tal wouldn't want it was a wife who would want to make headlines and cause gossip. Piper, while absolutely lovely and feminine, didn't possess the hard-edged conventional beauty associated with models, actresses, and jet-setting royals.

"Yes, I do believe she will be advantageous on many fronts." Self-satisfaction oozed from his voice. Tal got that tone when he negotiated a big deal or pushed through legislation he was proud of. "Now, why was she angry? Did you two frighten her?"

So he didn't know everything. "I told you before we suspected she was rather innocent. I can confirm that she's a virgin."

"That is excellent news."

"She doesn't want to be, and she's a little pissed off that she still is." And Kade's cock was definitely angry.

Rafe sent Kade his patented "shut the hell up and let me deal with him" look. "But we agreed that we would handle this following all of the traditions of our ancestors, including the fact that you must be the first to take our bride. Unfortunately, we could not explain that we'd whisked her away to be married to three princes and her maidenhead belonged to our oldest brother. I prefer to keep my head on my shoulders. I also was unsure if she would simply jump off the plane."

"She is a reasonable girl," Tal argued. "It's why I selected her. I doubt highly that she will throw a fit when she realizes she'll have three husbands to depend on and provide for her, and she will have a job unlike any she could have aspired to. Trust me. I know this girl. She never expected to have half so much. She will be grateful."

Kade very quietly slapped his hand to his forehead. His brother thought he knew Piper because he'd talked to her over the internet? He was wrong. He might know the business side of Piper, but he had no idea how sweet and hot the woman was. And how stubborn she could be. Kade had thought about her all night. Piper wasn't just going to let them walk all over her. She would fight for herself.

He wanted her. That was easy. Resisting was getting tougher every hour because he was learning to admire her. Even as she'd tossed him out of her bedroom last night, his dick had been hard, while his heart was getting soft. The last several days had been spent completely focused on Piper. He'd learned that she was quite smart and filled with resolve. She challenged him. Kade liked to be the playboy. His older brothers took care of the kingdom. They didn't need him, but Piper made him think he needed to take charge of something.

"I like this woman. I don't want her to be grateful," Kade said, aware his voice was more somber than usual. "I am grateful to her. I'll go along with this whole tradition thing, but I don't want her hurt."

Tal groaned a little, the sound coming over the speakers.

77

"How will she be hurt? This is a woman married to her job. We will give her that and more. She will have a family *and* a high-powered career. She will like being prized for her amazing brain. That woman knows more about the economics of energy than anyone I have spoken to. She has ideas that could change the way the world works. Trust me, when she realizes the power she wields, she won't care that we misrepresented ourselves a bit."

Rafe's eyes rolled. "I begin to doubt that. There is a quiet strength to her. I worry a deception could wound her pride."

"If we play this in anything but a traditional fashion, we leave ourselves open to Khalil challenging us in court." Tal's words dropped like a lodestone. "I know this seems archaic and barbaric and we should just negotiate with her, but the taking of a captive bride is our tradition and our law. Someday, we may find a way to refine it and bring it into the present century, but I've been more worried about our economy than our legal processes."

Kade couldn't disagree, but...

"Had we settled on a wealthy bride, she would have been prepared. Our marriage practices have been debated for decades." Rafe settled back in his chair. "Unfortunately, Piper knows nothing of our world. She could care less about pop culture. It will be up to us to wrap her in pleasure and affection so she does not wish to leave."

A long sigh came over the line. "She won't leave. I know what I'm doing. Just bring her here. I grow tired of waiting."

The line died. Kade leaned forward, so much falling into place. "He's never really seen her. He thinks she looks like that sad little photo on her driver's license. He truly believes he can bring her in, marry her, and then work with her like she's some sort of co-worker he won't have any emotional connection to. And that she will be so grateful, she won't care."

Rafe sat back in his chair, a weary look on his face. "You had not yet figured that out? I knew it the minute I realized who she was. She is beautiful, but does not possess the sort of beauty that shows up in a photograph. It's in her spirit, her smile, the way she moves. He has no idea what Piper is really like."

"What if she runs?" Kade couldn't stand the thought, but he would not bury his head in the sand. Anything was possible. Tal was right. They should have challenged the law long before now but many other pressing matters had taken precedence, and marriage had seemed a distant thing. And then Tal had been taken, upending their world. That week when the rebels held him had changed all their lives. Talib had left a happy, optimistic young royal, and he'd returned a cold, distant man. They'd all been merely existing since.

Now they had to deal with the real possibility that they could lose the crown—something their family had held for centuries.

They needed Piper for more reasons than simply holding on to their birthright. But perhaps Tal needed her most of all.

"It will be all right, Kadir." Rafe stood, straightening his suit. "We will convince her. But you and I must do it. Talib is no longer capable of truly loving a woman."

That so wasn't what he wanted to hear. "He's not dead inside. I know he isn't."

"I hope not. But we have to take care of her. I cannot allow Talib's cold heart to scar her. I care about her. I think I can love her. What happened last night nearly ripped me apart. We will manage this fucking travesty of a handfasting. Then she will be ours. We will give her every reason to stay. Are you in or out?"

There was a brisk knock on the door. Before he could answer, Rafe opened it, and Piper stepped through, her face a careful blank. She was gorgeous in the early morning light. Her brown hair shone richly. Her skin was a creamy pearl against the turquoise-colored dress she wore. The swell of her breasts made his cock hard.

"Do you have any information on how I can get to my apartment? I'd like a map, please." She said it with an even tone, but he couldn't help but notice that her hands shook.

"A limo will pick us up, Piper," Rafe replied.

"I'd rather take a taxi."

Kadir looked at her. She was solid. She wasn't some delicate flower, but her heart was far more fragile than anyone believed. He'd handled her all wrong last night. He'd acted like a child who'd had his toys taken away. He'd treated her like a plaything and not a beloved female.

Maybe it was time for Kadir al Mussad to grow up.

He followed his true instincts, the one that had nothing to do with testosterone and everything to do with his heart. He stood and crossed toward her, his heart lifting as her eyes flared. Yes, he wasn't always going to do what she expected. Rafe was right. It was up to them to keep her. Tal wanted her to save the kingdom. But Kade needed her to save him.

"What are you doing?" The question came out as a breathless huff.

He didn't give her a chance to move out of the way. He simply crowded her and wrapped his arms around her, hugging her close to his body, reveling in the feel of her against him. For the first time in his life, he simply allowed himself to enjoy a woman's softness for emotional reasons. It was funny. He might never have truly opened himself to her if she'd just been a girl he and his brother shared, but she was the one. He would be married to her and that meant he had a chance to sink into her. "You're coming with us, *habibti*. Don't bother complaining. I won't let you take a cab somewhere. Please, Piper, forgive me."

It took a moment. She was stiff in his arms, but then Rafe was there at her back, his hands on her, following Kade's lead for once.

"Forgive us, Piper," Rafe said quietly.

"There's nothing to forgive." Her words were soft, but there was a hard edge to them.

"We didn't mean to hurt you."

"I know. You just felt sorry for me."

He pressed her against his brother, trapping her between them. He pressed his pelvis against her stomach. "I feel sorry for me right now. I've been like this all night long."

"And me."

Piper's body nestled against his as Rafe pressed against her, too.

Her eyes were bright with unshed tears. "I don't understand. I wasn't going to turn you away."

Kade struggled to find the words to make her understand. "Piper, we care about you. We want you, but we want to make love to you when the time is right. Can you honestly tell me you had any thoughts of the future last night?"

Piper sighed, her body finally relaxing. She didn't wrap herself around them, but she stopped fighting. "I wasn't thinking at all. I was just feeling. And this morning, I'm glad we didn't go through with it. It would have been a mistake."

He forced her face up. She was so beautiful. "Yes, but I do not think we're on the same page yet. This is going to happen, Piper. We will come together when everything is as it should be. Do you remember how we explained last night that in our family, brothers must share a woman?"

Piper flushed. "Yes. It's not exactly the kind of thing a girl forgets."

"There are three brothers, *habibti*. Think about that." He kissed her quickly before she could pull away. Then he stepped back.

He deeply enjoyed the shocked look on her face.

The plane rolled to a peaceful stop, but he was pretty sure Piper's mind was still soaring.

"Come on then, love. It's time to meet your friend, Tal." Kade took her hand and started to lead her out of the plane.

"So I'm going to Tal's? Should I get my briefcase? Does he know I'm coming?"

Rafe walked behind them. "He knows. I have little doubt he

81

is waiting for you."

The plane door opened, and a blast of heat hit them. Piper gasped a little. He was sure it wasn't the last he'd hear of that sweet sound. She was in for a bit of a surprise.

* * * *

Talib stood in the heat, adjusting his tie yet again, wondering what he was doing. It was traditional to wait for guests in the receiving room, but Piper Glen was more than a guest. She would be mistress of this house if things worked out.

Three bodyguards stood behind him. All former US Special Forces. All recommended by his friend, Cole Burke. He almost never went anywhere now without his own small SEAL team. Every man was decked out for the occasion in a suit and those sunglasses that the US military seemed to hand out to their resident badasses.

"You have incoming, sir." Cooper Evans nodded toward the west hall.

Ah, his day was complete. He stared at his cousin, Khalil, a hungry beast if ever he saw one. Over the last few months he'd dropped some weight and the new gauntness to his features gave him the air of a jackal on the prowl. This handfasting to Piper must work out. Khalil was just waiting to pounce.

Alea frowned, moving from behind Landon Nix. The big former sergeant kept his eyes on Alea as though waiting for someone to make a move.

"I didn't tell him." Alea nodded their cousin's way. "But I think he suspects. I swear he has spies everywhere. I worry he has them even here in the palace."

It was probably a good idea to rerun background checks on everyone working in the palace. Once again, he worried that he was placing Piper in danger, but there was nothing he could do but try his utmost to protect her. He had to move forward.

To call Khalil a cousin was a misnomer. They were related

by blood in a distant fashion. Alea was his first cousin, born to his mother's sister. Khalil's family had branched off two generations back, his grandfather refusing to share a wife in the traditional fashion. He'd been given money and a place to live, but Tal often wondered if that was enough for the al Bashirs, who had been forced to give up the name al Mussad when their grandfather abdicated.

Khalil, the only living son left, gave Tal a polite bow, but there was no way to miss the daggers in his eyes.

No. Wealth and power weren't enough. Khalil wanted the throne. The question was how far would he go to get it? How far had he already gone? His suspicions about Khalil grew by the day. Tal just wished there was some way to prevent the bastard from ever meeting Piper.

"Can't you execute him or something?" Alea said, a frown on her face. She was dressed in a lovely skirt and blouse, but there was something stiff about the outfit that bothered Tal. Alea had always been a frilly bit of femininity in a house crowded with men. And then she'd been kidnapped. Tal often wondered if he would ever see that carefree girl again.

No, he would not, and he understood why better than anyone.

"We aren't barbarians, Alea. Though if I had any proof that Khalil betrayed his country, I would certainly plead for a swift trial."

"My sheikh." Khalil practically oozed menace even though his voice was perfectly even. "It is a glorious day, is it not?"

Patience. It required patience to weave a web. He could banish Khalil, but without proof of his perfidy, there would be a scandal, and the last thing he needed was Khalil to go to their enemies and stir trouble. Not when they were close to having a new queen and these green energy breakthroughs.

"It is, indeed," he called, then said more quietly to Alea, "You will recall our traditions regarding this event?"

She groaned. "And you say we aren't barbarians. Don't

expect me to help you."

"Alea," he warned.

"I know what's at stake, but I don't have to like it." She strode off.

Khalil watched her, his eyes too hot to be watching a cousin. "She is still pouting about the little incident in America?"

Patience. He only had so much of it. He moved forward, wrapping his hand around Khalil's throat after making damn sure they were out of view of the cameras. He shoved him against one of the lovely ornamental stone pillars that were so plentiful in the palace. Khalil's feet dangled. "She is not pouting. She was kidnapped, tortured, and forced to work in a brothel. If it hadn't been for the same man who saved me from radicals, she would still be there or worse. She would have been sold and used until she died. So if I ever hear you use the word 'pouting' again in relation to what our cousin suffered, I will prove to you that I can still be barbaric."

He set Khalil down.

"You are a pathetic dog, Talib, but I'll let it go for now." He straightened his suit. "I think I shall freshen up before I meet your future bride. We'll see if you can keep this one. I rather think not."

Khalil's thousand dollar shoes beat against the marbled floor as he strode off.

"You know, assassination gets a bad rap." Dane Mitchell was the largest of his personal security force and by far the most sarcastic. He was roughly six foot seven, with the build of a well-designed Mack Truck and a deep Southern accent.

"I appreciate the sentiment, my friend. Unfortunately, he has friends in the government." And mostly likely, well-placed contacts among the rebels. "Have you found anything out?"

In addition to being damn fine security, his little team was also being paid to track Khalil's movements and to try and find any dirt on the jackal that they could. Tal couldn't prove it, and hoped it wasn't true, but he was suspicious that Khalil had a hand in Tal's own kidnapping and torture six years before. If he ever had proof, well, assassination would be a blessing for Khalil. Tal had learned torture from the best. He would love to show his cousin just how quickly a strong man could break under the right pain.

"I found out he loves prostitutes. And not expensive ones. I have some pictures that would curdle your stomach. I kind of feel sorry for his wife. If you decide to get him thrown out of office, those pictures will do it. He spends all his time with prostitutes or doing some charity thing at a hospital. It's a 'save the children' thing from what I can tell. I guess he's trying to keep up a good image. It must be a great life for the fucker. Seriously, he's a total pervert."

Tal felt a little smile cross his face. He'd heard about his security detail's proclivities. There was a reason they fit so well in Bezakistan. "Many would say the same of us, my friend. Trust me. There has not been a handfasting ceremony here since my mother was captured by my fathers. Even in 1975, the press went mad, and they weren't as crazy then as they are now. The word perversion will be floating around quite a bit." He hoped it didn't deter or upset Piper.

Dane smiled, though on the big guy any smile looked a little like a shark baring his teeth. "We'll keep them off you and the little woman. Tell me something, Tal. Is any of this going to hurt her?"

He had to tread very carefully. Tal trusted these men, far more than he'd believed he would trust anyone past his blood again. But they had hard limits. They were deeply protective of women. And he hadn't missed the way they kept everyone off Alea. "She is going to be my bride. I would not allow her to be hurt."

"And you're sure about all this secrecy? I don't get it."

Tal didn't expect him to. Handfasting with a captive bride was a dumb, ridiculously old ritual. "Our marital customs are ancient laws, still on the books. Eventually I hope to have them, stricken or amended. But my country's government works slowly, and it's more concerned with ensuring our safety and economic well-being than fixing cultural problems."

A hint of a smile crossed Dane's face. "I actually rather like your government."

"Normally, I do as well. But now I must engage in this antiquated ritual or Khalil will inherit the throne. He will do anything he can to seize power. If he does, he will take over the oil wells and bleed this country dry. So, you see, my plan must work."

Landon slapped him on the back. "Then you better be damn charming, Sheikh. You better pull out your magic carpet and give her a ride, if you know what I mean."

He sighed. They made him laugh. They kept him somewhat grounded. It was often easier to be with them than it was his own brothers since they didn't remember him as he'd been before. "I will attempt to do this, but you should understand. I chose her for her brain. She is very smart, clever. I doubt that this will be some passionate match."

Cooper stared out of the open doors, his eyes going wide. "Who the hell is that? Dayum. That is the softest little bit of femininity I have seen in a while. Did this Piper intellectual girl bring along her hot sister?"

Tal stared out. The limo must have pulled up while he was wishing he could choke the breath out of Khalil. He couldn't miss the woman Cooper spoke about. She wore a sundress, the delicate material flowing around her knees like a handkerchief blowing in a summer breeze. On her feet were a pair of yellow heels. Stilettos. He was a sucker for stilettos. He especially loved them when they were settled on either side of his neck as he fucked his way into a soft, hot pussy.

His breath caught. His entire body stiffened, especially his cock. She was lovely. So soft. Her hair was brown, but shot through with reds and blondes that caught the light and practically gave her a damn halo. Except nowhere, in any ancient text, did angels have cleavage like hers. The dress had been selected to show off her plump, ripe breasts, the V-neck and the turquoise color of the gauzy material flattering her skin. She had on a pair of sunglasses, but even without seeing her eyes, he could tell she was gawking. Her gorgeous, full lips were slightly parted in awe as she took in the sights. Her mouth looked small. He would likely have to force his cock in, but she would have that same look on her face when she came.

Tal had to catch himself. What was he doing? His bride was here, and he was reacting to some bimbo his brothers had brought along. A gathering rage rode through his system. This had to be Kadir's doing. Rafiq wouldn't think to bring his latest girlfriend along when they were supposed to be focused on securing a bride.

Sure enough his youngest brother got out of the limo and was immediately all over the brunette.

His heart sank. Poor Piper. Had she been forced to watch Kade's behavior the whole trip? Was this how his brother meant to show him he wouldn't accept Tal's choice of bride?

"I will kill him." Piper deserved better than Kade's scorn. She might not be the most beautiful woman in the world, but she was sweet and smart and he was actually looking forward to having her as a companion. Over the last few months, he'd grown closer to the woman than any he had in years. He appreciated her quick wit and her soft heart. The woman with Kade was beautiful, but she likely didn't have half of Piper Glen's smarts. She might make his dick hard, but Piper would be his wife. *Their* wife. He would never allow his youngest brother to dishonor her this way again.

"Oh, wow. Uhm, boss, you told us she was kind of homely. We have two different versions of that word, man." Dane shook his head as Rafiq joined Kadir.

Rafe, his ultimately reasonable brother, the one he counted on, walked right up to Kade's little bit of honey-on-the-side and pulled her into his arms. He kissed her, his lips molding to hers before he broke it off and smiled. Rafe pointed up as he talked to her.

Tal knew exactly what his brother was saying. He was pointing out the architecture on the palace. He gave every visitor the same speech about the marble and arches, and the center of the palace that dated from the fifteenth century. But now he gave the speech with an intimate smile on his face as his hands tangled with the brunette's.

Rafe wouldn't dishonor their promised bride. Rafiq believed in his country's traditions. He was circumspect.

So…that gorgeous, curvy thing was his Piper?

Dane huffed behind him. "Holy shit, Tal. If she's your little smarty-pants bride, she doesn't look like an egghead."

Tal strode forward, his heart racing. No way. He'd seen her pictures. She was plain. She would engage his brain but not his heart. Careful. He'd been so fucking careful.

"Rafe?" He called out to his infinitely more reasonable brother. "The trip went well?"

Introduce me to my plain but brilliant bride. Tell me she's shy and still in the limo.

Kade's arm tightened around the brunette's waist. "Talib! It's good to see you."

He stopped, halting a few feet before her. "And you, brother." His youngest brother was the wild one. He loved Kadir. He did, but he worried about him, too. Still, he couldn't help but notice the way his youngest brother's hand slipped into the brunette's and her fingers curled around his.

"Talib, it is my greatest pleasure to introduce you to…" *Don't say Piper. Don't say Piper.* "…Piper Glen. I believe you two have been speaking. Piper, *habibti*, this is our brother, his Serene and Royal Highness the Sheikh of Bezakistan, otherwise known as Talib al Mussad."

She freed her hand and pulled her sunglasses off. Her blue eyes went wide and that truly magnificent chest swelled. "Tal?"

Fuck. Fuck. Fucking fuck fuck and a goddamn fucking duck. He'd only heard her voice a few times, but it was imprinted on his brain. That soft Texas twang with the hint of smarts and vulnerability. Piper. *His* Piper. His goddamn fucking virginal bride who would be his companion and who would rarely tempt his cock but never once move his soul.

Both were completely poleaxed because she was so beautiful.

"Hello, Piper. Yes, I am Sheikh Talib al Mussad. Or Tal, if you please." There was nothing else to do. He had to introduce himself. Funny. He'd thought this would be a prideful moment when he revealed himself to be so much more than she'd expected, and he found himself almost shy. He didn't show it, of course.

Her blue eyes took him in. "Talib. Of course. How stupid of me, but then I have been for months, it seems." She stopped, her shoulders slumping a little. "Or am I wrong? Are you my Tal?"

This was supposed to be a special moment, when she looked up to him. Instead, she looked betrayed. "Yes. I am Tal, Piper. How is your sister?"

He knew everything about her. He knew about her family and her love for Mindy. He'd already taken care of the girl's education, though Piper wouldn't realize that for a few days. He knew about his bride's upbringing. He knew what she liked and what she didn't.

Until now, he hadn't known how her eyes would pierce through him and see straight to his soul. He hadn't known how his cock would pound at the very sight of her.

Her whole face contorted as if in pain. "You're the third brother?"

Why did guilt roil in his gut? "Yes. It is good to meet you in person. I have enjoyed our talks over the internet. I am very eager to continue our discussions now that you are here."

Her eyes dropped away, studying the ground in front of her.

She didn't pull away from his brothers, but he could feel her confusion.

"You're the sheikh?" Her voice was a bleak monotone. "And you let me think you were just another researcher."

He couldn't let her win this argument. If he allowed his guilt to show, she would have the upper hand. It wasn't how he intended to begin a marriage. "Bezakistan is my country. I didn't lie to you, Piper. I work very hard for my country. This project means the world to me."

"Of course. I'd like to go to my apartment, please. When would you like my presentation? I need a few hours to settle in and get everything in order." She was cool and competent, that flustery feminine energy from before fleeing, leaving a somber woman in its place.

"Don't worry about that right now," Kade said. "You need to rest, *habibti*."

"I will show you to your rooms. Don't be angry with us. Let us explain about security measures. Talib cannot simply tell everyone who he is. And he really does the work he said he does. He has a master's degree in economics." Rafe's hand tangled in hers.

Her eyes went up, taking in the grandeur of the palace. "This is where I'm staying? Well, naturally." Sarcasm dripped, and she looked furious. Closed. "I'd like to rest now. I want to get my presentation ready. And what we discussed on the plane? It won't work. I'm not that girl. So you all need to rethink this because if I'm here for any reason other than the job, then I should just buy a plane ticket now and head home as soon as my presentation is over."

Oh, she was here for a job. She was here for the most important job he could think of. She was here to be their wife, to save his throne. It didn't matter how much she moved his cock. He had a crown to think of. She was going to be theirs. Her beauty and innate sensuality that tempted him so were problems he would deal with later.

He caught sight of Khalil, stalking behind the palace walls, his stare taking in Piper.

This was precisely why he hadn't wanted a woman who would move him. The idea of Khalil even looking at her as a potential way to get under his skin had his blood pressure rising. It would be hard enough to protect her with a cool head, but if his emotions came into play? He had to shield her from being a target for rebels and neighboring radicals. Everything rested on her soft shoulders.

He needed her wedded and bedded and pregnant as quickly as possible. He had no intention of hurting her, but he had no intention of letting her go.

"Please, allow me to show you to your rooms." It was time, perhaps, to play on everything he knew about her. "I apologize for the subterfuge. I wanted a thought partner in this process. Can you honestly tell me you would have spoken as openly as you did with me had you known who I am?"

Her eyes flared a little and then slid away from his. "Probably not. I think I called you an idiot on a couple of occasions."

He brought his fingers to her chin, forcing her to look up at him. "My math was faulty, and yours was correct. And you called me an ape with my head up my backside because I was being stubborn when you knew you were right." He sighed a little, letting his face fall, noting all the while that she utterly softened with every layer of guilt he heaped on her. "I loved our talks, Piper. Ask anyone in the palace. I set aside that time to work with you, and it was sacred. I walked out on a conference with the British Prime Minister because I had a call scheduled with you."

Yes, she was flustered again and that was right where he wanted her. And Rafe was a bastard because there was no doubt he'd dressed her for this occasion. The brilliantly colored sundress was lovely and modest, but he couldn't miss the swells of her breasts and the way her skin caught the sunlight. Rafe had trussed her up like a gorgeous bird ripe for the plucking.

"I would have waited," she murmured.

"But I could not." He let his hand drop. He was actually surprised that when he looked back on the incident, he meant every word he said. He could remember sitting there listening to the Prime Minister talk about deeply important issues and he'd been watching the clock, waiting for the seconds to tick by until he could talk to her, her slow accent soothing him. He sighed. "It does not matter. I will admit I brought you here for selfish reasons. I thought to dazzle you with everything I have to offer. I have obviously failed."

That gorgeous skin flushed, and he knew he had her. She just stared at him, clearly uncertain what to say.

"I will leave you be, Miss Glen. Again, I apologize for the deception. I can only hide behind my desire to begin a relationship on equal ground. Please allow my brothers to show you to the rooms I have prepared for you. I will leave you be until such time as we conduct business. I wish you good rest and please enjoy my country."

Tears pooled in her eyes, but he couldn't let those sway him. It was time to make his exit and allow the wonders of the palace and her own soft heart to work in his favor. He bowed politely and turned to go, Dane stepping in beside him, Landon and Cooper in flanking positions.

The big former SEAL had a frown on his face. "That was a pretty piece of manipulation if I ever saw one. You're a ruthless son of a bitch, Tal."

He walked forward. Dane wouldn't be the last person he pissed off. By the time this was over, he might lose everyone.

But he would keep his crown. One way or another.

Chapter Six

Three days later, Piper walked out of the conference room, her laptop in hand and her heart heavy.

Two days of meetings had been enough to tell her that everyone here took her opinion seriously. She'd met with CEOs, government officials, and a representative of the Kyoto Protocol's Clean Development Mechanism Executive Board. Tal had been with her in every meeting, deferring to her, allowing her to speak for the country. Gavin James had been present, introducing her as the representative for both Black Oak Oil and the country of Bezakistan.

And Gavin had been effusive in his praise for Talib al Mussad. Just the night before, he'd taken Piper to dinner and told her stories about the sheikh and his brothers. She didn't miss the fact that he spoke about his own lifestyle, too, and how much he enjoyed sharing Hannah with his brothers. Baby number three was due soon, and all three brothers were thrilled. They loved their wife. They had an amazing life full of joy and love. Piper was happy for the James family, but couldn't fathom why her employer had shared so much personal information about his marriage. He must not grasp that the al Mussad brothers merely wanted to take her to bed.

But she was sleeping alone, at least for now. Tonight, they intended to hold a banquet to both celebrate the official alliance between Black Oak and Bezakistan, as well as welcome her to their country. Rafe, Kade—and even Tal—had made it plain that afterward they would like it very much if she gave up her solitary bed for theirs. So far, she'd been demurring. But now… Piper sighed.

What was she doing? Was it really so important that Talib had hidden his full name from her? She actually understood why he'd done it, and it wasn't like her to hold a grudge. His subterfuge had hurt more than she'd believed possible, and she'd let that rule her actions since her arrival. Now, she was beginning to ask herself some hard questions. If he'd been anyone else, would she have been quite so upset? Had she been using her anger as an excuse to keep Tal at arm's length because she felt so out of her league? Piper wrinkled her nose. Likely so. And it probably wasn't fair to him. Or her. Coming to Bezakistan had been, at least in part, about opening herself up to new experiences. But the first thing she'd done was close herself off when fear gripped her.

With a sigh, Piper looked out over the balcony. Every turn in the palace was a surprise. She stopped and looked out over the city. She'd come so far from where she used to be. No more little towns or tiny office kingdoms for her. She'd been given actual apartments. As in more than one. She had a bedroom and a huge office space. And an assistant who constantly talked about how amazing Talib was.

"You are all right, Miss Glen?"

Tal's voice pulled her from her thoughts. She glanced back his way. He looked utterly perfect in his dark suit. The only hint that he wasn't completely civilized was the jagged scar that began under his ear and disappeared into his shirt collar along with the dark hunger that lurked in his stare.

She smiled. "Yes, sir. I was just watching the people go

by."

He stepped in beside her. It was the first time in days he'd willingly gotten close, and her whole system went on full alert. Rafe and Kade spent most of their days with her, but she could feel the distance now. They were polite, but more reserved than before. A sad atmosphere hovered around them because the al Mussad brothers were a take-it-or-leave-it deal. Accept one, accept them all, and she'd turned down the sheikh. Since then, she'd been firmly placed in the "look but don't touch" category and it hurt.

Piper didn't understand why Rafe and Kade had made an exception for Britney in Accounting. They'd taken her to bed without their eldest brother. Maybe Tal hadn't known about her. Or he hadn't wanted the woman. But Piper knew that, for whatever reason, he wanted her.

Still, she couldn't help but feel brutally manipulated.

"My ancestors built the palace to be at the center of the city. Much of this structure was redone, but the core has stood since the fifteenth century." A satisfied look passed over his handsome face. "Bezakistan is small, but we've withstood invaders from the Huns to Saddam Hussein. We did it with intelligence and efficient use of our natural resources. I hope we continue to do so. I pray we bring this country into a whole new world. We're on the precipice, Piper. We can do it. We can lead the world. Imagine it, a country utterly dependent on oil bringing about the change to green, renewable energy."

She had to grin because he was really good at selling the pure intentions stuff. "You'll make a fortune off the patents alone."

He turned, his smile flashing. "Naturally. I intend to be an innovator, not a fool. There is much money to be made, and I will have it for my people." He stopped, his expression turning somber. "Please tell me you are you coming to the banquet tonight. We are hosting it for you and your employer, you know."

"Of course I'll be there." As the only representative of Black Oak currently in the country, she didn't have much choice. With Hannah due soon, Gavin had returned to the States. "Rafe and Kade worked me over." In fact, they wouldn't let up. Everywhere she went, one of them was there to escort her. And to make her feel comfortable again. She looked up, and sure enough, Kade was standing at the door to the west wing of the palace. He didn't approach, just sent her a ridiculously sweet smile that made her blood pound. Before they had played naked games on the airplane, she never would have realized what that smile meant. Now she knew he was thinking about playing around, and in the dirtiest way. But at the moment, he wouldn't do a thing about it.

"I am sure they have tried to work you over, Piper. They would kill to work you over. I am the one holding them back. My brothers growl every time I walk in a room because they know that if it hadn't been for me, they would already be in your bed."

She flushed. She couldn't get used to how they talked openly about sex, especially between more than two people. Just the day before, she'd met their mother, and the lovely British woman had sighed when she talked about her four husbands. Four. Piper couldn't figure out where to put three men, much less four. Maybe they tag teamed, like in wrestling. "I don't think they're missing much by not being in my bed. I'm sure they told you that I'm not exactly experienced."

"They told me you were beautiful when you took your pleasure. They told me you were so hot they thought the plane would go up in flames. They told me they'd never wanted a woman the way they wanted you that night." His dark eyes held her. Of all three brothers, he was the most intense, the most magnetic.

Kade was the one who made her laugh, forced her to take everything less seriously...and made her think wicked thoughts. Rafe, with his sexy sophistication, was the one she could talk to about books and movies and all the sights she wanted to see, as well as the pleasures he yearned to give her.

And Tal? Tal was a mystery. He'd been her crush, but that man had been more down to earth. The Tal she'd known through instant messaging and computer chats had been teasing and playful and so smart, but she'd been able to argue with him. This Tal was intimidating, his features beautiful and slightly cold. And she couldn't stop looking at him, wondering what was going on in that head of his. He was pulling her in despite her best attempts to stay aloof.

He leaned in, his face softening so that cold edge to his beauty fled, leaving only the man behind. "Piper, you do not have a romantic interest at home, do you?"

She shook her head. She had the feeling he already knew that.

His fingers brushed across her face, skimming against her skin and making her shiver. "Then why won't you try seeing what could develop between us? Is it still me? I know you like my brothers. How can I convince you I will be good for you as well?"

Piper didn't know what to say, so she bit her lip and said nothing.

He moved in, invading her space, but she couldn't seem to move away. He was so close she could feel the heat of his skin. She had to force herself to breathe. It was insanity. She was a virgin. Not particularly by choice, but she'd never honestly cared enough about a man to go to bed with him. And that had been true of her fiancé, too. If she'd learned one thing since coming to Bezakistan, it was that she'd never been in love before. Being around the al Mussad brothers made her realize that because she was pretty sure she was falling head over heels for them.

"I want to kiss you, Piper. Don't tell me no." His eyes were right on her lips, looking down at them like he was a starving man and she was a ripe piece of fruit.

"But Kade..." His youngest brother was standing there, waiting for her. It didn't seem right.

"Oh, my lovely Piper, you don't understand us at all." He never turned away, merely kept those gorgeous dark eyes on her, but he spoke to his brother, his voice rising. "Kadir? May I kiss your girl?"

That sexy laugh of Kade's floated toward her. "Please, brother. Kiss her well. Make her ours."

Tal leaned in, his lips brushing hers. The first touch sparked against her skin, and she opened her mouth to gasp, but he cut off the sound, his tongue surging in.

Electricity pinged through her body. Piper lost the will to worry about what anyone would think. Her hands came up, clutching Tal as he pulled her close, drawing her into his heat. She would have to thank Rafe for forcing her into heels because otherwise poor Tal would be bent in half. Even with the four and a half inch stilettos, he still bent down to take her lips. He was the tallest of the brothers, his body the broadest as if he'd been built that way to wield authority. Through the rich material of his perfectly cut suit, she could feel how firm his muscular body was. Everything feminine inside her softened, yearned to get even closer. Ached to surrender.

His hands tangled in her hair, pulling it out of the staid bun she'd fashioned this morning. He didn't prevaricate. He didn't play. He tugged on her hair and dominated her mouth. She could feel the hard line of his erection against her belly.

Her breasts tingled, felt heavy—burned for his touch. And she was doing that thing again, getting wet and ready. It had practically become her default state since she'd met these men. Constantly surrounded by them, every day she endured a needy ache she didn't know quite how to combat. Every night, her solitary bed had become an exercise in broken sleep and frustration.

Tal gave her one last kiss, then released her. He took a deep breath, rubbing their foreheads together. His usually steady

98

voice was just the slightest bit shaky. "Piper, this banquet is meaningful to my brothers and me. Thank you for agreeing to come."

"You're welcome," she said automatically. Her brain was still mush after Tal's kiss.

"And afterward...will you come with us, allow us to see if we can make you happy? My brothers and I don't enter into relationships lightly, but we all want very much to be with you. I assure you, we will treat you like a queen."

She was on the precipice of something. Was it heaven or complete disaster? No clue. But could she live the rest of her life not knowing which it would have been? She'd always played it safe. She'd done the right thing and waited for something special.

If this wasn't special, she had no idea what the word meant. She realized this meant giving herself utterly to these three men, and she would never have imagined that she would want or care for all of them. But sometimes, she supposed, life took strange turns.

"Yes."

A slow smile crossed his lips, and he brushed his nose against hers. "I will do everything in my power to ensure you will not regret this. Now go and prepare for the banquet. I will look forward to this evening."

She took a step back and nearly fell on her backside, her heels wobbling beneath her. Tal caught her in his arms, pulling her back up and steadying her on her feet.

"Thanks," she said breathlessly.

"Pandora is back, I see." He smiled. "Yes, I know all about that. I think it's an apt nickname. You are certainly shaking up my world." He seemed satisfied that she wouldn't trip, and Kade now stood beside her, offering his arm. Tal graciously gave her up to his brother.

Kade took advantage. "Thank god, we're back to kissing." He thrust an arm around her waist and planted a perfect kiss on her cheek. "I've missed kissing you, cuddling you. And now I have to take you to Rafe. Maybe I won't tell him we're off the leash just yet."

Tal stopped at the door, turning to her. "And Piper, whatever happens, know that I will always take care of you."

* * * *

Rafe watched as Piper and Alea disappeared with the spa attendant. He rather wished he could go with her, watch as she was pampered and turned into the queen he knew she could be.

She'd said yes. Oh, she didn't know exactly all she was saying yes to, but such was the way of captive brides in Bezakistan. And weren't most relationships a bit like that anyway? When one started a relationship, there was no sure way of telling where it would go. Only this time, he knew damn well it would lead to marriage, and he knew he could make Piper happy. He would do everything in his power to make her so.

He turned and walked out of the lush spa. It catered to Bezakistan's elite and the wealthy tourists who visited. He nodded to the security team who had followed discretely behind him as he'd led Piper and his cousin to the spa. Three stayed behind and one peeled off to follow Rafe as he walked down the street.

Normally they all trailed him, but he wasn't about to leave Piper unprotected. Talib had been insistent on her security protocols. There was no way to miss how worried Tal was about Piper's welfare. His brother was a bit paranoid, anyway. It was understandable. After what Tal had endured, Rafe was surprised he went out at all.

"I see you are determined to take care of your last-chance girl," a distinctly sarcastic voice said.

Rafe sighed. He wanted to go and make his preparations for the upcoming night. He didn't want to deal with Khalil.

"Cousin," he acknowledged and tried to move on.

Khalil stepped out of the shop he'd been in and moved in front of Rafe. "Can't I offer my felicitations on your engagement?"

It was always a dance with Khalil. There was always some hidden meaning to his words. Rafe had begun to wonder if his cousin's words didn't often hide daggers as well. "We are not engaged."

"I am not naïve, cousin. The girl might be, but we both know this banquet isn't simply to celebrate a business relationship or to welcome her. I suspect some very quiet, sacred words will be exchanged during the event, will they not? Are you trying to hide her and your coming handfasting from the press?"

Of course they wanted to keep the press out of this as much as possible. Piper needed to be eased into her new role. Hell, they had to figure out a way to explain her new role, but they were all terrified she would run. Rafe's conscience plagued him. It wasn't a question of whether she would she feel betrayed, but simply how much. But it wasn't as if they intended to hurt her. Indeed, they would ask her to marry them...just later, after a few weeks of getting to know each other intimately. If the press wasn't involved, then Piper might not have to know she'd been more married than not all along.

"She is simply a guest of the sheikh, important because she is helping him with the Clean Energy Project, which could be a great boon for the whole nation."

Khalil's dark eyes narrowed. "And none of you are sleeping with the girl?"

Not yet they weren't. He could answer that question with complete truth. His aching cock was proof of how much he wasn't sleeping with Piper. "Though I admit she is quite lovely, we are not sleeping with her. You know as well as I do that we must find a bride, and look we shall. We are quite aware that our time is running out."

It was best to acknowledge the facts. If Khalil believed he was dodging, the man would get crafty.

A predatory grin crossed Khalil's face. He was almost too thin, and his eyes were marked with dark circles, making him look older than his forty-five years. "Yes, and the parliament also knows the clock is ticking down. Perhaps you would not have this trouble if you would open discussions to change our barbaric laws."

And the minute they did, radical religious groups would be all over it, attempting to rip out all language that made Bezakistan a secular country with a free market economy. Certain lobbyists would also love to challenge the way wealth was distributed, taking from the mere citizens and putting even more into their own already rich-beyond-compare pockets.

And Khalil would attempt to do what his father couldn't. Take back power and place it in his own tyrannical hands.

"Too late now, so we shall muddle through." Now it was time for a bit of deception. "Kade is going to talk to the Dutch ambassador about a possible meeting with their princess. We have a bit of time left. And we are not hideous trolls. We can always buy a bride if need be."

Khalil's shoulders moved in a lazy shrug. "You probably can, and I can see Talib doing that. He's a ruthless bastard. I'm certain he has a checklist and would simply order one off the internet if he could. Kadir just wants a pretty place to put his dick on a regular basis. But you, my cousin, you are the difficult one. You are the one who, what is the phrase? Yes, you are the one who thinks with your heart, not your head. Not so smart but true. You think I don't see the way you look at that fluffy piece of American ass?"

Before he could think, he had his cousin's shirt wadded in his hands, hauling him forward. "You don't *ever* speak of her that way. You will mind your manners around her or we will have a problem, you and I."

Khalil's voice was pure menace. "Yes, I can see she is just

102

an important guest for her knowledge of energy and economics. You would never be so foolish as to marry someone for anything but political reasons, and an American would be a terrible idea. You have certainly thought this through."

Rafe let him go. Damn, he'd made a terrible mistake. He'd lost his cool and given away something important. He took a step back, his mind racing, trying to find a way out of the trap Khalil had baited him into. "I won't have any woman treated with disrespect, especially one who is our guest. I confess, I like Piper very much. We discussed her as a potential bride, if you must know. But Talib will never marry a commoner. So I am thinking of making Piper my mistress. If the others are going to force me into a marriage I don't want, then I will find love where I can. I will pretend to be in love with our bride, but my mistress will always have my heart."

"If you say so, Rafiq." Khalil smiled smugly. "I will look forward to this evening. And I will be watching."

Chapter Seven

Piper looked down over the banquet space. The grand hall had been completely transformed from cool and elegant to a rich, decadent space. The lights were shining, shimmering. The room was beyond splendid. The smell of spice filled the air, reminding Piper that she'd skipped lunch. The food had been brought to her, a sumptuous feast laid out for her pleasure. As she'd thought the words, she'd realized they could apply to her as well. Later this evening, she would be laid out for the al Mussad brothers, and she'd worried she was a little too sumptuous for them.

Her hands shook. She'd spent a whole afternoon preparing, ostensibly for the banquet, but she knew what the whole spa experience had really been about. She hadn't needed a Brazilian wax to sit with dignitaries and talk economics.

"Are you all right?" Alea appeared at her side, wearing a long flowing dress in a midnight blue color. The draping of the dress perfectly suited her petite figure. She was a beauty with golden skin and deep brown eyes. Her rich chocolate-colored hair was chicly cut in a long bob that brushed the tops of her shoulders. She was so unlike the other women Piper had met.

Alea was kind but deeply aloof. Now that lovely face frowned at Piper. "I can get you out of here. You don't have to stay."

Piper's heart sank a little. Alea had been like this all afternoon, offering Piper transportation out of the country every time she made mention of her home or a little thing that was different between the two countries. Alea seemed genuinely fond of her cousins, but Piper couldn't overlook the fact that the girl seemed determined to whisk her away from them. "I chose to be here, you know. This is what I want."

Alea's eyes widened. "Are you sure?"

Piper didn't want to play all the social games others seemed to adore. She just liked things laid out. "I chose to come to Bezakistan, and I'll be staying for a bit. I don't know why you don't like me, but it shouldn't be because you think I'm some sort of social climber. Tal and I share a passion for our project, and I'd like to get to know Rafe and Kade a bit more, too." She felt her face flame and hurried to finish, hoping Alea didn't notice. "I promise I'll be good to them."

Alea glanced down at the ballroom where at least a hundred people mingled. "I know what they have planned tonight with you. They don't deserve you." While Piper was busy sucking in a shocked breath, Alea turned, her hard beauty softening for the first time. "Piper, I apologize if I made you think I don't like you. The last few years have been hard on my manners. I've become isolated and cynical. I like being around you very much, and I wouldn't want to see you hurt."

Piper frowned, trepidation tightening her belly. "You think they would hurt me?"

"Not physically. They would never do that, but I worry that our world is a bit less civilized than yours, filled with a tad more intrigue. And you are perhaps too honest and forthright."

"Look, I have no intentions of getting involved in palace intrigues. I just like your cousins a lot." *I might be falling in love with them.* A dangerous thought, but she didn't lie to herself. She was falling for them each because of their

105

individual ways.

Alea stepped back in the shadows, pulling Piper along, her voice dropping to a whisper. "If you become involved, there will be no way to escape the politics. My cousins think they can protect you, but I'm living proof they cannot. Tal especially should know better."

"What do you mean?" There was something about the desperation in Alea's voice that made Piper reach out to her, holding the woman's hand.

Alea was stiff for a moment as though the intimacy was wholly unwanted, but she relaxed and threaded their fingers together, a moment of sweet sisterhood. "You could be so good for them, but I worry for you. Do you know about what happened to Talib? Do you know why he has that scar on his neck?"

The long jagged scar was a ghostly white line that ran from just below his ear and disappeared under his shirt. She'd longed to trace that scar and have him tell her the story. She'd made it up in her head, a story of boyhood clumsiness.

"He was kidnapped by radicals, held and tortured for days."

Piper gasped. "Tortured?"

"They kept him in a warehouse just outside the country. Rafe was supposed to bring millions of dollars. He paid the ransom, but they wanted more. They wanted for us to declare our constitution dead. Rafe was forced to refuse. They set my cousin's execution date. They were going to televise it. Luckily, the US government wasn't at all interested in allowing our country to fall to radicals. A Navy SEAL team located and rescued Tal. They lost several men and one of the team members had to smuggle Tal back into the country."

"I had no idea." She wasn't up on world politics. She tended to stay in her own sheltered corner. What had Tal gone through? What horrors had he faced?

Alea's voice dropped to a mere whisper. "I was taken as well."

"By the same radicals?"

She shook her head. "By slavers, but I have my suspicions. My cousins believe that it was a coincidence, but I don't think so. I was lured to the place of my kidnapping by a note from the Bezakistani Embassy. My cousins think I was simply taken at random, and I don't have proof, but there are very few people with access to that particular stationary. I don't want to delve into what happened. Just know that the politics, the pain, are not limited to my cousins. The people who would take down this government will use anyone they care about."

"Princess?" A deep voice rumbled through the quiet, causing Alea to jump.

"Dane. You frightened me." She took a deep breath, but straightened up to her full height, a stubborn tilt to her jaw. "Since when does a bodyguard interrupt the royal family's private meetings?"

The enormous bodyguard's stark blue eyes narrowed. Piper had been introduced to Dane by Talib a few days before. He'd been pleasant and polite, but now he looked dangerous. "Since the princess became reckless and threatens her cousins' plans."

"Don't you dare question my loyalty to this family or my country, soldier. You know nothing." Alea turned and stormed away.

Dane seemed to deflate, his shoulders slumping. "Ms. Glen, I apologize for the scene. The princess isn't fond of me. She only really gets along with Landon. Coop and I are a little too Neanderthal for her tastes. If you would allow me to escort you, the sheikh requests your presence in the main hall. There are a few people he would like you to meet."

Piper was shaken by the conversation with Alea, but it had oddly crystallized her determination to go on with the evening. Clearly, Talib had his reasons for being aloof. He'd been through hell. Yet he was still gentle with her. The brothers had more difficulty to shoulder than she'd imagined, but they treated her with great care. The thought warmed her.

And Alea was wrong. She wasn't important enough to be brought into their politics. The relationship she was entering into would be kept quiet. She would almost be their dirty little secret.

But she was willing to risk it—and her heart—for a night or two with them.

She stepped forward and took Dane's arm, allowing him to lead her down the stairs.

"They're good men, you know," Dane said.

Piper glanced up at the rough former SEAL. "I've found them to be."

"They'll do everything they can to keep you safe. And so will I. After tonight, you'll be a high priority."

She blushed. Did everyone have to know about their fling? "I don't know about that. I don't need any added attention."

"Like it or not, if you follow through with what the sheikh wants, you will be important."

"Maybe for a little while."

"Forever, Piper. I hope I can call you Piper. Just know that we're going to be here to take care of you, the same way we watch out for the brat princess."

Piper sighed. "She's not a brat. She's been through a lot."

"We all go through a lot, Piper. How we handle the pain we've been dealt is the way we're measured in life. We can take it and let it mold us into better people or we can allow it to tear us down. The princess hasn't figured out which way she's going yet. I'm not the only one who would help her, but she shuts everyone out."

"Piper!" Kade's voice rang out over the ballroom floor. His face lit up as he strode across the room. His brother joined him, Rafe peeling away from the crowd. They were perfect in their tuxedoes. Kade was broad and so masculine she nearly sighed. Rafe looked like he'd just prowled off the cover of a magazine.

Dane smiled, his mouth quirking up. "I can see you're going to be in good hands. Just remember, Piper, my team is here for you should you need help. We take care of this family."

He stepped back as Kade and Rafe descended, both reaching for her hands. She wasn't family, but just for tonight, she felt like she belonged. It was a lovely feeling.

* * * *

Talib turned slightly as the American ambassador said something about trade agreements. It was the kind of thing he should pay close attention to, but Piper was walking down the stairs on the arm of his bodyguard. A brutal flash of jealousy split his soul. He had the sudden, almost overwhelming urge to plant his fist in Dane's face. His hand was on her arm, guiding her down the stairs. She was wearing a white gown that skimmed her curves and molded to her breasts, the fabric looking almost transparent in certain lights as it shimmered.

He was going to kill Rafe. No doubt his middle brother had picked the gown and now every fucking man in the place was going to look at their bride-to-be's breasts. Rafe might enjoy treating her like a Barbie doll, but after tonight she would be a much more modest doll.

His brothers met her at the bottom of the stairs. Piper's smile lit up the room, her blue eyes dancing happily as she took in the sights. Talib felt his heart nearly stop. Her hair was flowing over her shoulders, her skin glowing.

"Excuse me, Mr. Ambassador." Without a look back, he walked away from the man, but not toward Piper. He needed a moment alone. The last few days hadn't gone as he'd assumed they would. He'd been so sure when Piper arrived that he would see her, satisfy his curiosity, enjoy a few intellectual discussions, then put her to the back of his mind until she became their concubine. After that, he meant to continue his day-to-day life without really thinking about her.

He strode past the throng of people, needing some air. Nothing was working out as planned. He wasn't supposed to be obsessed with Piper, or burn to pin her body under his and fuck her half the night. But he couldn't fool himself for a minute longer. He'd spent the last six years with his emotions buried deep, and they seemed to be bubbling to the surface now. Because of her.

He opened the French doors that led to the balcony and overlooked the garden where he and his brothers had played as children, their mother watching over them with her gentle smile. He was far from the child he'd been.

He caught sight of Landon's broad figure at the door, a silent sentinel. This was his life now. Guarded constantly. How could he think about bringing Piper into this? If his enemies ever caught wind of the unexpected depth of his desire for her, they wouldn't hesitate to use her against him.

But he had no choice and he knew it. He had to hold himself apart from her, make everyone, even Piper, believe he was indifferent. He wasn't going to lose years of progress because he was worried he might break her heart. He had to harden his own. What he was feeling wasn't love, just a perfectly normal sentiment for the woman he was about to marry, coupled with a hearty dose of lust.

Once he'd fucked her, he would see that she was just like every other female, and he could settle into a pleasant friendship and leave her heart to his brothers.

He glanced around, realizing that he was being an idiot. Alea was distracting Khalil at the moment, as planned. Now it was time. He pulled his phone out and texted Rafe to bring Piper to him. Rafe knew what to do.

Mere minutes passed before the door opened and Piper walked through. Her eyes widened as she took in the garden. This hadn't been part of her tour. It was a very private part of the palace connected to his rooms. Piper had been shown much smaller guest rooms, but after tonight she would reside in the family rooms, a set of opulent apartments fit for a queen. And he would visit her there often until he was assured his line would continue.

And otherwise they would live separate lives.

"This is so beautiful," Piper said, looking over the gardens. The silvery moonlight gave the space an almost haunted look.

She was a beautiful thing. How could he have ever thought her plain? He'd taken one look at a picture on a government document and decided she wasn't lovely. Her features taken one by one were unremarkable, but she practically glowed in person, her loveliness a function of her personality and kind spirit.

"We used to play here as children." Rafe didn't seem to have Tal's reticence. He wound an arm around her waist and cuddled his front to her back, his chin resting on her shoulder. "Kade tried to climb the palms from the yard to the balcony. He got stuck there once and our fathers had to rescue him."

Piper was turned away from him, but Tal could hear the smile in her voice. "It's so odd to hear you talk about having four fathers."

"They were great men, happy men. I miss them all dearly. They have all passed on now. We didn't get away with much, but we were always taken care of." He paused for a moment. "And our mother always knew she was loved."

His mother had been the daughter of an English aristocrat. His fathers had taken one look at her and known she would be theirs. They had actually stolen her, smuggled her out of the country, almost causing an international incident, but by the time she'd emerged from their concubine period, she'd been sated and happy and ready to play the gracious queen.

He had to hope Rafe and Kade could do the same with Piper.

The doors opened again, and Kade walked in with their secret guests of honor. Two men. The head of Congress and the country's highest appointed judge. Both were necessary for the ceremony to be legal, and both would be very discreet.

Piper looked up, pulling away from Rafe when she realized

they weren't alone.

They were doing the right thing. If they sat her down and tried to talk to her in a logical fashion now, it would take too long. Her natural caution would win that war. If she thought for a moment that the world would know about her relationship with three men, she would likely run. She wouldn't be able to handle the pressure all at once, but after she'd been eased into it and shown how good it could be, she would end up happy, like their mother.

Though he would be nothing like their fathers.

"Sheikh, it is my deepest honor to officiate at this grand day." The judge shook his hand. It had been his father who had married Talib's parents. He spoke in Arabic, the same language that would bind Piper to them in mere minutes. It was a language she didn't understand in the least, making everything so much easier, especially since her consent wasn't required for thirty days. By then they would have wrapped her in pleasure and luxury, and she would never leave them.

"Thank you both for coming and for your discretion. My brothers and I would love to keep this quiet until the actual wedding day. If the press got hold of this, our bride could be hurt, and we would like to avoid that." He spoke in Arabic as well.

The Prime Minister nodded. "We all agree. And no matter what Khalil says, she's a perfect queen. I've found her to be incredibly intelligent, and she has an endearing manner. She can be taught to deal with the press."

Fucking Khalil. He cursed the day his cousin had been elected to a seat in parliament. He'd been a pain in Tal's ass ever since. "Is his chief objection that she's a commoner?"

Tal knew what his real objection was, that she would ensure the al Mussad line continued to rule. But Khalil needed a logical argument, so he'd tried to invent one.

"I believe he's upset that she's an American. Some suggest they already have too much influence here. Between Black Oak

Oil and your security team, you surround yourself with Americans, Your Highness."

Tal shook his head. "And Americans have saved our asses time and time again. I'm not going to let my cousin's bigotry influence my security force or my choice of a bride. As for going into business with Black Oak, no one complains when the shareholder checks come in." There were some in Bezakistan who lived off shareholder checks alone. It was a moot point. "Can we finish the ritual quickly? I have a bride to claim."

The other men laughed, and the Prime Minister nodded.

His cock hardened at the thought of Piper naked in his bed, spread out for his pleasure. Not that it spent much time in a relaxed position anymore. Since Piper had come to the palace, Tal found himself in a constant state of arousal. He glanced back and found his brothers each watching Piper with a hungry look in their eyes.

She was in for an interesting night.

He reached out, gesturing for Piper to come forward. Both of his brothers tensed, well aware of the gravity of the moment. He switched to English. "Piper, my dear, come here. I would like for you to meet His Honor, Judge Nejem and you've met Prime Minister al Feid."

Her smile was wide with none of the easy pretension of a longtime socialite. "It's so good to see you again, Prime Minister. And Your Honor, it's a pleasure."

Judge Nejem took her hand in both of his, his eyes getting a little misty. "She reminds me of my own sweet girl," he said in Arabic.

Kade stepped up. "Sorry, *habibti*, the judge only speaks Arabic, but he's pleased to meet you as well. He says you remind him of his daughter. She's a lawyer following in her father's footsteps."

Piper blushed. "Please tell him he honors me."

The judge spoke the Queen's English with a perfect accent, but now he merely nodded and played his part. Tal kept Piper's hand in his while Judge Nejem spoke to the brothers, intoning the ancient words that would bind them together. "Princes of the Desert, do you take this woman as your concubine with the promise to make her your wife in thirty days should she assent? Do you promise to make her the center of your world, the sun that warms your family? Do you promise to protect her and ensure her happiness?"

Kade stepped forward, placing his hand on Piper's shoulder. He was solemn as he replied in his mother tongue. "I do so promise."

Piper looked around as though figuring out something important was happening. She frowned, but remained silent.

"I do so promise," Rafe said, pressing a kiss to her temple.

All eyes shifted to him. His throat felt almost unaccountably swollen. He had to push the words out. "I do so promise."

The judge squeezed her hand. "So be it. Take your concubine. Bind her to you. Make her long to be your wife. I will be back in thirty days for her answer. The best of luck to you all."

He let Piper's hand go and nodded, turning and walking out.

"Uhm, did I offend him?" Piper asked.

The Prime Minister laughed, the sound booming. "Absolutely not, dear. He welcomed you to Bezakistan. He was honored to meet you. I wish you all the best. Your Highness, please let me know if I can help you in any way."

He left and they were alone with their brand new concubine. Their almost wife.

According to all the laws of their country, she was theirs. Theirs to care for. Theirs to protect.

Theirs to fuck.

The banquet went on behind him, but Tal was only thinking of one thing. His cock pulsed in his slacks.

"They were so nice," Piper said, turning to Kade. "I'm

hungry. Can we try the tabouli?"

They walked in, talking about the dinner yet to come.

It was going to be a long few hours before they could sequester her alone with them for the night.

Chapter Eight

Piper seriously thought about running. She could just shuck the Givenchy shoes Rafe had insisted on and run like hell.

But where would she run to? Her crappy apartment? Her lonely life?

She stood in the doorway of Talib's master suite and everything in her felt electric. Her heart pounded. Her breath shuddered. Her female parts throbbed. This was it.

"Piper, please come in." Tal stood in the hallway, his smile warm, his hand gesturing her inside.

She forced her feet to move. The wine she'd indulged in was a pleasant warmth in her belly. Twenty-five years and she hadn't managed what would happen next. Twenty-five lonely years without male flesh pressed against hers. The night she'd spent with Rafe and Kade had been one of the best of her life. She could still feel the way her whole body had tightened, the blood pounding through her system, reminding her she was alive.

She wanted more.

A hand pressed against her back. "*Habibti*, you're here."

Kade's smooth tones soothed her, reminding her she

wouldn't be alone with Talib, who both intrigued and scared her. Not because she was worried he would hurt her, but he was so charismatic, she worried about her heart. Kade was different. Kade had spent days and days convincing her that he wanted her. Of course it wasn't long term, but Kade's desire was real and she'd grown comfortable in his presence. Same with Rafe.

She wasn't so sure about Tal. She knew he liked her. She knew he and his brothers shared. What if he was only willing to make love to her because Rafe and Kade wanted her? Tonight should be simple, but her pride kept complicating matters.

She felt another hand on her waist. Rafe. "Piper, beloved, please come with us."

How could she possibly deny them? They were so sweet. Rafe had spent days teaching her how to fit in. Kade had made her laugh even when she'd been so stressed she'd thought she would break. And Talib had been her friend for months, trading barbs online about their research and making her feel like she had something special to contribute. Even this week, he'd deferred to her on economic matters. It would have been so easy for him to take control of the meetings, but he'd allowed her the power.

She wasn't sure he would give her any power tonight. She'd lost her power the moment she'd said yes. Now she would belong to them for the night.

Two hands cradled hers. Rafe and Kade. They gave her such strength.

"Did you enjoy the banquet?" Rafe breathed the words against her ear.

She'd loved every minute of it. It had been worlds away from anything she'd ever experienced. She'd eaten new food, talked to interesting people. It had been a wild magic carpet ride, and she'd loved every surprising turn. "Yes, I did."

"I didn't," Kade said. "I spent the whole time wondering when the hell the damn thing would be over."

Talib chuckled. "You should know Kadir is the most

impatient of us all. He will make you crazy."

She could enjoy Kade's kind of crazy. Especially since she had Rafe's perfect patience. "I can handle him."

She could handle both Kade and Rafe. Her smile fell. Talib was another story.

"You certainly can." There was a rumble to Kade's voice that made her skin sing. His hand came up and turned her chin toward him, his face glancing down. "You handle me quite well, *habibti*."

His lips smoothed over hers. Heat infused her, making her heart rattle and surge. This was what she'd been waiting for. Connection. That was what she felt when they touched her. She'd never known just how alone she was before Rafe and Kade had pulled her into their world. The sense of belonging was so much stronger when they both had hands on her.

What would it be like when Talib touched her?

He'd been so careful, only kissing her that once. But she couldn't forget it.

"I'm a little scared." She couldn't seem to take her eyes off Tal. He stood there looking so gorgeous and remote. He'd removed his tuxedo jacket and tie, exposing the long line of his throat and the terrible scar Alea had explained. Golden skin peeked out from where the snowy white dress shirt had been unbuttoned.

Tal took a step toward her. "There's nothing to be afraid of Piper. I have no desire to hurt you." A little grin ticked his lips up making him look decadent and sinful. "Well, not in any fashion that won't enhance your pleasure. I like to play games, Piper. Do you understand what I mean?"

She was pretty sure he wasn't talking about checkers. "Sex games?"

A chuckle rumbled from his throat. He was close now, his hand coming out to cup her face. All three men had a hand on her. "Yes, Piper. I enjoy sex games. Sex should be fun, no?"

It should be. It should also have meaning. This had a lot of meaning for her, and it went beyond how much she adored the three men in the room. This was proof that her life was starting. Finally. Mindy was happy in school, and now it was time to truly live, even if it meant her heart would ache when this affair was over. At least she would have felt. And she was going to be brutally honest, with them and herself, about it all.

"I hope sex is fun. I don't actually know much about it." She hoped that didn't sound too stupid.

Talib's eyes warmed as his hand moved down her body, fingers trailing toward her chest. The touch was light, causing her to shiver. Already her body was heating up. "Yes, my brothers mentioned you are a virgin. Is that why you're afraid?"

Honesty was painful sometimes. And hard to keep track of. They were distracting her. Rafe was nuzzling her ear, licking at the shell. She'd never thought of an ear as particularly sexy, but wow, she felt that touch in her female parts. In her pussy. They were right. There was no place for silly euphemisms here. Rafe's tongue traced the line of her ear and the sparks went straight to her pussy. Kade pushed her hair back and kissed the back of neck. So sensitive. The play of his lips sent shivers down her spine. And with one finger, Tal traced the *V* of her bodice. The dress Rafe had selected left a generous amount of her skin on display, and Tal seemed intent on exploring it all.

"Piper?" Tal's deep voice pulled her out of her thoughts. "Darling, I asked you a question. You should answer me. Unless you want a spanking."

Piper took a long breath. He was talking about games again. What had he asked before? Why was she scared? "I'm worried I won't be able to please you."

She knew next to nothing. The evening she'd spent with Rafe and Kade had been about them pleasing her. She wanted to learn, wanted to be more than a doll they passed between them.

Tal's mouth was a sensual line, just the slightest hard edge of desire making him look ruthless. "You wish to please me?"

She wanted to please them all. Pleasure, romance, sex—

that was a whole portion of life that had been closed off to her before this moment. "Yes."

"You want to please the sheikh?"

That question felt like a landmine, and she wasn't exactly sure why. She answered as honestly as she could. "I want to please Tal."

Her friend. Her secret crush. She knew he'd never really existed. He'd been a facade to protect the sheikh, but she'd dreamed stupid girlish dreams of him for months.

An almost sad look crossed his face. "Sweet Piper, they are one in the same."

He took a step back, unbuttoning the rest of his shirt as he moved. He shrugged out of it as he walked past the arched doorway that led from the living area of the suite. She hadn't been past this gorgeously decorated set of rooms before. This was Talib's private sanctuary, and it consisted of an entire wing of the palace. The most she'd seen of the bedroom was the balcony, and even that had been from the outside. The sheikh's bedroom opened to a huge sun-dappled courtyard. Rafe had given her the tour and explained that when he and his brothers had been born, each was brought out on to the balcony and presented to huge crowds of cheering citizens.

She was just a girl from a dusty West Texas town. When she was born, she'd been presented to a herd of farm animals.

The marbled floors under her feet felt cool and too unfamiliar.

"All is well, Piper," Rafe promised. "We will take care of you."

"Don't be afraid." Kade hugged her from behind.

"Present her to me." Talib commanded to his brothers as he disappeared behind those arches.

She pressed her lips together to hold in a gasp. Her stomach knotted. *Present her?*

Rafe moved to her front so they enveloped her. "Let us show our brother how beautiful you are."

"He will be so crazy about you, *habibti*." Kade's erection brushed against her backside. "Trust us."

She did trust them. They'd been nothing but kind to her. Sometimes she didn't understand their customs, but she had come to care about them very much. She was in love with them. It was stupid to lie to herself. She might only have a few stolen days, a month at most before she had to return home and they got on with their royal lives. She wasn't going to beg off now because she was afraid. "Just tell me what to do."

Rafe touched his nose to hers. "Be your beautiful self, love."

"Follow our lead. We'll have the sheikh at your feet in no time at all." Kade took her hand and led her down the hall.

She followed, her heart racing . There was no turning back now. She'd come so far. She had to see where this led.

Her heart threatened to burst out of her chest when she finally entered the room. Bedroom didn't seem to cut it. It was a magnificent slice of the palace. With high ceilings and columns, the "bedroom" was larger than her parents' entire house. An enormous, curtained bed dominated the space. The flowing curtains were tied back, and the bed had to have been custom made because she'd never seen one so big. It surely fit three or four people. Maybe five.

There was a sitting area just to the left of the bed. The room was lit with soft candles and a small buffet had been set to one side, complete with everything they could need for a romantic evening. Despite the beautiful nature of the room, the man sitting on the chaise was what really took her breath away.

Talib al Mussad, Sheikh of Bezakistan, reclined on a wide, plush lounger. He'd shed his confining clothes, and his body was laid out in all its glory. He looked up as she walked into the room, his eyes narrowing. He was built on bigger lines than his brothers, every inch of golden flesh muscled and toned. Her eyes caught on his erection, and she tried to avert her gaze. It was too intimate.

"No," Rafe commanded, his voice going hard. "Do not turn away. Look at his cock. It's for you, as mine is for you. As Kade's is. You are woman enough for us all. Never think yourself anything less."

She gulped and forced her gaze up. She wasn't a girl anymore. She hadn't been for a long time. The minute she'd taken responsibility for her sister, she'd left girlhood behind and become a woman. Sex didn't make a woman. Responsibility, devotion, sacrifice. Those things already marked her, and she'd done a damn fine job. Rafe was right. She was woman enough for them.

Piper stared boldly at the sheikh. He was a gorgeous predator, every line of his body hard but graceful. And he was definitely interested in her. If she'd been worried he was just going along for his brothers' sake, his erection put that idea out of her mind. His cock stood straight up, thick and long, reaching almost to his navel.

"I hope you like what you see. My brothers are right. This is for you." He wrapped his hand around his cock, stroking from base to bulb. Tal's cock swelled, growing thicker and longer right before her eyes. "Now show me what belongs to me and mine."

She started a bit as she felt a hand on her zipper.

Kade steadied her or she would have fallen. He righted her, holding her hand. "Don't be afraid. Let us show him. This is tradition."

"You traditionally show off naked women to your brother?" She sometimes didn't understand this place. And she wondered just how much stuff they made up to get her to do things she otherwise never would.

Kade slowly dragged the zipper of her dress down, every inch a big step toward that moment when he and Rafe would unveil her. "Yes, we do. When brothers take a concubine, the younger ones present her to the eldest. She is a gift to be shared."

"Concubine." She knew the word. Mistress. Lover. It seemed so much heavier than girlfriend or momentary hookup.

"Yes, for now," Rafe said. "Relax and let us show you off. We think you are beyond beautiful, Piper. Let us share this lovely view with Talib."

The straps of her dress slipped over her shoulders as Kade finished unzipping the garment. She was suddenly grateful for all the spa treatments. Earlier in the day, they had buffed her skin to a dewy glow and taken care of those pesky extra hairs on her brow line. They'd also rid her of every single strand of hair below her neck. Sure, she'd screamed at the time, but now she could stand there with some small amount of confidence.

Her hands shook as the bodice of the dress was lowered.

"You selected her clothes, Rafe?" Tal's voice was deeper than before, his eyes on her. His hand continued to move up and down his cock in a slow, sexy rhythm.

"The dress is Marchesa. I love how the white makes her skin luminous. She did not care for the deep V-neck at first, but it shows off her lovely breasts."

He'd known she'd been worried about the dress? It was so much sexier than anything she'd ever worn.

"She looked stunning. But every man in the room was staring at her breasts." Tal frowned, sitting up, his eyes accusatory.

Rafe chuckled, kissing the curve of her shoulder. "Perhaps, but they did not touch. They can look at our beautiful concubine all they like and merely wish they were the ones in her bed."

"But the minute they touch, well, we have traditions for that as well," Kade promised.

Piper was pretty sure she wouldn't like those traditions. They likely involved blood.

"Show me the corset," Tal commanded.

The lines of the dress hadn't allowed for a traditional bra. She'd squeezed into a white satin and silk corset that forced her breasts up like ripe melons being displayed for sale.

"I strove for perfection on the lingerie." Rafe pushed the dress off her hips, and Kade whisked it away. "La Perla. I think you can agree she looks exceedingly lovely."

She looked half naked. More than half, actually. She was left in her corset and a tiny white thong, along with stark white stilettos that elongated her legs.

She gasped as Rafe's hand cupped her backside, his fingers snapping the thong.

Tal stood, staring down at her. "She glows like a pearl. You have an eye for dressing her, brother. But I need to see more. Show me her breasts."

She felt caught. Trapped by Rafe and Kade's hands. Captive to the dirty promise in Talib's dark eyes.

Cool air caressed her skin, causing her nipples to tighten even before Kade and Rafe went to work on the corset. In mere seconds, they were lifting it away from her, and she was left in nothing but a tiny thong and her shoes. She bit her bottom lip, forcing herself not to cover her breasts with her hands.

Tal simply stared, his eyes on her nipples. He didn't move toward her, just stroked his hard cock and looked. "They are beautiful. Like the woman herself. Lift them for me."

Kade sighed from behind her, his arms sliding around her torso. His big hands cupped her breasts, lifting them up. His thumbs flicked her nipples, making her shake in his arms. Piper held her breath to trap in her moan.

"She has the loveliest breasts in the world, and they're so sensitive." Kade demonstrated by pinching them lightly and watching them bead tighter. "See. She responds beautifully."

Tal sat up and leaned closer, his fingers lightly touching her nipples. "Tell me something, beautiful girl. Have my brothers played with your breasts?"

"Yes." The word came out on a breathy moan. She had two sets of hands on her. While Kade's lifted her breasts, Tal's fingers continued to toy with her so-sensitive nipples. He stroked lightly at first and then caught them between his thumbs and forefingers, twisting just a bit.

"Did you like it? Did you like it when my brothers licked and sucked your nipples?"

She was shaking, a dizzying ache coursing through her. Embarrassment rapidly drowned in a sea of want. Being put on display should make her angry, but nothing about this felt wrong. In fact, the hunger in Talib's eyes made everything about this feel good and right. "I loved it when they touched me."

Rafe stood behind Tal, watching with a smile on his face. "Our pretty concubine has trouble with dirty words, brother."

His fingers tightened, making her moan again. "Does she now? Tell me what they did to your breasts, Piper. And your pussy. I want to see that, too. I think, perhaps, my brothers made a meal of you. I might need a taste."

Kade immediately pushed the thong off her hips as Tal stepped back, the loss of his touch making her cold. Kade held her hand as she stepped out of the thong, and Tal took in a long breath, his smile dangerous and predatory. Then she wasn't cold anymore. The raging heat in his stare made her shiver and swelter with need.

"Rafe, you've been at work here, too. That is a lovely pussy. Spread your legs, Piper. I can already see those lips are wet. I want to see them as you tell me the tale."

They expected her to talk? She was lucky to be standing.

Tal edged closer and loomed over her, a patient expression on his face. "I need to make something clear. When we are in the bedroom, you follow my rules. I won't hurt you, but I will spank that gorgeous ass if you don't obey. Indulge me. I love to give a good spanking."

"He does," Kade affirmed. His hand slipped to her backside, cupping a single cheek. "He would love to get this ass a sweet pink. And he'll make you love it. Before we're done with you, you'll love many things you can only dream of now. We'll have you bound and blindfolded so all you can concentrate on is the sensation of our tongues and our cocks. And we're going to make you love it when we're all inside you. But not tonight. Tonight should be gentle. Don't tempt Tal's beast tonight. Give him what he wants. Tell him about our night together."

Spankings and bondage? She couldn't say she was completely terrified by the thought, but daunted at the moment, yes. She just needed to get through her first time. Right now, Tal wanted words.

"It will be all right." Rafe's soft tone soothed her. He winked at her as he dispensed with his shirt before working his way out of his slacks. "I'll help you. We were in the plane, and Piper kissed me. I love the way you kiss."

Nervous laughter bubbled up. "I didn't think I was very good at it."

"Well, let me remind you." Rafe strode over to her and cupped her face in his hands, tilting her head back. His lips descended on hers, a sweet melding of flesh that soon sent heat zipping through her. She relaxed, almost drugged by the desire he coaxed from her.

"I will remind you, too." Kade pulled her out of his brother's arms and kissed her himself. As always, Kade's kiss went wild. Where Rafe took things slow and sensual, Kade immediately invaded, sending heat sizzling through her system. Kade pulled her body flush against him, his erection nuzzling her belly. "Tell my brother how we kissed you that night."

"Passionately," she sighed. "It was the most erotic experience of my life." Though she was pretty sure tonight would top it. Tonight, she would finally know passion in every sense of the word.

"Now tell him where we kissed you." Kade touched a finger to her lips, giving her a wicked smile.

"My lips." She watched as Kade's fingers moved down her body to her nipples. "My breasts and nipples. I loved that." In fact, she'd fantasized about having both men at her breasts and

Tal devouring her pussy. Kade's fingers moved again, this time dipping in between her labial lips, skimming over her clit once, twice, until she gasped.

"Rafe kissed me there," she murmured. A hard pinch to her clit had her panting. "My pussy. He kissed my pussy."

Tal interrupted them, gesturing for Kade to move away. "I am sure Rafe did much more than kiss your pussy. I'm sure he ate it like the ripest fruit. Now go lie on the chaise and spread your legs for me. It's my turn to inspect that delicious bit of flesh my brothers so seem to love."

Before she had a chance to protest, Rafe lifted her up, his arm going under her knees and hauling her to his chest. "I would not want you to fall, *habibti*."

He strode across the floor and placed her on the lounger. The plush material felt decadent against her naked flesh.

"Spread your legs, Piper." Tal stood at the end of the chaise, his big body looming above her.

"Do it now," Rafe added to his brother's command as he got on his knees beside her. "He will insist on inspecting your pussy. He will do nothing more until he does. Let us see if I can erase a bit of your shyness."

His lips closed over her left nipple, sucking her deep inside his mouth. Kade was on the other side, his clothes gone now. He, too, dropped down and sucked a nipple into his mouth.

Desire overwhelmed her as she looked down at the two dark heads working over her breasts. They suckled and laved affection on her sensitive peaks as each man slid a hand down to her knees and gently pried her legs open, revealing her pussy to the sheikh. She didn't have time to feel overwhelmed or embarrassed. She was far too busy squirming under their knowing lips and tongues. It was everything she'd dreamed of.

Tal took a deep, luxurious breath. "She is responsive. There's nothing cold about her. How did you stay a virgin for so long, Piper? You're obviously a sensual thing."

She felt like it now. She was restless, writhing, wanting so much more. She wanted Tal to touch her. She wanted all of her men to shower her with pleasure so she could return it. "I didn't have time. And the one man I thought wanted me didn't really. I waited for a year, but he said I wasn't sexy."

Tal lowered himself to his knees, leaning onto the chaise and placing his face close to her pussy. "He was an idiot, this man. He has no idea what he lost. And what we gained. Tell me, Piper. Did you enjoy the way my brother ate your pussy?"

The thought could still make her weak and now it brought on that rush of arousal that coated her flesh in her own cream. Tal, like his brothers, seemed fascinated by it. His fingers played in the folds of her pussy, applying light pressure. It wasn't enough. "I loved it. Please touch me, Tal. Give me more."

"I will. But you must be still, concubine. This is our time."

"I want to learn, too." She didn't just want to lie there. "I want to know how to please a man."

A single finger pierced her pussy, slowly invading. "You want me to teach you how to fuck so you can please some other man?"

She shook her head back and forth, thrashing at the foreign, wonderful sensations making her pussy tingle. "I want to know how to please you. All of you."

"That's better. I think you will discover none of us likes hearing you speak of other men while in our bed. Piper, I understand that this relationship seems odd to you, but you should understand that while we share with each other, we will never allow another man in. I didn't even like them looking at you tonight."

Rafe suckled her nipple again before his voice tickled across her sensitive skin. "He is quite possessive, Piper. Freakishly so."

"Like you're any better," Kade scoffed.

A mischievous grin sprawled across Rafe's face. "Perhaps not." He turned back to her. "You will learn to deal with him.

128

With all of us. Now stop wiggling. We promise to teach you how to please us later. Tonight, the way to please us is to obey."

Obey? She wanted to move, to kiss them, put her hands all over their dark satin skin, feel the heat and hardness of their cocks. She reached for Kade with a moan and turned a beseeching gaze on Rafe.

"Settle down." Kade's hand was on her belly, a command to stay put. "Let us make you feel good. Later, I will to teach you exactly how to please me. I'll teach you just how I like to have my cock sucked. But first, I want to watch you come again."

She tried. She really tried to stay still, to let them have their way. Kade and Rafe bent to play at her breasts again, the sensation sparking across her skin, sending livewires down to her pussy where Tal awaited with ravenous glee. He was evil, too, teasing and caressing, his touches light and nothing like what she needed. Instead, he did exactly as he'd threatened. He inspected her, running his hand over her recently waxed skin and praising its softness. He parted her labia, running his nose there before lightly kissing her clitoris. His finger taunted as he playfully pressed in, rotating inside her core.

The stimulation was only enough to drive her crazy, but not over the edge. Her whole body wanted, aching for that finger to go deeper, to move faster. She pressed down, trying to force Tal's finger further inside.

"Brothers, stop." Tal hopped off the chaise. "Turn her. Ass in the air. She must learn some discipline."

Piper found herself on her hands and knees before she could breathe. Then she couldn't breathe at all. Anticipation slid through her, and she felt so vulnerable. Their gazes raked her; she knew it. She tried to suck in air, but it was no use. "What?"

"Hush," Kade admonished. "You didn't obey, so there will be some discipline. Tal, I think we should go easy on her this once."

"What a surprise," Tal shot back. "I'm sure Rafe agrees."

Rafe chuckled. "I think we should give her what she wants. She wanted to learn. This is an erotic lesson in giving and receiving. Kade, lie in front of her. Give her your cock."

Kade slid in front of her, his massive cock rising up. It was so close she could feel the heat coming off it. There was a pearly drop of fluid just beginning to seep from the tip.

"It's semen, *habibti*. You've never tasted it before, have you?"

She shook her head. "No." She'd never tasted a man before, and she'd never had her naked backside in the air either. "Do you want me to kiss it?"

She'd once seen a about a minute of a video where a woman sucked on a man's cock. Her fiancé had quickly turned it off and pretended he hadn't been watching the kind of porn that would make the old biddies in the town spew insistent speeches about fornication and sin. But in that brief minute, Piper had seen the way the woman moved her lips up and down on her lover's erection while the man had groaned in pure ecstasy. She wanted to give that to Kade.

"You will pleasure Kade while you also learn to obey your Masters. That's what we are in the bedroom, concubine. We're your Masters. Out of the bedroom, treat us with respect, but we want you to have your own mind. I don't know how I would get through a meeting without you arguing with me at least three times," Tal said.

"I don't mean to argue." She gasped when he lightly caressed her clit with a fingertip before pulling away again. She sighed in frustration. "You're just wrong an awful lot."

A loud smack cracked through the air, and then Piper's backside was on fire. The sting flared across her skin, and she cried out. Heat lashed her, the sensation seeping into her system. That smack had hurt, so why was her pussy aching?

"Yes, that is exactly what I mean, darling. I never want you to think you're submissive to me in the boardroom. I need that glorious brain of yours to keep me in check. But here, you'll be a proper concubine." Tal's hand smacked the other cheek, the heat sinking in quickly this time. "Now be good. You will take your discipline while you pleasure Kade."

Kade smiled at her, his cock in hand. "Please be careful, *habibti*. I really don't want to explain any terrible personal injury to our physician. He remembers me in diapers. We're having dinner with him in a few days. Let's not have his latest memory be reattaching my dick."

Just like that, he made her laugh, her anxiety dissipating. Tal smacked her ass again, once on each cheek, then rubbed the heat into her skin with his broad hand. She could deal with the spanking. She was actually kind of getting into it. Her bottom felt so wildly alive, her skin hypersensitive. "I'll be careful."

"Lick the head." His voice went guttural. His hand wrapped around his cock, pointing it her way.

The next smack moved her closer to Kade's cock. She managed to stay on her knees and did as Kade bade. Her tongue came out, licking the bulbous head, drawing that bead of pearly liquid into her mouth. Salty. Kade tasted complex and woodsy. She liked it.

She sucked the head gently into her mouth, following her instincts. She let her tongue discover the edges and ridges of the head before she dipped even lower. Velvety skin filled her mouth, and she wriggled to get closer to Kade…and to try to relieve a bit of the tension building in her pussy.

Piper felt the hint of air that came right before Tal smacked her cheek once more and forced herself to remain still.

Discipline. This was what he meant. It required her to think. About her body. About the sensations. This was a conscious choice, to take and give pleasure. To put herself in their capable hands and trust that they knew all the best ways to enjoy their shared pleasure.

She found a rhythm, her whole body engaged in the act of moving and flowing around them. She played with Kade's cock in her mouth, enjoying the freedom of exploration. She loved the way he tasted and the clean masculine scent he gave off. She adored the sounds of appreciation and pleasure he made as he pushed and pulled in and out of her mouth.

And she was rapidly becoming addicted to the feel of a hand on her backside. Heat suffused her, making her skin scream and then sing with every fall of Tal's hand.

"Talib. Please." Kade's voice was desperate.

She felt Tal's hand still on her cheek. "Her ass is a lovely pink. Yes, I think we can be done. Teach her what she needs to know."

Kade's hands tangled in her hair. "I need to fuck your mouth, *habibti*. I'm so close. You're a natural. Just suck me."

Piper sucked hard, hollowing out her cheeks, following his lead. Her jaw ached, but she wasn't going to give in to the discomfort. She wanted to be the one who brought him pleasure. She wanted to make him feel so good that he would be hungry to seek her out again.

She whirled her tongue around the head of his cock and tried to swallow as he began to press further and further into her mouth.

"Breathe through your nose." She felt a hand on her back. Rafe's, she thought. They were all watching her. "Concentrate on Kade. I plan to play a bit. Nothing like the spanking. This is not for discipline, but to prepare you."

Kade settled into a rhythm, his thrusts deep and smooth. Piper felt a hand on her bottom again, this time parting her cheeks. Cool liquid dripped on the forbidden flesh there, her back entrance contracting at the sensation.

"See, that will not do. Rafe, you must prepare her," Tal growled as he spread her cheeks wider.

They were looking *there*, while she had a man's cock in her mouth? When Piper Glen decided to lose her virginity, she also lost her damn mind. And there was nothing to do but ride the delicious, maddening wave.

Suddenly, a finger pressed against her backside, rotating

and flexing, trying to coax her to open up. And the cock in her mouth swelled, hardened even more. Kade groaned loud and low as his cock jerked against her tongue. Then salty juice coated her tongue, taking her mind off the jangly sensation in her rear as she swallowed him down. Slowly, his cock softened in her mouth, as did his hands on her hair.

"So good. You were so good, Piper. You don't need lessons. You just need men who care about you." He gently disengaged his cock. Kade slid down, bringing his mouth to hers and kissing her lightly. "Thank you so much."

Piper panted because something hard was right at her back entrance. It twisted and turned against her flesh, seeking entry. "What is that?"

Kade sighed, the sound one of pure contentment. "It's a little plug for your asshole."

"I don't think I need a plug. Everything works just fine down there."

They chuckled, saying something in Arabic before Tal came to stand before her. "How did you think you were going to accept all of us, Piper?"

"Tag team. Won't that work?" She winced as Rafe pressed the plug in, gaining ground with each little thrust. It wasn't pain exactly, but it wasn't pure pleasure, either. It was an odd mix of fullness and pressure, with a blend of pleasure and discomfort that made her want to twitch to increase the sensations, make them better. Something. But she held still because it would please them.

Tal gripped her chin in his big hand and turned her face up, a wicked gleam in his eyes. She'd never seen him look so young and carefree. A smile of pure bliss crossed his face. "Tag team?"

She loved that she'd brought that out in him. He needed someone to tease him and bring him back to earth. He needed it so badly. "Like wrestling. If you haven't watched it, then we should. You've made me deeply aware of your culture. Well, it's time you knew mine. We might need to sit down and watch a whole season of *Redneck Island.*"

His face went blank before his laughter boomed through the room. It filled her, making the spanking and the plug in her backside seem worth it because she'd never heard Tal sound so happy. "I will watch this show for you. Later. But for now, you should understand that soon we will take you in our way. All three at once. One in your pussy. One in your ass. And one enjoying the sweetness of your mouth. But tonight, we will be gentle. Try not to lose the plug."

Rafe helped her to her back. She had to clench the muscles of her bottom to keep the plug inside. Despite her apprehension, Piper couldn't deny that the idea of having all her men at once deeply intrigued her. The thought of them filling her every hole and pleasuring her at once deepened her ache and made her moan with need.

"Not here. I want to take you on the bed." Tal leaned over and picked her up, cradling her to his broad chest. "This is the bed where our fathers first took our loving mother. Where our family was born. Don't ever think we don't care for you, Piper. This is sacred for us."

That they would treat her first time with such reverence made tears prick her eyes as he laid her out on the bed. It was sacred for her, too. She'd waited so long and now she was happy she had. Rafe and Kade joined them. Rafe positioned himself behind her, lifting her up so he could cuddle her back to his front.

"I am ecstatic to be here with you in this moment," Rafe said against her ear.

Emotion overwhelmed her. She was ecstatic, too.

* * * *

Tal looked at the woman on the bed. His concubine. His bride. Soon, his wife.

He had expected to want her. He'd expected the excitement to come. He hadn't expected to need her with every breath he dragged into his body and every beat of his heart.

His bloody hands shook. What the hell was wrong with him? He wasn't supposed to want her like this. She wasn't supposed to move him all the way down to his soul. He'd laughed at her antics, his whole body relaxing in a way he hadn't in years. His cock had been harder than ever before from the moment he'd seen her beauty in all its glory. His fucking heart was pounding.

He'd thought he'd lost his heart long ago.

Now, as Tal looked down at his concubine lying on the bed where he'd been conceived, he wondered about his own family. Always before, it had seemed a far-off reality. Sons and daughters were something he'd given little thought to. Now he couldn't get them out of his head. He could make a baby with Piper. Tonight.

While she might well be furious, he would fucking make it up to her because he didn't intend to allow her to leave. He would give her the best life possible, but he could not let her go.

His cock pulsed. She was spread out before him, his brothers lovingly presenting her to him.

She was theirs.

Their concubine. Their queen.

So why did he hesitate? Because his heart ached looking at her. Because he wanted to be a better man for her. That man she could have loved had been burned away long ago. He'd died in a warehouse rife with refuse and the stench of piss, when the old Talib al Mussad had broken under torture.

The new Talib was ruthless enough to steal her virginity and hope to plant a seed in her womb.

She would never, ever know that she made him ache to be the man he used to be.

He touched her cheek, the skin so soft beneath his fingertips. Every inch of her was perfection, from her gorgeous silky brown hair, to her pert breasts with their dusky tips, to her petite legs. Her pussy had been perfectly waxed, revealing her lush, feminine flesh and the pink pearl of her clitoris.

He couldn't fucking help himself. He needed to take her, to claim her virginity, but he hungered to taste her first.

He got to his knees and lowered his head. The scent of her arousal hit him, charging through his system, making his cock twitch and ache. She smelled bloody good, feminine and spicy. And no other man had ever spread her silky thighs and taken that tight cunt. The idea that he would be the first thrilled him in a way it shouldn't.

If he had half a brain, he would let Rafe take her before him. Tradition demanded he go first, but such a deep responsibility went with the act. Even so, the primitive side of Tal knew he wouldn't allow it. The very thought made him want to growl and tear his brother's head off. He could share, yes. That was tradition. But he would be her first.

He breathed her in, letting her scent fill his lungs. She was his, the one he'd been promised. Reverently, he licked at her pussy, gathering cream and letting it soak into his tongue. So sweet. She was sweet and lush and so responsive.

Her little gasp went straight to his cock. He licked at the seam of her pussy, loving the way her cream pulsed forth for him. As he swallowed her flavor, it infused his body like a drug, pinging through his bloodstream. She was pure and innocent. While he enjoyed the idea that her hymen was intact, what he prized more was that her soul was pure. She gave and gave without asking for anything in return.

"Tal! That feels so good," she breathed, thrusting her fingers in his hair.

Every word jolted him. He could bring her pleasure. He could make her a great queen. She would be everything they needed her to be. No question. What could be more perfect?

He let his tongue explore her thoroughly. Every crevice was a delight, soft, tight, and responsive. She was far past anything he'd dreamed.

"Do you like how Tal eats your pussy?" Rafe asked.

Tal lifted his gaze to find his brother toying with her nipples. They were rosy brown between his fingers, elongating under Rafe's ministrations. Nipple clamps. He wanted to see her in clamps, her nipples dragged down by the weight of the jewels he would place on them. She was his to fuck and adorn and love.

Not love. He couldn't love. The things he loved could be taken away and broken, destroyed. She didn't deserve that.

"I love it. I can't get enough. Please, don't stop. I wouldn't be able to take it if you stopped." Piper squirmed under him.

He let his tongue fuck into her virgin cunt, every inch a pure pleasure that would soon belong to his cock. He ate at her pussy, lingering over her sensitive spots, laving her with sweet delight. Finally, he made his way to her clitoris, the little pearl bulging out and begging for attention. He sucked it into his mouth, glorying in the way her body bowed and her moan filled his ears.

"Give it to him, Piper." Kade's voice whispered into the hush. His brothers were backing him up. Rafe held her down, pleasuring her nipples, while Kade had a hand over her belly, anchoring her. This was his family. Everything after would flow from this night.

The al Mussads would rise or fall from their attention to this woman's body.

He sucked her clit in, laving the little nub with his tongue. His fingers played in her pussy, reveling in how tight she was. Her taut muscles clenched around his finger. God, he would die when he got inside her.

Over and over he sucked at that little nubbin of flesh until she shook and a wave of moisture coated his fingers. Piper writhed under his mouth, cried out, her body shuddering as her arousal coated his tongue. She gasped and moaned as she came, panting his name.

He drew his body up, his breath sawing in and out of his chest. He couldn't wait a moment longer. His cock ached. He needed her. It didn't matter what his fucking brain wanted. His brain wasn't in charge anymore. His cock was in command, and it had to have her. It had to take Piper Glen and begin to make her Piper al Mussad, a queen. His wife.

He pushed her knees apart even as Rafe kissed her sweetly, and Kade cuddled his head to her breasts. His brothers loved this woman. That much was clear. He couldn't love Piper. He couldn't. But he would make her theirs with all the passion in his body. He would protect her at all costs.

Tal pressed her legs up with his thighs, making a place for himself at her core. His cock lined up to her pussy, masculine to feminine, dark to light. The head of his cock nestled at her slit like it belonged there. Every muscle in his body tightened. He'd never actually fucked a virgin before. He had to be careful. He had to be patient enough to make her like it. This was his life, and his brothers', on the line. Their happiness.

Gently, holding back his darkest instincts, he pressed forward, slowly piercing her. Her cunt was still swollen from her orgasm, and every inch of her was a delicious pressure. She tightened around him, her legs pressing against his sides.

"You feel so good. Tell me I'm not hurting you." He couldn't stand the thought. He wanted her to love everything about the way he possessed her body.

Her head shook. She reached around his neck, arms linking and trying to pull him closer. "Please, Tal. Please. I need you so much."

He pressed forward and felt a barrier. Her virginity. God, it was right there, the proof that no other man had taken her. No other man had tasted her sweetness, altered her innocence. He paused, the moment overtaking him. She would be his. His and his brothers'. She wasn't some woman to play with. She would be their wife, and it moved him.

With a deep moan of pleasure, he pressed forward and sank

deep, taking her virginity in one long thrust of his cock.

Piper panted underneath him before she tensed, crying out for a jagged moment. He drove into her body with his own, loving the feel of his chest pressed against her breasts. They fit together like puzzle pieces.

He held himself still, giving her time to adjust to his hard presence deep inside her. "Tell me, are you all right, *habibti*?"

Her breath was hot on his skin. "I think so. It didn't hurt too badly. But I'm so full."

Relief swamped him. He'd worked so damn hard to not hurt her. He knew the plans he'd set in motion were ruthless and manipulative, but he sought to shelter her at the same time. To shower her with pleasure. The orgasms they'd given her had softened the blow of losing her virginity, and he was thankful.

But nothing could soften the way she felt around him. The walls of her cunt gripped him without mercy, hugging him close, surrounding him with heat and slick moisture. She was so damn tight, the plug in her ass squeezing him even tighter than she normally would. One day she would be full of all of them.

One day she would be round with their baby.

He was deeply aware of the fact that he wasn't wearing a condom. He'd never not worn one. Not once in his life. He knew she was too far gone to realize it. He should have protected her, but he didn't because he wanted her so fucking bad. He was desperate to tie her to him. She was his future. His hope. If he got her pregnant, she couldn't run, couldn't deny the connection between them. She would be theirs forever, and he would make being their wife worth her while.

She didn't know it yet, but as far as he was concerned, they were married and this was forever.

He pulled back just a little, the sensation making him quake. He had to keep his composure, not lose his head. He forced himself to slow down when all he wanted to do was fuck her like the animal he really was underneath the veneer of urbane suits and polished manners. He wanted to let himself off the leash, but he managed to find a smooth rhythm to please her instead. "Better?"

She'd relaxed back against Rafe who looked perfectly content holding her and whispering to her. "Much better. It feels good, Tal."

Tal raised himself up on his arms, adjusting his position so Kade could play at her breasts. They were all a part of this. She needed to understand that she had three Masters, three husbands to rely on. Two who would open their hearts and give her everything inside.

Tal would give her the world, but he had no heart to share anymore.

He let the thought go. All that mattered was consummating his marriage and making sure she would give her assent to stay at the end of thirty days. They had a month to make her so deliriously happy that she would be convinced to stay. Four small weeks to drown her in pleasure and affection and pray that she forgave them when she finally learned what they had done.

So little time to make her love them.

Tal thrust in, her snug channel fighting to keep him deep. He forced self-control and eased inside her with long, smooth strokes that brought him closer and closer to paradise.

Fucking Piper was unlike anything he'd felt before. Sex had always been a fun game before the incident, and then it had been a need he'd fulfilled with women who wanted nothing more from him than money and access to a lifestyle they could only dream of.

Piper didn't want either. She wanted more.

What the hell was he doing? It was wrong. He should stop. But there was no going back.

"Help me, brother." The command came out as a low growl. His whole body was set to go off. He needed to ensure her pleasure first.

Kade sucked a nipple into his mouth as his hand came

between them, rubbing her clit with just the right amount of force.

"Come for us," Rafe whispered in her ear. "You are beyond beautiful when you do."

Piper's eyes widened, a look of shocked surprise on her face as her pussy clamped viciously around him. Her body shook as she screamed and came, her hips grinding up helplessly.

And he couldn't stand it a moment longer. Kade's hand disappeared, and Tal lost all sense of decorum. He fucked into her hard, spreading her legs even wider so he could delve deeper, force her to take every inch of his cock. He needed more of her. He needed every fucking bit of her softness.

His whole body lit up, pleasure coating him in a hazy fog as he thrust in again and again. He covered her body with his, needing to feel her silky skin everywhere around him. In the haze of his lust, he heard her come again, her pussy pulsing around him, milking him.

He couldn't hold it off a second longer. His balls drew up, shooting off in grateful jets. He came, his body bucking over and over, her name on his lips.

He gave her every drop of semen he had in his body, holding her close and reveling in the intimacy. He laid his head on her chest, his cock still deep inside.

"Thank you, Tal." Her hand found his head.

He didn't want a "thank you." Fuck. He wanted an "I love you."

He was in deep trouble. Tal knew it. He needed to keep his distance, but he found his eyes closing, resting for the first time in years, content in her arms.

Chapter Nine

Piper stretched, every muscle aching deliciously. She opened her eyes just a bit and caught sight of Talib's gorgeous face close to hers. He was so beautiful laying there, the harsh lines of his countenance softened by the morning light. There was just the hint of scruff on his face. She longed to touch him, to feel that light beard against her skin. He would likely get rid of it. She'd never seen him looking anything but perfect, but now with the hint of beard and his hair mussed, he was an approachable god.

"Go back to sleep, darling."

She loved his deep grumble. "Okay."

He sighed and snuggled down, obviously not ready to face the day.

But Piper needed to stretch, and she couldn't do that here. She felt the press of another warm body against her back. Kade, she thought. It was hard to remember. They'd each taken her the night before, their faces over hers, each man loving her with his mouth and his cock and his hands.

She'd never imagined such pleasure existed. And she doubted she would find it again.

But having three lovers did leave a girl with a quandary. How did she extricate herself from the bed without waking them? She kind of wanted to clean up before they woke. And brush her teeth. And her hair.

She was probably a mess. And she really hoped she hadn't snored.

Piper scooted out, the silky sheets aiding her in her quest. The good news was they had completely destroyed the sheets last night so she slid out of the bed. The bad news was she landed on the carpet, on her rather sore backside. She stifled a giggle. Really good sex hadn't made her any more graceful. And she was naked.

She stretched, her arms going over her head. Despite her sore muscles, her skin still hummed. Her body felt achy and sore—in a good way. She could still feel their hands on her, caressing and loving every inch of her body.

It was a night she would never forget. Piper got to her wobbly knees, still reveling in their affection, along with a pleasant sense of power she hadn't expected. She'd handled all three of them. They'd gone to sleep with smiles on their faces. Her lips turned up a little as she looked back at them. Kade had turned on his stomach, his well-muscled backside on display. Rafe was on his back, an arm outstretched. And Talib had taken his own advice. He'd gone back to sleep, his hand over the spot where she'd lain next to him.

Her men. Maybe not forever, but they were hers for now.

Contentment lulled through her. Smiling, she wandered toward Tal's balcony. She wanted to breathe fresh air, feel the warm breeze and sunshine on her face before the day got too hot. Afternoons in Bezakistan were as bad as Texas summers, but the mornings were usually lovely, with a gentle wind blowing in from the sea. She loved the mornings here.

She slipped her arms into Tal's dress shirt. It was huge on her, coming almost to her knees, but it covered her as well as any robe.

There was a tray of coffee and breakfast breads on the table. She winced. Talib's servants had already been in here. She hadn't thought to draw the drapes on the bed the night before. Gosh, what must they think of her now? Her skin flushed, but she would just have to brazen through it. This certainly wasn't the first time they had seduced a woman to their bed, and it likely wouldn't be the last. They were too well-practiced in the art of taking a woman together.

And they had the routine down. Piper poured herself a cup of rich-smelling coffee as she thought about the night before. After the first time, they'd adjourned to the hot tub in the monstrosity of a bathroom. That was where Rafe had taken her, sitting her in his lap, his cock finding its way home. After they'd bathed her, Kade had carried her to bed where he'd gently made love to her before they'd all fallen asleep together.

She moved toward the balcony, a muffin in one hand, a mug of coffee in the other. She had plenty of time to shower before anyone would expect her to begin work for the day. For now she would look over the palace gardens and soak in the moment.

This was the start of her new life. Free and brave. That was what she was going to be.

She breathed in the fresh air as she set her coffee and muffin aside for a moment and stepped out onto the terrace. A cheer rose up. Flashbulbs exploded.

Piper screamed.

The palace grounds, almost always deserted at this time of morning, were filled with people. And cameras. She was nearly blinded as more flashbulbs went off. There was a whooshing sound and the heavy thud of helicopter blades. A sleek black chopper swooped down, and a man with a camera, complete with a long telephoto lens, leaned out the window.

The crowd erupted in another huge cheer. A thousand people jumped up and down shouting the al Mussad name.

Piper turned, trying desperately to get back inside, but she got caught in the filmy curtains, twisting and turning around. It was a labyrinth of linen and silk, trapping her.

"What the hell?" Tal's voice rang out. "Rafe, get up. We've got a problem. Get on the phone and deal with the press." There was a momentary pause. "Piper? Darling? If you stop moving, I think I can extricate you from the curtains."

"Sheikh!" The swelling crowd chanted for Talib.

"I think I'll just stay here." If Tal got her out, she would be standing in front of a whole bunch of people wearing only Tal's shirt, which she was pretty sure had blown up when that damn helicopter had swooped down. She might just stay right here forever, and then she wouldn't have to deal with the possibility that her hoohaw had been caught on film.

"Darling, I'm very sorry this happened, but I need you to come out now." His big masculine hand reached in, trying to catch her.

Piper dodged him. She wasn't coming out until she had some answers. "Who are those people?"

The curtains moved, jostling her around, and then she heard Kade's voice. "They're just citizens, *habibti*. They gathered because they heard we have taken a new concubine."

"God, can you not just say girlfriend? That word sounds so...medieval." She sniffled, tears threatening. They had taken pictures of her half-naked, looking her absolute worst. Was this the Bezakistani version of the paparazzi?

"We're going to have to tell her now, Kade," Tal said, his voice heavy. "Khalil did this. I just know it. I swear I'm going to have his head."

Kade's head poked through the curtains. "Piper, we need to talk, explain a few things."

"Why does anyone care that we slept together? Does this happen to all your girlfriends?" She wasn't even sure she could call herself his girlfriend. She'd only slept with them once. They hadn't made her any promises.

Kade's face tightened. "Tal, shouldn't Rafiq be the one to

explain? He's the smart one."

Tal seemed to be trying to force the curtains open. Piper held them shut. On the one hand, it was hot and slightly suffocating in all this fabric. But on the other was total embarrassment on a national scale. Maybe she could listen to their explanation from here.

"Rafe is currently speaking to the press," Tal argued. "And I have little doubt they're getting anxious and beginning to wonder exactly what is wrong with our concubine."

"Wrong with me? Why do they care about me at all?" Piper asked, panic creeping into her voice .

Kade took a long breath, muttering something that she would bet wasn't a polite thing to say in his language. "Piper, my dearest, a concubine means something a little different here. You know the word to mean a lover or mistress. Here in Bezakistan, it's always meant the woman the sheikh and his brothers will marry. As Rafe and I explained, it's tradition in our country to steal a bride. We don't do that in precisely the same fashion our ancestors did, but…the practice is still both accepted and expected."

"What does that have to do with concubines?"

"Well, even though we steal a bride, she must still agree to marry us. According to our laws, she has a month to decide. During that month, she is called the concubine."

Her mouth dropped open. "Oh my god. They think you're trying to marry me."

It was horrific. How could anyone think they— unbelievably rich and powerful men—would want to marry her? It was a mistake of historic proportions.

Kade's hand finally made it through the yards of curtains. He cupped her face. "Yes, they think that. We tried to keep our interest in you quiet so this wouldn't happen."

She'd screwed everything up. "We'll just explain that there's been a mistake."

"That would be a much greater scandal, *habibti*. And I

personally have no interest in correcting anything. I'm crazy about you, Piper." He got his hands on her hips, pulling her close.

Tal finally tore through the curtains, his face flushed. "There is no mistake, Piper. We are going to marry you. I would never have taken your virginity had I not been prepared to marry you. This is not at all how I intended to start our lives together, but we must deal with this fiasco now. The press is here, and they are wondering why the hell my concubine is hiding."

Piper heard their words, but they weren't computing. They couldn't be. Because everything they said made almost no sense. They couldn't possibly be saying what she thought they were saying. "But...there must be a mistake. You didn't ask me to marry you."

Talib's face tightened, his jaw a hard line. "Piper, will you marry me?"

"Oh, no, I can't do that." No way. No how. It would be a horrible mistake. She wasn't queen material. She had important work to do, and they needed someone far more polished and pretty to fill that role.

He huffed, his eyes rolling. "And now you see why I did not ask. Could you please stop hiding in the curtains? Every moment you hide, the press writes something about your unsuitability. You're an economist, darling. What is this little episode doing to our stock?"

Who cared about stock? Except that Bezakistan made an enormous amount of its money off stock and so did Black Oak Oil. And Black Oak was heavily invested in Bezakistan. Her mind rattled off numbers. Tal was the head of the country. The country was dependent on stocks and oil futures. If the future wife of the sheikh was a complete idiot, the stock might fall.

And they had lied.

"I don't understand any of this."

Kade leaned in, his face close to hers. "I know. I'm so

147

sorry. Forgive me. Please come out and smile and wave for the citizens and the press. Once we've done that, we can sit down and I will explain everything to you. Piper, I don't want this to come between us."

The enormity of what they had done slammed her squarely in the chest. "You lied."

He shook his head. "Not really. I just didn't tell you everything."

"Are we married?"

"Not yet," Tal said, his voice clipped. "You now have a month to decide. But you should understand that we only have a few months before the crown reverts to Khalil, who will bring in radicals and change the face of this country forever. He's counting on you to run. He's the one who brought the press down on our heads."

She didn't understand a darn thing except that they had kept her in the dark about something that affected the rest of her life. And still, there was a lot riding on her. She had made friends here. She cared about Black Oak Oil. She couldn't let them down. "What should I do?"

She asked the question of Kade. She couldn't look at Tal yet. Some events that had made her scratch her head over the past few days now snapped into place and made sense, including the reason Rafe and Kade had refused to sleep with her on their journey to Bezakistan. Her virginity had belonged to Talib. To her future husband.

Together, the three of them had colluded to marry her to a man she didn't really know. Because the Tal who had been her co-worker had been nothing but a pretense, just like their entire reason for bringing her here.

Tal didn't seem to care that she was talking to Kade. "I need you to walk out with me, hold my hand, and smile." Tal said the word smile, but he was frowning. "If you don't, they will assume you have already rejected us. If that happens, Khalil will be meeting with his lawyers to challenge us and our claim to the throne within the hour."

Her head was spinning, and all the ramifications of their deception swirled in her head. But the stakes were terribly high, too. The decisions she made now would affect their futures—and hers. Even if she didn't remain their concubine, if Khalil overtook the country, all her work would go down the toilet. "Can't I get dressed first?"

Tal's frown deepened. "Rafe is talking to the press. He's going to schedule some photo shoots for later this afternoon. You will look your best then, and those are the photos we will circulate. For now, Khalil has left us with no choice but to put you on display. If you would just walk out onto the balcony and allow me to kiss you, I believe we can stem the tide of scandal."

She laughed, a little hysteria tingeing the sound. "I can stem the tide of scandal if I walk out half naked and kiss a man in front of a bunch of cameras?"

"You aren't in America anymore, Piper."

She wasn't. And she didn't have much of a choice now. She turned, ignoring Kade's attempts to hug her. His affection hadn't come with an ounce of honesty. She wasn't sure exactly what was happening, but she needed to buy everyone a little time. Then she could make some decisions.

She allowed Tal to pull her free. The sun hit her face, but this time she felt the heat instead of the soft glow. Flashbulbs blasted all around her as Talib pulled her into his arms.

Unlike the night before, now there was no gentleness in his face. There was a hard, possessive look in his eyes as he drew her against him. Her heart raced as he cupped her cheek, and his mouth came down on hers. Arousal flooded through her, but there was a cool distance to Tal that she couldn't ignore.

As he took her mouth, a cheer went through the crowd, the sound nearly deafening her.

When Tal turned, Rafe and Kade were immediately at her sides, grasping her hands, gazing at her with affection before they turned to the crowd with triumphant smiles.

149

Though surrounded by people, Piper had never felt so alone.

* * * *

Rafe watched as Piper walked out of the bathroom. Her robe had been double knotted as though she was desperately afraid the tie might come open and expose her. Her face was set in tight lines, so unlike the happy, sensual woman who had ridden his cock the night before.

All in all, this was not how he'd imagined the morning would go. He'd thought he would feed Piper while they lay in bed and made love well into the afternoon. Now was their concubine time, damn it. Instead of enjoying his bride, he was fielding questions from fucking reporters. The story would be splashed across every magazine in the free world.

His cell phone trilled again, and he seriously thought about throwing it out the window.

Tal stared at him. "Are you going to answer that?"

"No." He was in charge of dealing with the press. He would not allow Tal's impatience to screw up his plan. "I will let them stew until tomorrow. To the outside world, we are in seclusion now. It should be expected since we're meant to bond with our future bride."

Piper turned suspicious eyes his way. "That whole meet up with the judge and the Prime Minister last night wasn't just a greeting, was it? There was a reason you invited them to join us on the balcony. They asked you a question, and the three of you all gave the same answer. That was some sort of ceremony."

Sometimes, she was too clever. He looked to Tal, who frowned his way.

Piper picked up on that, too. She stood in front of Rafe, blocking his view of his brother. "You have a mouth, Rafiq. You can answer me without Tal telling you what to say."

This proved she hadn't been properly prepared for the job

they had selected her for. He'd let her down. His heart twisted in his chest. "At times like these, Piper, he is not my brother. He is my sheikh."

Rafe might have enormous influence, but Talib made the decisions. He'd known that his whole life. While he and Kade were able to traipse across the globe, Tal had a country to run.

"So you and Kadir just do what Talib tells you to?" Piper sounded more aggressive than he'd ever heard her. "That's the way this works?"

Tal groaned, his eyes rolling. "Yes, Piper, they never give me a single moment of trouble. Damn it. Consider this family like a corporation. I'm the CEO."

She frowned, her lips curling down. "I don't think I want a family like that."

Why was Tal taunting her? Rafe reached out for her hand, happy that she didn't totally reject him. She didn't curl her fingers into his, but she didn't pull away. "Give this a chance. Our life will not be like this all the time. I promise the press will settle down."

"Before or after I have to make a decision I never thought I would, with your entire country watching?"

Now it was Rafe's turn to frown. Yes, he had deceived and failed to prepare her, but his intentions had always been good. "You never once considered you might marry us? Our relationship was not even remotely serious for you?"

Now she pulled away, drawing her hand back. "Don't be ridiculous. You're royal. I'm from a town of two hundred rednecks in West Texas. Why would I imagine marriage was even possible?"

"You're also one of the world's experts on green energy economics," Tal shot back. "It's a skill my country can use."

Rafe wanted to hit his brother. Even if that argument had swayed Tal to consider Piper in the first place, this wasn't the time to point out all the practical reasons she worked as their bride. "Piper, I knew I wanted you from the moment I saw

151

you."

But she turned, rounding on Talib as though she knew he was the one who would give her the fight she so obviously wanted. "Is that why you sought me out? Is that why you befriended me?"

Tal didn't back down an inch. "It's why I sought you out to help me with the project. You had the knowledge to help me and my country. You also turned out to be a suitable wife."

Rafe let his head hit his hand. Tal might have his respect as his sheikh, but as his brother, Rafe wanted to kick him.

"Suitable?" Piper asked, the word a hiss.

Kade chose that moment to walk in carrying Piper's clothes for the day. "You can put these on for this afternoon. A stylist is on her way to assist you with hair and makeup before the photo shoot. Then servants will move all of our clothing and things into this wing by nightfall."

Piper, who had been staring down Tal, now turned on Kade, who stopped, his eyes widening. "Why would they move me in here? Why can't I stay in my own room?"

Kade's jaw dropped. "*Habibti…*"

"Don't you *habibti* me." She turned to Rafe, ignoring Tal altogether. "I told you that I didn't want to marry Johnny because I didn't want to be an asset; I wanted to be loved. Yet you brought me here, knowing Tal's motives. Did you think I'd feel differently now?" Her words stabbed him like a knife. The blade twisted when her face closed up. "I'm going to my room. And I intend to stay there until I've decided what to do."

"The servants talk, Piper." Rafe felt for her. She was reeling, confused…but he could not give in. There was far too much at stake. "I intend to figure out exactly who decided to not wake us this morning when the crowd began to gather, but we could be in trouble if the press gets wind that you refuse to share the traditional rooms with us."

Her face flushed. "You can't expect me to just go along with this…this farce. I don't want to be some sort of pampered princess, cloistered and coddled and pointless."

"*Shaykhah*. That is what we would call you. She is the wife of the sheikh. She is the one who binds our family and forms the center of our universe. We have sought our *shaykhah* for some time. Only once have we been able to agree on a woman for us all. You, Piper." Let her stew on that. Tal was wrong to try to explain with logic just now.

She stopped, her body language softening, her expression crumbling. "It wasn't fair to not tell me."

Rafe crossed to her. "I know you do not wish to hear this, but it is our way. Piper, can you not find it in your heart to believe that we care for you? To forgive us for being fools? Did we make a mistake? Yes. But we did it because we feared losing you. I know that's an excuse, but you are more special than we ever hoped to find."

"I think it's interesting that you've decided I'm so special just a few months before you'll lose your crown if you fail to take a wife." Suspicion flavored every word.

"I could have bought a bride, Piper." Tal stared out the window, no doubt seeing the reporters who were prowling around the periphery of the palace. His brother was beyond restless, his face stark and angry. "It would have been simple. You are not exactly an easy bride."

"I apologize for being difficult." Her face fell, and Rafe could see that she looked somewhere between torn and stricken. "I don't understand any of this."

Rafe did what came naturally. He took her into his arms. She stood stiffly in his embrace. "We intended to protect you from all this."

"Were you ever going to tell me we were married? Or would I have found out a couple of years down the road?"

Kade dropped her clothes to the bed and came to her other side. At least one of his brothers was being smart. Piper would be unable to resist affection for long. "We were going to ask you to marry us as soon as we'd all eased into our relationship.

We picked out a ring and everything. We thought it would be good to propose the American way. We wanted it to be very romantic."

"Why me?" She glared at Tal's back. "If you truly care about me beyond the knowledge I can bring to your country, then explain why."

Rafe sighed. "Because you're special, Piper. Because you move me."

Kade nuzzled her cheek. "You move me, too, *habibti*. You move my cock. It's moving right now."

Piper scoffed, but Rafe heard a laugh buried in there. "I'm glad to know that." She sobered a little, pushing out of his arms. "I need some time. You've just turned my whole world around."

Tal turned, his face a blank mask. "What did you have in Dallas, Piper? What did we take you from that was so cruel? A ratty apartment? A low-paying job? A constant struggle to make ends meet? No love life to speak of?" She winced, but Tal plowed on. "We're offering you the world, Piper. We're offering you a palace and more money than you could dream of. We're offering you enormous power to chase your own ideals. Free reign to pursue this project you love. You will have to explain to me why I'm suddenly the bad guy."

"Do you love me?" Piper's shoulders squared, obviously waiting for a hard blow.

Rafe could answer that easily. "Yes. I loved you from the moment I laid eyes on you. I followed you down a hallway hoping that you would turn so I could ask your name."

She flushed. "I fell instead."

He would remember the moment forever. "Yes. You fell. But I promise from now on that I will be there to catch you."

"I love you, Piper. I know it must seem sudden, but believe me, *habibti*, I've been with enough women to know how I feel," Kade said.

Rafe shook his head in agreement. "He is right. He has

slept with most of the females in the Western world. He should know this is different."

Kade growled his way, but Piper smiled just a bit.

Until she turned back to Talib.

"I'm offering you everything I have, Piper. If it is not enough for you, if my brothers' love and devotion isn't enough, then you should say so now." He stepped forward but didn't touch her. A cold ruthless will poured off his brother. "The time is coming when I must take a wife or step down. I selected the bride I thought would be the best for my brothers and my country."

"What about for you?" Piper asked.

"My needs are inconsequential. I like you, Piper. I enjoy your company. I admire your mind, and I crave your body. That will have to be enough for you."

Her face fell, her eyes finding the floor as though she couldn't stand to look at them. "It isn't."

Tal straightened up, looking every inch the sheikh. "Then you have a decision to make. Think long and hard, Piper al Mussad. Your decision affects the lives of millions. And it affects your friends. Black Oak Oil is heavily invested in this country. If the throne goes to my cousin, he will not honor our contracts. He will simply take everything from them. Think about Hannah and her children when you decide whether or not to stay. You're not a girl anymore, Piper. And this love you want is a naïve dream. I'm offering you a life, a chance to make a difference to my people—hell, to the planet—and you wish me to understand that you won't be happy until I cut my heart out and serve it up on a silver platter? It won't happen. We will be partners. That is my offer. Take it or leave it. My country awaits your wisdom."

He turned and strode out the door, leaving a stunned Piper in his wake.

Rafe thought seriously about killing his brother. "Piper, you must give him time. You cannot fathom what he has endured, the pressures he's under."

Piper's eyes were still on the empty doorway. "I should give him time? Why should I give him anything? He didn't even give me the courtesy of asking me if I wanted this responsibility, Rafe. From what I can tell, everything the three of you have done has been to manipulate me into a position where I have no options."

"You have options." Just none he wanted her to take.

"Yes. To capitulate or seem like a selfish witch." She sank to the chaise, the very one they'd laid her out on the night before when he had lovingly presented her to Tal. Now, she looked weary, her eyes full of tears. "Go away. Both of you. Please. I need some time. I'm not saying no. You three have boxed me in so tightly that I probably can't. So give me space for now."

Kade looked at him, misery awash across his face. "*Habibti*, I am more sorry than you can know."

It was time to give her what she needed. Until now, they had done very little of that. "We will remain on the palace grounds should you require us."

They retreated. Rafe felt hollow as he walked down the corridor, knowing that he had left his heart and soul behind with the woman he'd betrayed.

Chapter Ten

Piper took a long breath, forcing back tears. Hours had passed. The photo shoot had been a blur, and now the day was waning. Two separate buffets had been laid out for her, but she hadn't touched a thing. Soon someone would try to make her eat dinner. She could hear people milling around outside, but at least the curtains were drawn properly again. Just a few minutes before, a small army of servants had brought her clothes and things in, depositing them neatly in a closet that seemed to have been emptied out just for her. And it wasn't just her clothes. There was a never-ending parade of designer wear she'd never seen before.

Someone intended to dress a princess.

A *shaykhah*, she amended.

What on earth was she going to do?

Her computer trilled, the sound of a call coming through. Before she'd come to Bezakistan, she'd made sure her sister knew how to use her computer to call her. Or it could be one of the James brothers calling to point out that she was seriously screwing up their business. And the country's. So many people depending on her.

She'd never imagined that her vagina had the power to destabilize a whole country.

With grim resolve, she sat down in front of her computer and clicked the button that connected the call.

Her sister's face filled the screen, her blue eyes wide. "Oh my god, Piper. You're on TV. Like everywhere. Seriously. You're on the *Today* show."

Heat flashed through her system. "Tell me they're not showing my backside."

Mindy got the same look on her face she used to get right before she lied to Piper about her report card. "Not at all."

Piper felt tears cloud her eyes again. She seemed to have a never-ending supply of them today.

"Piper, it's okay. They totally did that thing where they blurred out that part of the screen. And the rest of you looked hot. That was some serious sex hair, big sister. So don't worry. No one has seen your privates. Wait. Do you ever get on YouTube?"

"No."

"Then no one has seen you," Mindy assured her.

"Oh my god." She'd done some stupid things in her time, gotten into some dumb situations, but this took the cake. "Does everyone in town know?"

She hadn't been back to her small town in over a year. She'd been very happy to be able to visit Mindy in Lubbock instead of having to go back to that place where she'd been judged for her every move. Her college years had been one long tightrope because the old biddies of the town had been like hawks watching her every move, waiting for the moment when they had a reason to take her sister away. It had been a sick game for them.

Mindy's grin filled the screen. "Well, the townsfolk here have figured out a couple of things. One, that you're marrying godless heathens who apparently take you three at a time."

"Oh my god." Her sister shouldn't know that.

Mindy was utterly nonplussed. "Two, said godless heathens are totally gorgeous and kind of rule the world because they have all that money. My friends back home say it's a standoff. Half the town wants to ask for a loan and the other half thinks you're going straight to hell, but even that half is sure you're heading there first class."

Piper let her head find the desk.

"Sis? Why are you so upset? In those pictures, you look so happy that you're glowing. I'm thrilled for you. Hell, I'm kind of thrilled for me."

Piper sniffled, looking up at the computer. "Why?"

Her sister was leaning in, a soft smile on her face. In the background, Piper could see a display of red and black Texas Tech logos on the wall. "Because I was told today that my tuition and books and room and board have been paid for the rest of my time in school, Piper. You did that, right? No more freaking out every six months. No more working at the pizza place for grocery money. I can really do this. I can be a doctor."

Now tears filled her eyes, but for something other than self-loathing. "I didn't. I'm sure it was Rafe."

She'd talked to Rafe about her sister. She'd opened up and let him know how worried she always was.

Mindy shook her head. "They told me the man who signed the check was named Talib al Mussad. He's the sheikh, right? I just thought you strong-armed him into doing it. Except you didn't use your arm. You used that part of you that is absolutely not all over YouTube."

She laughed. There was nothing else to do. "At least tell me I didn't look wretched."

"Like I said, you looked hot. Although I have to admit, I really didn't look at you once the hottie walked out without his shirt on. And then the second one. And the third one. Holy crapballs, Pipe! You hit the jackpot. Those men are superhot, and I saw the way they looked at you. I am totally jealous, and tell me I'm getting to come to the royal wedding thingee."

She'd missed the wedding thingee, but then so had Piper. Although according to everything she'd read this morning, it hadn't been a wedding, more like a promise to marry. "Sweetie, I don't know that I'm marrying them."

Mindy's mouth dropped open. "Are you kidding me? You landed in a country where no one blinks an eye that you're marrying three hot billionaires."

How did she make her sister understand? "It might be fine here, but what will everyone else think? What will the people at home think?"

"Who cares? Piper, the people at home made your life hell. Don't you dare think you have to live by their standards. Do you understand what you're being given? You're being given the chance to not give a damn what anyone thinks."

Her sister was a little naïve. "Oh, sweetie, that's just not true. That's not what a princess is. Or a *shaykhah*. Don't you know that every eye will be on me?"

It would be just like it had been at home, but on a global scale. Everyone would watch her. Everyone would be waiting for her to make a dumb move. The press would live for her mistakes. They would be splashed across the tabloids.

Mindy threw her arms up in obvious frustration. "Who cares? Piper, they can't do anything to you. Who cares what they say? You have the power. You just have to take it. You'll be a queen."

But was she ready for that? No. Not at all.

And still, with her heart yearning for the sense of belonging and connection she'd felt last night, she wasn't sure she could walk away.

"I don't know, Min. What the press didn't tell you is that those incredibly hot men didn't bother to tell me they were pledging to marry me. They thought they could just sort of fool me for a while and then they would ask me."

Mindy groaned. "God, it is so good to know that men are dumbasses all over the world. Look, do you care about them,

Piper?"

She was in love with them. After last night, she was pretty sure she would never love anyone else. But they had lied. How could they start any sort of meaningful life together like that? And Talib had been so cold this morning. The heat and desire of the night before had been gone. The man she'd made love with, given her virginity to, had fled, and she'd been forced to deal with a sheikh instead.

"I'm crazy about them, but I don't know that it's enough."

Mindy sighed, sitting forward, her hand on the screen. "I love you, sister. I'm going to give you the same advice you gave me that day so long ago. Do you remember? Our parents were gone. You stayed home with me. I didn't want to go to school because I knew everyone would pity me. What did you say to me?"

Piper remembered the day. It had been so hard to let her sister go. She'd been so young, but the responsibility had weighed on her. Mindy's first day of high school. Their parents should have been there. Piper had tried to come up with something her mother might have said. Piper put her hand to the screen, the need to touch her sister so strong, she couldn't resist. "I told you to be brave. I told you that this was your world, and you were the only one who could build it."

Her sister nodded, the words heavy between them. "Build your world, Piper. Build it strong so no one can tear it down. I'll be there no matter what."

"I love you." Her sister had turned into a strong woman. She'd done one thing right.

"You, too. Call me later. And if you can, make sure this little camera thingee catches those hot hunks in various states of undress." Mindy grinned just before her hand moved and the connection was broken.

Piper shut the lid on the computer, her sister's words ringing through her head. Build her world. It had been a silly thing to say. She'd struggled to find the words to give Mindy strength that day, but they had proven true. She'd managed to build a world for them both and then, when Mindy no longer needed it, she'd started building her own.

Was she willing to shut Rafe and Kade and Tal out because they hadn't said the right things? Before she truly knew what was in their hearts? Or should she try building a world and then tell them how to live in it?

"Miss Glen?"

Piper turned, startled at the deep voice that cut through the quiet. A man stood in the doorway. He wore a perfectly cut suit and the maroon tie that every member of the senate wore. A politician. "Yes?"

He bowed slightly. "I am a member of the parliament. I represent one of the western districts. I wanted to welcome you. I actually just came from the parliament building. We had a special session in order to discuss the sheikh's new situation."

She stood, wishing she hadn't been caught crying. The man before her was polished and smooth, his dark eyes assessing her. He was a gaunt man, almost stark, but he was being excruciatingly polite. And she was well aware that she was the sheikh's new situation. "I'm sorry. I wasn't told to expect visitors."

He smiled, but there was no humor to it. "I apologize if I offend."

She wasn't going to anger the parliament. She rallied, calling on every lesson in etiquette she'd ever been given. She stepped toward him, offering him a seat on the couch. "Of course not. Please come in. Should I call for refreshments?"

It would make the servants happy. They'd been waiting to be given something to do all day long. One hovered just outside of the door.

His head shook slightly as he lowered himself to the couch. "I already rang for tea. I hope you don't mind. It should be here in a minute."

With perfect timing, a young man in long, formal robes

strode in carrying a tray with a lovely silver tea service. With an elegant hand, he poured two cups and then bowed, leaving them alone again. Piper let the spicy scent of the hot tea fill her senses. Everything was decadent here. Even the tea. She took a little sip.

"I thank you for receiving me," the parliament representative said. "I merely wished to call upon you. I was at the banquet last night, but I did not get the pleasure of an introduction."

She tried to recall him from the night before. The evening had flown by in a flurry of new faces and names. She took another sip of the tea. Rich and fragrant, it reminded her she hadn't eaten all day. "I apologize. Last night was my first big reception. I didn't get to meet everyone."

"My name is Khalil al Bashir. You have heard of me, no?"

She put the tea down. Khalil. Yes, she'd heard of him. Nothing good. "You're the cousin."

He inclined that perfectly coiffed head. "I am, indeed. But I hope you don't believe everything you've heard. I'm afraid my cousins don't like me much. My grandfather decided to buck tradition long ago. He loved my grandmother. He did not wish to share the bride his brother had selected for them."

"He gave up the throne for a woman?" It was an interesting story. She didn't like the word "selected," however. As far as she knew, Rafe and Kade had been involved in the process.

He held his cup, and she couldn't miss the slight shake of his hand. "Oh, yes. Theirs is a great love story, and one I understand. I have to admit that I find the whole idea of sharing a wife a bit distasteful and barbaric. It is an old tradition and one I have tried to see eradicated."

"Shouldn't people be allowed to decide what they want?" The idea of sharing a wife was odd, but she couldn't really see why it was wrong if everyone involved agreed to it.

Khalil's hand waved in an imperious motion, dismissing her thoughts. "Were you allowed to decide, Miss Glen?"

There were landmines everywhere. This man might seem perfectly pleasant, but everything had changed, and she couldn't count on appearances. "I have every option open to me, sir. I can call this whole thing off when I wish to."

That much had been made clear to her. She hadn't spent the whole time crying. She'd used her computer, looking up everything she could find on Bezakistani marriage laws. Apparently the tabloids were fascinated with the royal brothers. If only she'd paid attention to a magazine other than *The Economist*, she might have been more ready for this morning.

"This isn't about love, Miss Glen. The reason the brothers marry a single woman is that they do not wish to split the wealth. It is a way to keep the property intact. This way, they need only give their daughters dowries, and meager ones compared to their wealth. My grandfather was given next to nothing when he chose to marry my grandmother. Al Mussad blood ran through his veins, yet he was treated like a commoner." Khalil's face had gone red, but he stopped as though realizing he was losing his temper. He took a long breath and that charming mask slid over his face again. "There were five brothers then." He smiled a little. "You should be glad you need only deal with three."

She couldn't even imagine five. Of course, a couple of weeks before, she wouldn't have been able to imagine three. But they were all so different. Each so appealing in their way. "I think you should probably talk to your cousins."

"I am not here as family, Miss Glen." He sighed, leaning forward. "Please relax. I truly do not bite."

She sat back, holding herself apart. "I don't think this is a good idea. Talib wouldn't be happy that I'm talking to you alone."

"Talib would be quite upset, but then Talib doesn't always tell you what he is doing, does he?"

"Obviously not." But she wasn't a complete fool. "You were the one who told the press."

He shrugged. "What they did was not only not fair to you, it was not fair to this country. You will have enormous influence over the sheikh. We depend on him. Can you not see how important your position is?"

Again, she felt the weight of her new position on her shoulders, and she didn't even truly understand the scope of a *shaykhah* yet. "I think I would only have the influence Talib allowed me to have."

Khalil huffed, an aristocratic sound. "So that's the way he's decided to go. I wondered why he selected you. Please don't get me wrong, dear Piper. You are lovely. I really do understand what they see in you. But I was surprised when I learned of your background."

She sent him what she hoped was a nasty little smile. "Am I a little common for your tastes?"

His eyes flared. "Not at all. You misunderstand me. I am common now, Piper, and I am quite proud of my status. What my grandfather did, he did for love. He gave up his crown for my grandmother because they were the only two people in the world who mattered to them. I was merely pointing out that all the women he has vetted before now have been royal or very wealthy. But I'm afraid Rafiq and Kadir have always shot them down."

"How many women?" She knew the answer to that question. The internet had been a treasure trove of pictures of her men with various beauties. She hated the fact that she was one in a long line of willing women.

"Many. They have been searching for a very long time." He leaned forward, his eyes soft. "Are you ready for this?"

No. Absolutely not. Nope. But she wasn't going to say that to him. In fact, it was time to start using that brain of hers. She wasn't exactly sure why Khalil was here, but she knew darn straight it wasn't for her benefit. She might be angry with the al Mussad brothers, but she wasn't going to sell them out. "I'm as ready as I can possibly be. You're right, of course. I didn't grow up with a ton of money, but I understand this economy in a way all those pretty debutantes can't. I believe the sheikh was simply looking for his version of perfect. He's a picky man, my Talib."

Her stomach churned. She wasn't used to these games, but she also wasn't ready to give up. If she hadn't decided to go home, she better start playing the game, and that included a little deception.

"You understand that Talib was ready to marry any one of those women, Miss Glen?" Khalil's mouth turned slightly cruel. Finally she was seeing a bit of the real man.

"I understand that he didn't marry them. He's chosen to marry me." He just hadn't bothered to tell her. But then Khalil knew that. Khalil had been the one to contact the press, and most likely he had many spies in the palace. And that made her a little mad. "And you should refer to me as Mrs. al Mussad."

He stood, his eyes going cold. "You are just a concubine at this point. Nothing is settled until the marriage is celebrated in public four weeks from today. You will learn a lot in those weeks. You will learn that you are not capable of being a sheikh's wife. My country doesn't need more American influence."

As her daddy would have said, that man was completely full of bull crap, and he needed a serious cleansing. "The people in the square didn't sound unhappy this morning." She stood up, ready to be done with this unctuous man. Maybe Mindy had been right to remind her of a few things. She'd stood up to scrutiny before. The worldwide press couldn't possibly have a thing on Miss Adeline Hawkins of the First Baptist Church. She'd survived a bunch of old women who wanted nothing more than to destroy her. "They were quite happy that the sheikh and his brothers have decided on a bride."

She gave him her most polite smile. It was the one she'd learned to use on every single woman who came by to make sure Piper was taking proper care of little Mindy. Most of them had called her Cindy because they didn't really care about anything but causing trouble. "I appreciate your coming by. It's so good to meet my husbands' family."

Piper was deeply pleased to see the way Khalil's cheeks flushed, and he stood, his fists at his sides. "We'll see about that, Miss Glen."

He strode out of the room.

"That's *shaykhah* to you, sir."

A burst of applause caused her to turn, her heart nearly stopping.

* * * *

Kade watched Piper turn, his whole body filled with pride for her. Rafe stood at his side, silent, but Kade could feel his emotion.

She'd stood up to that fucker. She'd been a queen, so much stronger than he'd imagined. It wasn't that he'd believed her to be weak. He'd just thought she would need more time. Not his Piper. She'd risen to the occasion.

"Where did you come from?" Her voice was breathless, so unlike the commanding tone she'd used the moment before to completely dismiss his cousin.

The day had dragged on, every hour pure misery. He'd talked to the press, plastering a fake smile on his face as he talked about their courtship and how happy he was, all the while praying she didn't simply flee.

"There is a separate stairway. It leads from the rooms below. They're usually used as nursery rooms."

Her skin flushed, a sweet pink coloring her cheeks. "Oh."

Rafe stepped forward. He'd been Kade's partner in misery. "We thought you might be sleeping. We did not wish to disturb you."

She frowned. "Your cousin disturbed me enough. I don't like that man. He was trying to run me off. He doesn't know how hard it is to run off a Texas girl. We can be stubborn."

Thank god for Texas pride. "He's wrong about Talib. Tal was never serious about the other women. He's been putting this off for many years because no woman moved him."

Her arms crossed over her breasts. "I don't know about that. Khalil might have ulterior motives, but he was right about one thing. This marriage is Talib's duty. I don't know that I like being a duty."

Kade wanted to hold her. The early evening light brought out the gold and reds in her hair. "It was not a duty to love you last night. You can't imagine that. No man could have performed as we did for simple duty."

Rafe frowned. "We made love all night, Piper. There was nothing of duty in that."

"It's too fast," she said, her head shaking.

Frustration welled. "Do you have a timetable? How long should I wait to love you? How many more days or weeks before you'll believe me?"

He nearly took back the words, afraid that he'd frightened her with his harsh comments. But she didn't move an inch.

Her eyes narrowed. "How about giving me the courtesy of honesty, Kadir? Then maybe I'll give you a timetable." She sighed and turned, dismissing him as easily as she'd dismissed Khalil.

He stared at her, his blood pressure rising. She thought she could dismiss him?

Rafe walked after her, passing her and disappearing into the hall. What the hell was he doing? Kade prayed he wasn't getting Talib because this was his fight.

"I was honest with you, Piper. I told you I love you. I would never have made love to you if I didn't intend to spend my life with you."

She turned back slightly. "Oh, I seriously doubt that. Do you think I didn't look you up, Kadir? I'll admit I've been naïve up to this point, but I did a quick search earlier today. You seem to prefer blondes. Lots of them."

He really wished he'd been more circumspect in his younger days. "I cannot change my past. I am just a man."

"Did you ask all of them to marry you? Wait. You don't ask. You just take advantage of the fact that your women don't speak the language. Is that why you like the Swedish girls so much?"

She was pushing him. Anger started to rattle his cage. "I can only apologize for my past."

"And the present? Do you apologize for that as well?"

"No. Had we been honest, you would have run. You would never have even tried. But Piper, can't you see how well you handled Khalil? You have nothing to be afraid of."

"I'm not afraid, Kade. If I decide to be a *shaykhah*, I will be the best I can be. Don't you ever underestimate me. I know I come off as a little naïve, but I've been responsible for myself for a very long time. I had to raise my little sister, work a job, and put myself through college. I think that's what bothers me the most. I can't see how you can possibly love me when you think so little of me. You tricked me into this. You didn't even think I would be smart enough to ever figure it out."

"That is *not* true. We were just desperate. How can you think that? And how can you not see why we wanted to avoid this? Not even a day into our concubine period and Khalil is trying to persuade you to leave. He won't be the only one." Why couldn't she see? She didn't know this world the way he did. "I wanted to spare you the trouble."

"You weren't going to spare me anything, Kade. Trouble like this isn't something you can hide from. It was just waiting. This would always have happened. You can't just sneak a new bride in and expect no one to notice."

They were standing toe to toe, her face turned up to his, a pretty flush on her cheeks. Even her frown turned him on. If he moved just an inch closer she would be able to feel his erection. The minute he'd entered the room, his cock had hardened and pointed her way. He was addicted to her. And she was challenging him. "It isn't their business."

"It's their country, too, Kade. You can't treat it like your private playground. And you can't treat me like a toy."

"You're my wife. I will treat you anyway I like."

"I am not your wife, and quite frankly the more you talk the less likely it is that I will ever be your wife."

"Yes, so please stop talking, brother." Rafe strode back in, three servants moving behind him. They carried platters of food and pushed a cart of drinks. Rafe walked right up to Piper and got down on one knee. "*Habibti*, please eat. I've heard from the servants that you wouldn't touch a thing. I am begging you. I fear for your welfare."

She looked down at him, her lips curving up slightly. "I don't think I'm in danger of starving anytime soon, Rafe."

Kade watched in horror as his brother put his cheek to her hand. "Please, my darling. I've brought all of your favorite foods. And I brought the wine you enjoyed the other night. It will help relax you. It, perhaps, will take your mind off the fact that my brother is acting like a caveman."

"Well, you're acting like a lapdog." What the hell was Rafe doing? They needed to fight this out with Piper.

"I am trying to act like a husband," Rafe shot back. "I believe it will work better than yelling at her."

Piper's eyes narrowed, casting a suspicious glance at Rafe. "Is this how you get me to agree that none of this disaster is your fault?"

Rafe shook his head. "Absolutely not. It is entirely our fault. We made terrible mistakes and can only hope that somewhere in your heart you can forgive us." Rafe kept spitting out loads of crap, but Piper was following him as he got up and began to lead her to the couch. When he offered her a seat, she took it. Rafe was right back on his knees, her delicate foot in his hand. He quickly tossed off her shoe and began rubbing. "I intend to spend the rest of my life making this up to you."

It only took a moment before Piper's eyes closed, and she

relaxed against the couch, practically purring. "God, you really are the smart brother."

Kade sighed. Rafe would probably be the only one in her bed tonight, too, if Kade didn't take his cue. He walked around to the back of the couch where her lovely face was turned up and stroked her hair. "I really do love you. I know I haven't shown it as well as you might wish, but I do. Can you give me another chance?"

She didn't open her eyes, but she didn't turn him away either. "It won't work without Talib."

He knew that, but he wasn't sure how to fix it. "He needs time."

"We're almost out of time, Kadir." Now those gorgeous eyes opened and kicked him straight in the gut. "I have to make a decision in a couple of weeks. I don't think he's going to fall in love with me that quickly. I understand what's at stake. I do. But I don't think I can marry a man who doesn't love me."

"Rafe and I can love you enough for all of us." The thought of losing her made his stomach clench. For the first time, he had to really think about what he would do if she said no. Would he truly be able to let her go? Would he ever be able to accept another bride? There was no time left. They would be forced to choose from one of the women they had overlooked for Piper. He was sure one of them would be willing to sell herself for the wealth of the al Mussad name, but suddenly Kade wasn't so sure he would do the same.

"I don't know, Kade. I don't know anything right now." She sat up, her foot coming out of Rafe's hand. "Can I have the tea, please? I don't know that I need alcohol right now."

Rafe grabbed her tea cup, placing it in her hand. "Anything you want, Piper. And you don't have to make a decision today."

He sat on the couch beside her. Kade decided to follow his brother's lead for once. Rafe had played this so much better than either he or Talib. And maybe it was time to tell Piper a little about her wayward sheikh.

Kade lowered himself to the sofa beside her. "You need to get to know us better."

She huffed a little. "It was easy to get to know you. I just had to search your name on the internet to come up with a thousand and one al Mussad girlfriends."

He deserved that. And it was probably more than a thousand and one, but he appreciated the irony. "I wasn't talking about that. I want to just spend time with you. To hear your stories and to tell you mine. Though I won't be telling you the dating stories since you already know them."

Rafe gave her a smooth smile, the one that let Kade know he was about to be thrown under the bus. "I did not date as much. I was too busy with school."

Kade let his eyes roll. "Yes, he's the perfect angel, Piper. Whatever you do, don't look up the words Rafiq and Spanish night club."

His brother huffed. "You did not have to tell her that."

"Already seen the video." Piper sipped her tea, calm once more. "I can't believe you didn't get arrested."

Rafe shrugged. "The police in Barcelona are very forgiving when the bribe is big enough. And I could not know they had cameras behind the DJ booth. I thought we were alone."

"Yes, it was just him and three girls. Totally alone." Kade grew serious. "No. I wasn't talking about our past scandals. I was thinking about what happened to Talib and how it still affects him today. Piper, if you would just give him time. He's been through a lot."

She turned to him, her face blanching a bit. Her hands shook lightly as she put the tea back on the tray. "Are you talking about the rebels taking him captive?"

It was inevitable she would read about that. The family had attempted to keep it quiet, but the radicals had released videos of Talib al Mussad broken and battered and silent.

"Yes." Kade sighed. Though it happened years before, he could still feel the panic of the day. "Tal had gone to one of the drill sites. He used to do it once a month. He prefers to be hands on, and he enjoyed being with the workers. Our fathers had us working rigs by the time we were sixteen. Tal especially enjoyed getting his hands dirty. They found out where he was going to be and they showed up with twenty men. They killed Tal's security detail and many of our employees. They took him and his personal assistant."

Lily. A pretty British girl he'd met at University. Kade had brought her back to Bezakistan. He'd never been serious about her. She'd been too needy for Kade, but he'd known what she could give his brother right away. What he didn't tell Piper was that Lily had been more than an assistant. She'd been Talib's submissive for many months before they had been kidnapped. After his release, Tal had never spoken of her again, but Kade had read the reports.

"She died." The words fell out of Piper's lips like a lodestone pulling her down. She shook her head. "Sorry. I got a little dizzy just thinking about it. Do you think he had to watch?"

Rafe took her hand in his. "Yes, *habibti*. I believe they forced my brother to watch her torture. It was part of his own."

"Did he love her?" Piper asked.

Kade shook his head. She picked up on much more than he gave her credit for. "Not at all. He cared about her, felt responsible for her. He had a relationship with her that went beyond mere employment, but he didn't love her."

She put a hand to her head, her voice trembling just a bit. "The articles I read about the kidnapping all said Tal was fine."

"We kept the press far away. The American military helped. A SEAL team was sent in. They fought their way in, lost a few men. When it all shook out, my brother and one of the SEALs, a man named Cole Lennox, got separated from the team. They were pursued for days until Cole was able to get him back into the country."

"He wasn't being held here?" Piper asked.

"No. He was taken to a neighboring country. It's why the American military was so willing to keep it quiet. No one wants this part of the world to destabilize," Rafe explained. "So the story the press got was that Talib was able to escape on his own about two weeks after his actual rescue. We cleaned him up, and he didn't go in front of a camera until he could smile and be something like his old self."

Kade thought about the hollow shell his brother had been those days after his rescue. He'd sat in his bed, silent and unblinking for days as though trapped in a private hell. "I don't think he's recovered even today, *habibti*. So, please, give this some time. Please give us a chance."

"I don't know." She tried to stand. "I need a minute."

Kade stood with her. "Piper, sit back down, please. You look so pale. Rafiq, she needs to eat."

"I can't. Oh, help. I think I'm going to…"

She never finished the sentence. She passed out, her body dropping like a marionette puppet that had just had its strings cut. Kade caught her in his arms as Rafe shouted for help.

Chapter Eleven

Talib looked down at his concubine as she lay sleeping. She was frail, more fragile than he'd ever seen her. He realized one of the things he loved about Piper was her strength.

Liked. He liked that about her. He wasn't going to love her at all, damn it. He couldn't.

"She is fine, Your Highness." The doctor who had delivered him stood at the head of his bed. Dr. Haumoud was someone Tal trusted implicitly. "I took some blood. I'm going to have it tested for toxins, but I believe she has just had a couple of very stressful days. Her heart rate has returned to normal. She is resting now."

Yes, she was resting, but he doubted this was anything so simple as stress. The future *shaykhah* becoming violently ill on the day after her betrothal was far too coincidental for his tastes. "Thank you, Doctor. We will take very good care of her. Please contact me the minute you know anything at all."

Piper's chest moved up and down in a graceful symphony of life. Tal couldn't help but stare down at her and wonder what she was dreaming. Was she wondering what her life would have been like if they hadn't brought her here?

He stepped back out into the living area of the suite he now shared with his brothers and Piper. It was full. Rafe and Kade paced, both of his brothers pale with worry. Alea stood near the window. Dane and Cooper were talking quietly, conferring together. Landon leaned against the wall, his eyes on Alea. The big guard didn't seem to be able to focus on anything except Alea.

Tal couldn't even think about that problem right now. He moved toward Dane, Rafe and Kade joining him the minute they realized he was there. Dane looked up, his shoulders squaring.

"Sir."

"What have you discovered?"

Dane's mouth was a flat, straight line. "Not much. By the time we got here, someone had cleaned everything up. Landon went down to the kitchens, but even the dishes had been washed and put away by then. I don't think we would get anything off them even if we knew which ones had been used."

Rafe paled. "I'm going to kill him."

And thereby set off a huge political incident. "We don't have any proof Khalil was responsible."

Kade's fists were clenched at his sides. "He was sitting in here with her when we came up. The bastard just walked into our apartments and talked to our wife without bothering to confer with us. We don't need fucking proof."

Talib took hold of his temper since his brothers seemed so determined to lose their own. And they needed several facts pointed out to them. Facts that had been running through his head from the moment they had told him Piper had taken ill. "The press is watching us, Kadir. All eyes are squarely on this family. Do you see the headlines? She isn't our wife yet. They will talk about the barbarians who killed a man because he merely spoke to their concubine."

Khalil had a hand in this. Tal didn't care what the doctor said. She'd been perfectly fine all day, stressed, yes, but not ill.

He just couldn't prove anything yet.

"We've questioned the staff. No one remembers who brought the tea up here," Dane said

Rafe scrubbed a hand across his face. "Ahmed put together the food for the *shaykhah*. He has been with us since we were children."

"It wasn't Ahmed," Tal returned. "And I've just informed the staff that the *shaykhah* doesn't eat anything that Ahmed doesn't approve."

Alea stood, her hand over her heart. "Khalil usually brings one or two servants with him when he comes to the palace. It would have been easy for him to slip someone into the kitchens. Most of the high-ranking politicians bring their own servants."

Tal felt like snarling. "Not anymore they don't. I can't close the palace, but I can keep the extras out. No more servants. They will have to make do with our staff."

He knew every single member of the staff by sight and name. If he saw a single person who didn't belong, he wouldn't be responsible for his own actions. Piper was still breathing, but Tal was sure this had been an attempt on her life.

"Can't we keep Khalil out?" Kade asked.

"We can keep him out of the private quarters. I've already given the orders. No one except family is to be allowed in the private quarters. I cannot keep a duly elected member of the government out of the palace. Do you understand what that would look like to the press? Give me any evidence and I will work with it." Darker thoughts took over. He could act now. His eyes met Dane's, and he knew the American wasn't averse to handling the problem. Dane would do it quietly, but Tal worried that there would still be talk.

He couldn't do a damn thing without proof until after the marriage. He had to wait until the press coverage died down. Then no one would care that a minor member of parliament who had connections to the royal house had been murdered in his bed. Tal was forced to shake his head at his lead guard.

Dane frowned, his brow furrowing like a predator denied a snack.

"I want a security detail on her," Kade declared.

Dane nodded. "I've called some friends in. They'll be here in a few days. Until then, Landon is on the case."

"And Cooper," Tal said.

"Tal?" Dane started to argue.

"She is more important." Tal would brook no disobedience in this. "They will watch her and take care of her. She is more important than me. If she dies, I will have no crown and no throne because I don't intend to take another wife. Do you understand me?"

Kade sighed. "Thank god. That makes me feel better."

"What do we tell her?" Rafe asked. "Are we even doing the right thing? I'm afraid for her."

Tal was afraid for them all. He knew damn well what could happen to a woman an al Mussad brother cared about. He could still see Lily's body, broken and twisted. She'd cried, begging him to give something that wasn't his to relinquish. He hadn't loved her. She hadn't invaded his fucking soul the way Piper had, but he'd felt her death. The guilt of it weighed on him.

And he still couldn't let Piper go. "She'll be fine. Once our marriage is settled, Khalil will have no recourse and he will cease to be an issue."

Once their marriage was settled, he would have Khalil very quietly assassinated. It was funny. He'd avoided it all these years. He had his suspicions about his cousin, but the instant Piper was in danger, he threw out all sense of justice and simply wanted the fucker out of the way.

What was happening to him? He hadn't been able to get her out of his head all day. He still felt her gripping his cock, milking him for every ounce of come he had in his body. He'd never felt like he had when he'd made love to Piper. Had sex. Damn. He'd had sex with her. It had been a simple physical function, a consummation of their coming marriage.

So why did his heart threaten to beat out of his fucking chest when he thought about her? Why did he stop breathing when she walked in a room? He'd been a different person when he'd talked to her over the computer. It had been easy. He hadn't needed to be a sheikh. He could talk about what he loved—the economics of energy. And she'd spoken his language. A true friend. A partner.

It had been a near betrayal when he'd found her so fucking desirable.

She wasn't supposed to arouse him. She was supposed to fucking soothe him. Theirs was supposed to be a partnership, but he didn't feel like her partner. He felt like her husband, her pissed off, possessive as hell husband.

"I don't know that he will stop." Alea moved away from the window. Her face was grim as she looked at her cousins. "I don't think the marriage being legal will have an effect on him. He will only try to kill her again."

Rafe turned to her, his hands cupping her shoulders. "We don't know that he tried to hurt her, sweetheart."

Alea's face flushed, crimson marking her skin. "Don't patronize me, Rafe. You think I don't know what's going on? You think I don't know who was behind Talib's kidnapping?"

It was Talib's turn to flush. His whole system went on emotional overload, but he tried to present a calm front. He had his suspicions, but he hadn't voiced them to his brothers. But Alea wasn't finished.

"And I blame him for what happened to me, too. I can't prove a damn thing, but no one knew where I was going that night except for the consulate. I received a message from the consulate telling me where I should be and when, and surprise, cousins, the only person to meet me was the man who kidnapped me."

"Alea?" Dane stepped forward, a fierce look on his face.

She put a hand out. "Don't. I can't handle it. Whatever Khalil did to me, it doesn't matter now."

"It fucking matters to me," Cooper said.

Tears pooled in Alea's eyes. "Nothing matters now, not when it comes to me. But Piper is another story. She shouldn't have to deal with this. Why did you choose someone like her? She doesn't understand the exchange. She just wants to be loved. She shouldn't have to worry about being killed because she married one of us."

Landon, Coop, and Dane all looked ready to surround his cousin, but Tal needed to shut that down. Alea wasn't ready for anything like a relationship, much less one that involved three hardened soldiers. "I'm not going to allow anything to happen to Piper, Alea. And I will have Dane look into any connections Khalil has with the consulate in New York."

"Oh, I will absolutely look into that," Dane said under his breath.

Tal turned to him, keeping his voice low. He needed to talk to Dane, to make him see that Alea wasn't ready for all the things Dane wanted from her. "See that is all you look in to, my friend. Never forget that she is royalty."

Dane's eyes hardened, and he took a neat step back, his stance purely professional now. "Of course, sir. Since royalty never, ever falls for a commoner. Your *shaykhah* is so very royal, after all. Coop, Lan, let's patrol for a bit. I can see we're not needed here."

His guard, the men who had been his closest friends for the last several years, turned and walked out. They would be professional, Tal knew, but he worried that in his rage and fear, he'd broken something between them.

So much was breaking in his life. His peace. His friendships. He didn't want to think about the heart he was certain he didn't possess.

And Alea's words had cut him to the bone. Hadn't he learned his lesson? Hadn't Lily's death taught him that there would be no peace for any woman he cared about?

Alea took a deep breath. "Tal, forget I said anything. I'm

sorry. Carry on and don't give up the throne because Khalil will try to hurt any woman you marry. You can't let him win like that. I just really like Piper. She's so kind. I hate the thought of her being hurt. It feels like our family is cursed."

"We aren't cursed," Rafe said, his voice harsh. "But we do have some housekeeping to take care of. Talib is right. We can't kill him now. We don't have any proof that she was poisoned at all. The doctor said it could be a case of nerves. I don't believe it, but we have to follow our own laws."

"To a point," Kade said.

A small feminine sound escaped from the bedroom. Piper. His brothers dropped everything and practically ran into the room, leaving him alone with Alea.

"You should go and see to her," Alea said. Her eyes trailed to the door where Landon was now posted. He stood outside, only a bulky arm evidence that he was there.

Tal knew he should be in there with his brothers, but he also knew what would happen. He would crawl into bed with Piper and cuddle her, falling deeper into a pit he had no intention of ever giving in to. "They will care for her. I have meetings to attend to."

Alea's brow arched over her dark eyes. "Really? Tell me what's going on, Talib. I'm not stupid. I know you have a thing for that girl. You talked about her incessantly for months before you brought her over. Now you're pulling away?"

He wasn't pulling away. He'd never really been with her in the first place.

Liar. Fucking liar. You were with her in every way last night. She gave you a precious gift and you want to toss it in the trash because you can't stand the thought of her knowing who you really are. You don't deserve her. You should have bought a bride and forced your brothers to accept her or leave the family.

Self-loathing was like bile in the back of his throat. If he was half a man, he would tell her to go now, but he couldn't. He would protect her. He would allow his brothers to love her and adore her and be her true husbands. And he would be what he had become since being held in the pit and forced to face his true self. He would be the sheikh.

"I talked about her in relation to work, Alea. And don't try to get me to open my soul." He wasn't sure he had one anymore. "Unless you would like to talk to about what happened to you? No? Don't treat me like the freak, cousin. We're in the same boat, you and I. You think I don't see how you look at my guards?"

Alea's eyes widened. "I don't look at those Neanderthal he-men of yours."

"Oh, you look all right. You devour them, cousin, with your eyes. And in the same breath you send them away. So until you're ready to face your own situation, stay out of mine."

Tal turned and strode out of the room, his gut a churning mess. He longed to go into Piper's room, to be with her and his brothers, to begin to settle into his little family.

But he didn't deserve a family. The sight of Lily's tortured, lifeless eyes haunted him.

He would protect Piper at all costs. Even from himself.

* * * *

Two days later Piper was damn sick of being treated like an invalid. She'd been a little sick, and now Rafe and Kade wouldn't let her out of bed. They'd waited on her hand and foot, making her completely crazy. She'd felt perfectly fine the day after her fainting spell, but they had insisted on her convalescence.

"Can I get you anything?" Rafe asked, his eyes soft as he looked down at her. Kade stirred beside her, his face nuzzling her right arm. It was odd to not be surrounded by them. Neither man had left her side for days.

But Talib had only come in to make sure she didn't need

anything. He hadn't slept with them at all.

"You could get me a schedule of meetings." She tried to give him a brilliant smile.

He frowned. "I think not."

Fine. She could frown right back. "Rafe, you won't let me work. Is this how you view a marriage?"

A long sigh escaped his chest. She could see the weariness on his face. "No, Piper. I am simply trying to take care of you."

And he'd done a wonderful job. She let her hand slide over his. "I can't stay in bed forever, Rafe. You have to let me be me. If all you want is some sweet little thing you can keep in bed, then you don't really need me." She let her lower lip pout out because she remembered the previous night. "Not that you seem interested in doing anything fun in bed."

His lips curled up, his hand cupping her cheek. "Is that what you're upset about?"

Kade was suddenly awake, his arm curling around her waist. "I don't think we should upset Piper further. I believe you were right, Rafiq. We should give her everything she desires."

She could feel the hard length of Kade's erection nestled against her hip. Her whole body heated up, her core turning warm and soft. But she needed more than sex. For two days she'd toyed with the problem of Talib, and she needed answers.

"I think I desire a little talk." But she let her head drift back so she was in Kade's arms. Intimacy. It was her new favorite word. After years of deep loneliness, she reveled in their touch, surrounding herself with them. She should probably still be angry with them, but it was damn hard when they made her feel so adored.

Kade's lips brushed her cheek. "What do you want to talk about, *habibti?*"

Rafe joined them, though he had dressed for the day. He crowded her other side, his nose brushing against her hair. He sighed as though the scent of her settled something deep inside him. "We will talk about anything with you."

"Talib."

The name seemed to be a landmine between the three of them. The brothers stopped but didn't pull away. Even though there was no physical distance between them, Piper could sense the emotional divide that had just opened up.

"I think you should talk with Talib," Kade offered.

"Yes, because Tal is just going to open himself wide to me." Frustration welled. "Look, I'm trying to give this a chance, but it's hard when Tal will barely look at me. I don't expect him to be in here every minute of the day. He's busy. I get that. But is this the way a marriage would be? I'll be married to you two and Tal will just join in the sex?"

Kade groaned a little. "No. You will be married to Tal. I assure you he's going to take that vow seriously. He won't cheat on you if that's what you're worried about. As for Rafe and myself, we don't want another woman. We're too busy trying to get inside you."

And they weren't really hearing her. "I didn't say I'm worried about him cheating. I'm worried about having three husbands, one of whom doesn't really know I exist unless he's on top of me."

Most women wouldn't care. They would count themselves lucky that all three were rich, handsome, and good in bed. But Piper couldn't stand the thought. She'd gone through one engagement where her groom hadn't really wanted her. He'd just been trying to please his parents, and Piper had possessed a sterling reputation. Piper also suspected that her almost mother-in-law thought she would be easy to control.

How was Tal any different? He was marrying her because his country needed him to get married. She'd been selected because she had the right education and the right ideals, and his brothers thought she was kind of hot. She was crazy about Tal. She had been for many months before she'd met him. Even when he was just a low, sexy voice over the phone or a bunch of smart words and a quick wit coming over her computer, she'd been mad about him. She hadn't needed to see his face to know how much she liked him. That man was buried somewhere inside him.

But he, it seemed, just wasn't that into her. And she wasn't sure she could live like that for the rest of her life.

"He needs time," Rafe urged.

"I don't have any time. I have to make a decision," Piper replied. Every time she thought about it, her heart constricted because she was pretty sure there was no real decision to be made. She'd been placed in a terrible position, but Tal was right. Was she really going to subject the men she loved to the chaos of being forced to find a new bride in mere days or lose their throne? Was she willing to plunge a country into chaos because she wasn't being loved the way she wanted to be?

God, she'd just thought it. She loved them. She'd tried to stay away from the L word, even in her head, but it was right there. She might never say it out loud, but the truth was already in her heart.

"Would you really leave us?" Kade asked.

Rafe put out a hand. "This is her decision. Let her make it."

She huffed, a sound she was making a lot these days. "I don't really have a choice and you know it."

A slow smile spread across Kade's face, and he settled back down, this time placing his head on her breast. He cuddled her close. "Good."

She looked down at that black silk capped head and couldn't help but run her fingers through it. "It doesn't bother you that I feel manipulated into this marriage?"

She felt his chuckle along her skin. "Not at all, *habibti*. We were smart enough to catch you. We'll be smart enough to make you happy to be caught."

"I always knew you could learn, Kade." Rafe's warm breath played across her ear, making her shiver. "My brother is perfectly correct. We have our whole lives to make sure you never regret being tricked into becoming our wife."

"Tricked? You didn't have to try too hard. I sort of fell in." She sighed in contentment. At least this felt perfect. But she was still worried about Talib. Maybe she could set a trap of her own. "I want to know what Tal likes."

"He likes you, Piper," Rafe replied.

"I definitely like you." Kade had a hand on her breast, tugging at her silky nightie and releasing a nipple.

"What does he like in bed?" Piper murmured, her skin lighting up as Kade started to suckle a nipple. Heat shot to her pussy. Yes, she'd missed this.

"You need not do anything but be your sweet self." Rafe palmed her other breast.

They were distracting her. "I want to know how to seduce Talib, and you can tell me now or I'll put a stop to all this fun. Now tell me about this spanking stuff."

She didn't want to, but she would pull a power play if they didn't start talking. It was too important to ignore. Tal had gotten off on slapping her backside. What other things made his blood pump? How could she use his own dark desires to set a trap for him? One intended to push him past this polite mask he wore. A trap to help him fall in love.

Rafe settled his arms around her. "My brother enjoys playing...certain games."

"BDSM." She wasn't stupid. Along with looking up the marital laws of Bezakistan, she'd typed the word spanking into her search engine and came up with a shocking amount of pure pornography that might have given her computer an STD, along with some very informative articles on BDSM.

Rafe raised a brow, and Piper was happy to have surprised him.

"Yes," he admitted. "We all enjoy it to some degree. My brother is more interested in the Dominance and submission portion of the lifestyle."

Thank god she had Rafe because Kade already had another purpose. He seemed intent on making her crazy. He sucked on her nipples, getting them hard and sensitive. He bit and played with them, seemingly ignoring her conversation with Rafe.

"Has he taken a sub before?" She asked, remembering the words that had been used in the articles.

Rafe shut down. Kade stopped what he was doing. And the pieces fell into place.

"Lily?"

"Yes," Kade replied, his voice low. "She was his submissive, but you have to understand what that means."

Piper was pretty certain she knew. "It means she played with him. It means they followed certain rules. Were they twenty-four seven?"

Kade looked startled. "How do you know this? And no, they were not. They came together for play, but Tal didn't want the responsibility outside the bedroom. I wasn't interested in giving Lily what she wanted at the time."

"Kade met her in London at a club," Rafe explained.

"A fetish club?" She nearly laughed because the surprise was apparent on both their faces. "I can read, guys. I looked it up. Spanking seems to kind of go along with the lifestyle thing. So Lily wanted more than even Tal was willing to give her?"

"When I first met Lily, she was happy to simply play," Kade explained. "She was very independent. She had a good job as a personal assistant to a high-powered CEO. She was fun. And she wanted to see the world so I brought her back home, and Talib immediately hired her."

Piper could fill in the blanks. Lily had fallen for the handsome sheikh and wanted more. "Did she ask to be his slave?"

She'd figured out it was the BDSM equivalent of a marriage. It was a deep and lasting connection, or it should be.

Kade stiffened, guilt clouding his features. "I thought it would be fun for them both. I knew she wasn't for me, but she could have made Tal happy for a while and she would get something out of it, too. But six months in, she was making him miserable. She was clinging and jealous of everyone, including me and Rafe."

Kade put his head to her breast again, but this time he seemed to need comfort. She let her hand find his hair, smoothing it back.

"It's all right. You didn't mean for her to get hurt," Piper said.

Kade seemed to calm a bit. "Tal felt responsible for her. She'd played some before, but she claimed he was her first Dom. We know now that was a lie, but at the time he felt a deep sense of duty toward her. He'd taken a few submissives before, but never a slave. He was planning on letting her go. He just needed to find a way to do it with kindness."

Tal would likely take the responsibility of a slave seriously, even if he wasn't in love with her. Though she couldn't be sure he hadn't been. How could his brothers really know his heart? Tal believed in sacrifice, for his country, for his brothers. He would have sacrificed his own love if he'd been certain his brothers couldn't accept her as their wife.

"So she died before he could end their relationship."

A long look passed between Rafe and Kade. They were thinking about hiding something.

"If we wish her to be a member of this family, we must treat her as one," Rafe said. "She should know everything."

Kade nodded shortly. "We kept much of the incident out of the papers. What got through was bad enough. They took Lily along with Talib. He doesn't talk about it. I believe she was tortured in his presence in an effort to break him."

Tears pooled in her eyes. Talib would hold that guilt in. It would hurt him more than any physical pain. "How terrible for them both."

Did he miss Lily? Had he loved her deep down? Was he still in mourning? And was that why he couldn't open up to Piper?

Rafe turned, his face close to hers. "Piper, it was a terrible time, and I don't know that he's fully come out of it. He hasn't taken another submissive. I don't think he has played at all, and I believe this has created a void in his life. He needs a place where he is in control. I know it sounds crazy. He's the sheikh, but his whole life is dictated by his country, by laws and traditions, by the press and our economy. In his playroom, he needed only to think of his own needs and those of the women who brought him pleasure."

"It was more than pleasure." Kade sat up. "It was about trust. He needed that perfect trust he got from his subs. I don't need to control the way Tal does, but I've played enough to understand how that bond of trust would appeal to him. His life is hard. He works all day. He needs to relax, and he won't allow it. The night of our bonding was the first time I've seen Tal relax. He slept. He never sleeps anymore. I know you're angry. I know you feel we betrayed you."

She gave him the slightest smile, touching his cheek. "I think you took the quickest path to success. It annoyed me, but we all know I'm not going anywhere. I think you knew that if you got me here, I wouldn't be able to back down."

Because she cared about the people around her. Because she loved them. Because she'd loved them since she'd met them. Because this was the journey of her life, and it had led her to three amazing men. She wasn't going to walk away because she was scared. She was going to fight. Tal thought she was a safe choice. Well, maybe it was time for her to prove that he'd met his match.

Rafe put his forehead to hers. "I know I should apologize, but if I get to spend the rest of my life with you, then it was worth it. I would commit the worst of crimes if it meant bringing you into my family because I think you can save us. Kade and I already love you. I think Tal does, too. Be strong enough to hold us together."

Strong. It was a word she never would have used to describe herself, but now she saw Piper Glen through their eyes.

Through Mindy's eyes. She had been strong enough to save her tiny family, to be true to her parents. She could be true to her own heart, too. She could form her family, her new world. She just had to be smart enough and brave enough to make it happen.

She kissed Rafe, forgiveness flowing. It was silly to be mad when she loved them, too. They had played a game, risked a lot to keep her close. They were offering her something extraordinary. Love. A crazy bright future. A whole country to build. How could she turn that down?

Rafe's hand sank into her hair and his tongue surged in, rubbing against hers. Tal wasn't the only one who seemed to need a little dominance. Rafe pulled back on her hair gently, his mouth controlling hers.

Kade went right back to her breasts, sucking and tugging and nipping again.

She let go of all her worries. There was no place for them here.

Chapter Twelve

Piper eased the key into the lock and slipped inside the door. Dark. This room was so dark when almost every other room in the palace was lit with sunlight. She did as Rafe had instructed and closed the door before she started to look for the switch so no one would notice when she turned on the light. She ran her hand across the wall to her left and, sure enough, there it was. She flipped the switch.

Wow. So this was what the guys meant by dungeon.

The whole room was paneled in dark wood, the floors covered in a black marble. She was glad she hadn't worn shoes. Almost any sound would reverberate in this room like the crack of a whip. She feared that even breathing too hard would sound loud.

She tried to look at the room logically. She'd spent the night before in Rafe and Kade's arms, but this morning had been spent studying Talib, or more specifically, this one piece of Talib. She'd really delved into researching BDSM and all its accompanying toys online. She recognized a spanking bench. It was a padded bench-like piece with places for the submissive's arms and legs to be tied down while her backside remained in the air for the Dom to torture. There was a large cross on the wall. She searched her memory. St. Andrew's Cross. She'd watched a short video where a woman had been whipped by her Master while tied to the cross. He'd been an expert with the whip, leaving not a single welt on his sub's flesh but sending her to some euphoria called subspace that puzzled but intrigued her.

Was that what she had felt the beginnings of that first night with Talib? Subspace? After a while, the pain of the spanking had seemed muted and every slap of his hand had an almost calming effect. She hadn't needed to be in control. She hadn't even wanted to be. She'd simply wanted to please him and to gain pleasure in return. It had been relaxing to utterly let go, trust him, and not worry about how she looked or acted or what others would think.

She kind of longed to get back to that place, and she worried Talib was the only one who could take her there.

"Would you like to explain why you're here?"

She nearly screamed at the sound of Tal's dark voice cutting through the silence. "Oh, you nearly scared me to death."

He frowned at her, his hawk-like features in pure predatory mode. "You should not be here."

"How did you know I was?" Piper asked, surprised he'd gotten here so quickly. Was the door on a silent alarm?

"I followed you. I caught sight of you as I came out of a meeting with the press. I wanted to make sure trouble didn't find you." His narrowed eyes told her he wasn't happy. In fact, he looked furious. "I see you sought trouble instead. This door is locked. How did you get inside?"

Talib's fury wasn't simple. Maybe this had been a huge mistake. She'd wanted a little peek into his soul, but he looked almost volcanically angry. His face had flushed to a deep crimson, his hands in fists at his sides.

"I'm sorry." Her voice seemed to squeak through the room.

"I did not ask for an apology. I asked for an explanation. This door is locked. Besides me, only my brothers have the key, so I would like to know which one of them betrayed me."

She held her ground as he stalked forward. He was wearing his normal dress shoes, and they definitely echoed through the dungeon as he crossed the floor to her. She wasn't about to get Rafe in trouble because she was curious. She held up the set of keys. "I stole them while he was sleeping. I wanted to know what was in here."

Tal came to hover over her. He used every inch of his height for pure intimidation. "You thought you could simply walk into anywhere? Without permission?"

Piper sucked in a breath, reaching for her courage. The last few days with Rafe and Kade had been lovely, but she'd missed Talib's utter dominance. But now, being in this room alone with him, doubts crept in. Would she be enough woman for him? Could she hold even a little piece of his heart? Or had it been locked away when Lily died? She couldn't know unless she risked herself.

Ultimately, she was either in or out, and she had to decide now. She couldn't really leave Bezakistan and her men so she couldn't back down either. "Well, I was told this all belongs to me now. Or is marriage different in Bezakistan? Please inform me, Talib, because I seem to be ignorant of so very much."

He moved even closer, the heat of his body rolling off him. "You have yet to agree to our marriage, so I don't think you can lay claim to anything."

Suddenly, she wasn't so scared of him. If he was truly disinterested, there wouldn't be a huge erection in his slacks. He'd only been in the room with her for moments, but his cock had stiffened and pointed at her. She made a move of her own. She wouldn't win Talib al Mussad with shyness. She let her body brush his. "You made your points very clear, Tal. You know I'm not going anywhere."

"I know nothing of the sort."

"Only because you've been avoiding me for days."

His eyes flared and he backed off slightly. "I have not. I've checked in on you. I could not spend every moment with you. I had business to attend to. And even if you have made your decision, there is no reason for you to be in this room."

She turned, surveying the dungeon. It was a huge space for just two people to play in. She would bet Rafe and Kade had spent a little time in here, too. She could picture them in leather pants and nothing else. She couldn't help it. Ever since the spanking Tal had given her, she'd been unable to stop thinking about it. "I think I have every reason to be here. Unless you're planning on a very open marriage, I should be the only woman in this room. I like it. I want to play in here."

She stepped away, letting her hand touch the fine leather of the spanking bench. It was beautifully made, completely unlike some of the manufactured ones she'd seen on the internet. This one had been lovingly crafted with hand-carved wood. The leather straps had been lined with soft cloth so the submissive's wrists never chaffed. These were men who would take care of a woman, even if they didn't love her.

Tal followed her. "Damn it, Piper, you don't even know the meaning of that word. Play means something different in this room. You should leave. I plan to have this room redecorated as a family room."

She turned her head, looking at him over her shoulder. She winked his way. "I can imagine what the family will do in here. And I know quite well what it means to play."

She headed over to the wall. The dark panels had gilded doors in the center. She slid one open. Her eyes widened. It was a wall of sex toys. And someone had arranged very tasteful lighting to illuminate the plethora of vibrators, handcuffs, paddles, and whips. There was a whole drawer full of jewelry. They looked a bit like earrings.

She picked up a particularly lovely set. They looked like emeralds but she noted they dangled from the end of small clips. She opened the clip, pressing down on the tops. Little biting notches covered the sides, like an alligator opening up to take a bite. "You torture a girl's ears?"

He stared at her, keeping some distance between them as though he didn't trust himself to come closer. "They aren't for your ears, Piper. They're nipple clamps."

She nearly dropped them. "Nipples? Why?"

He sent her a nasty smile. "They make the nipples exquisitely sensitive. And they're a form of erotic torture."

"Did you buy these?" They were gorgeous, diamonds and emeralds. The idea of adorning parts of her body no one but her husbands would ever see held a certain appeal.

"I did, though no one has worn them. I enjoy clamping my subs. I like the way the jewels swing and how they glow against a sub's skin. Or I did. This part of my life is over now. I have no intentions of this lifestyle entering our marriage."

She replaced the jewelry on its velvet-lined drawer. Rafe had been right. This was a huge piece of Tal's sexuality. He'd carefully chosen everything in this room. He'd likely designed the interior himself. According to his brothers, he'd once spent hours in here playing with subs, women who trusted him with their pleasure. Since his capture, he'd lost this part of himself. Piper suspected he wouldn't be whole without it. "What if I want to try it?"

His voice came out as a low growl. "Get out of here, little girl. You have no idea what you're doing."

It was time to prove she did know a thing or two. As gracefully as she could, she sank to her knees, spreading them wide in a slave pose. Her skirt pooled around her. She hadn't expected to see Tal, so she wasn't dressed for the occasion. She'd come here merely to get a lay of the land, but now that Tal had followed her, she wasn't giving up this chance. She let her head drift down in a submissive position and waited.

The waiting was the hardest part. Silence reigned. She could hear the sound of her own breath, the roar of her heart, and the movement of Tal's shoes against the marble of the floor. It was hard and cold against her skin, and she was pretty sure that was why Tal had installed marble, not for its beauty but for the way it would keep a sub deeply aware of her surroundings.

"You're overly dressed for a sub, Piper."

"Do you want me to undress, Tal?"

"Sir. In here you call me Sir. Look at me."

She let her eyes drift up. His face was hard, no tenderness at all in his eyes. And his slacks sported a magnificent erection. "Yes, Sir?"

"Do you have any idea what you're asking for? Do you understand what you seek? I never meant to come down this path with anyone again."

Tears pooled in her eyes because she suspected Rafe and Kade didn't know the whole story. "Because you loved Lily so much you can't stand the thought of another sub?"

His eyes narrowed. "My brothers have been talking."

"Please, Talib. I would rather know. I have to know what the boundaries of this marriage are."

"I suspect I could tell you and you wouldn't respect them at all. Perhaps you're right. Perhaps you do need to see this part of me. Maybe then you will understand. You have one chance to get out of this. Get up and walk away, and we can simply be friends and lovers and partners in our intellectual pursuits. If you stay here, you will belong to me in ways you cannot imagine. You'll be mine to command, to torture, to fuck as I please." His hand tangled in her hair, drawing her head back, forcing her to look up at him. He towered over her, a dark, menacing, entirely sexual presence. "I will not go easy on you. Never imagine that because you're my bride that I won't make you scream for me."

Every word that came from his mouth was a promise of dark pleasures. She was a little afraid, but refused to walk away. "I want to try this, Talib."

"There is no trying. Yes or no."

Piper drew in a shaky breath, hoping she could handle him. But really, she had no choice. Deep down, she trusted that he would never truly harm her physically. Knowing that, she could put her body in his hands and hope that his heart followed. "Yes."

"Then take off your clothing. You aren't allowed to be dressed in my dungeon. You will fold your clothing, come back, and present yourself to me. Slave pose, but with your arms locked behind your back."

Piper stood, feeling awkward and ungainly. It wasn't easy to get up. Tal's hand came out to steady her. "Thank you, Sir."

His face was like perfectly sculpted granite. "I expect you to practice. You will practice every day until you can rise with exquisite grace. Your grace speaks much about your Master."

She flushed, embarrassment flooding her. "I'm klutzy."

"But capable of learning, Piper. Now remove your clothing and present yourself to me."

Her shaking fingers went to the buttons on her blouse. He watched her every move with dark eyes that missed nothing. She was caught between apprehension and anticipation as she carefully folded the blouse, then pushed the skirt to her hips.

"Slowly. This is a show for your Master. It is a delicious reveal of what you're offering me, and I can either accept or reject it."

It. He was talking about her body. He was talking about her heart.

She slowed, her hands skimming down her body as pushed the light skirt past her hips. The minute he forced her to slow her movements, she became aware of what she really was doing—and her effect on him. This was a dance for her Master. Maybe she didn't have to be good at it yet. She only had to show him all she offered.

She turned to him, letting him see her body. It wasn't something to hide. Her body was his. It didn't matter what he felt now. Maybe he was only looking for sex. Piper suddenly realized that she couldn't control Tal's heart. She could only do this, offer him everything she had. She loved him. She admitted to herself that she'd probably loved him even when he was just a name on a computer screen. Those months of computer exchanges had bonded her to him. Deep inside him, that man existed, and she couldn't let him go without a fight. But the only heart she controlled was her own.

Tears pricked her eyes. Deep inside her soul, she could hear Rafe and Kade whispering to her as they did when they had made love. They'd promised her they loved her. They told her she was lovely. Her heart was a worthwhile gift, and Tal was a worthwhile man. The whole sheikh thing, she'd decided, wasn't everything it was cracked up to be. She'd watched as Talib gave and gave to the people around him while they just asked for more. He might have everything money could buy…except life's treasures that were free but priceless, like moments of pure respite with a woman who would give all to him whenever he wished.

She folded her skirt, grateful for once that she was wearing the frilly underwear Rafe had bought for her. The white lace clung to her curves, and she could practically feel Tal's eyes rake her as she bent over. She slipped off her sandals and added them to the neat pile.

"Next time you will wear heels. I know my brother bought you some. He has perfect taste. He knows what will look good on you when you wear nothing but the shoes." Tal's voice had gone deep. "Your answer is always, 'yes, Sir.'"

"Yes, Sir." She couldn't help but see that he'd relaxed. He might not even realize it, but his shoulders had softened and his eyes were filled with that languid darkness she now associated with Tal and pleasure.

"Finish the job I gave you." He leaned against one of the dark columns that dominated the room, just waiting for her to take off the rest of her clothes. "Show me."

The bra had a front clasp. She was grateful for that. Rafe had made it very easy for her to unsnap it, but she let her hand trail down first, breathing softly, allowing his eyes take it all in. She cupped her breasts, thinking about the way Kade would palm her, rubbing his thumb over her nipple, getting it hard and ripe for his mouth. She let the pads of her fingers gently skim her nipples before finding the clasp. The lacy bra came undone and her breasts bounced free.

She'd always thought she was a little too chunky, but she felt different with Talib's eyes on her.

"The underwear now. Your pussy belongs to me. I don't like you hiding it. I know my brothers have a thing for silky lingerie, but when you're with me, you will not wear it. That pussy will be bare, ready for my use whenever I wish it. I will be able to raise your skirts and fuck you anytime, anywhere. Do you understand me?"

She knew the answer he expected. "Yes, Sir."

Hooking her fingers under the waistband of her undies, she slid them down.

She placed them on the pile and stood, waiting for his approval.

Tal stared for a moment, then he straightened, closing the space between them. "You seem to have picked up a few tricks, Pandora. You're not as charmingly graceless as you seemed just days before." He stopped mere inches from her. "Turn around. Place your hands on the seat of the spanking bench. I want your ass high in the air. Arch your back."

She did as he asked, leaning over and trying to find a good position.

"Spread your legs wider. Never try to keep me out."

He was behind her, his feet between her legs, forcing them farther apart. Her legs were spread wide, leaving her pussy on full display. She could feel cool air on her hot flesh. Tal's hand traced the line of her spine.

"This is how you present yourself to me. When I ask you to

greet me, you sink into your slave pose. When you present yourself to me, you will find the nearest flat surface and take this position."

Piper closed her eyes. She knew what she must look like to him. Wanton. Ready. Her pussy was begging to be filled with cock. His.

"Are you wet for me, concubine?" His hand was close. He was right at the base of her spine. Any minute he would find the valley of her ass and his fingers would go past it, straight to her pussy. She wanted more there than just a few fingers, but she was aching. She would take anything.

A loud smack cracked through the room and the skin of her backside exploded with a sweet heat. She couldn't help but gasp at the sensation of his hand spanking her ass.

"Answer me."

"Yes, Sir." Days ago she would have been too embarrassed, but now she understood. There was no place for shame in a loving relationship. Her pussy was sopping, desperate for his touch. She could admit everything to him. "I'm so wet."

Another smack, this one to the other cheek, spreading out the erotic pain. "Don't ever lie to me in this room. This is my room. No one but the two of us exists in this room. I might share you with my brothers everywhere else, but here you belong only to me. Now get on your knees. Greet me. Show me what you've learned."

She pushed herself off the bench and turned. Every nerve ending under her skin was alive. She sank to her knees, the cold marble hitting her flesh. She remembered what she'd seen and spread her legs wide. There were several variations of the slave pose. Tal had asked her to place her hands behind her back, thrusting her breasts out. Threading her fingers together, she spread her knees wide so her pussy was on display.

Tal stood before her. She stared at his ridiculously expensive shoes. She could feel the heat of his body, but for a moment, he didn't move. Then his hand cupped her head, fingers sinking in. "I want to feel your mouth, concubine. Take me deep. Swallow me down."

His hands went to the fly of his trousers, working rapidly to unleash his cock. He pushed them down, the slacks hitting the floor. He wasn't wearing briefs. His cock bobbed, the large plum-shaped head pointing toward her.

She didn't bother to bring her hands to him. She was pretty sure that would get her spanked, and she wanted to taste Talib. His hands pulled her head forward.

"I will to teach you how to suck my cock. Lick the head. Run your tongue all over it." He took his cock in hand and pointed it toward her. It teased her lips, his salty masculine flavor hinting at what was to come.

She peeked her tongue out, licking at the tiny slit. A pearl of fluid pooled there. Lapping it up, she swallowed, glorying in the deep groan that erupted from his chest. She'd done that to him. Before he'd been angry, every muscle in his body a study in tension. Now he was tense, but for another reason altogether, and she was pretty sure he wasn't thinking about business or his kingdom. He was focused on her.

Primal instinct took over, leading her to suck the entire head of his cock into her mouth. Even that bit filled her.

"Yes. Good. You'll have to practice." He moved his hips. Little thrusts that gained ground with each twist. "Your sweet mouth is very small, but before long you'll take every inch of my cock. Oh, my concubine, I'm going to fill every fucking hole you have. Your mouth, your pussy, your ass. In this room, they are all mine. When you enter this space, you're my slave. Take more."

He pressed in, forcing her jaw open. Her lips curled around the thick stalk. Her tongue played around the ridge where the head gave way to his long shaft. Smooth. The skin covering his cock was like warm velvet, her tongue moving over the rock-hard flesh underneath. She was lost in the sensation, smooth against hard, submission yielding to dominance. It was a sexy little game Tal liked to play. She was the one on her knees, following his commands, but she'd never felt more in control. This was her choice, to give him exactly what he needed.

He pulled out of her mouth abruptly. "I don't wish to come yet. That hot mouth of yours won't win this time. Stay in position. You want to be my slave, you'll have to dress the part."

His feet echoed across the marble floors as he kicked off his pants and shoes, discarded his shirt and made for the jewelry case she'd been looking at before. Piper turned, watching his muscled backside. He hadn't bothered folding his own clothes, tossing them aside while hers were neatly arranged. He moved briskly, opening drawers and pulling out items.

Abruptly, he turned, meeting her curious gaze with a censuring stare. A frown crossed his face. "I told you not to move."

Yikes. She'd wanted to watch him. She'd been mesmerized by the way he moved, and she'd forgotten he'd given her a very direct order. A flush of embarrassment went through her and she turned back around, taking up her previous position, eyes on the floor.

"It won't work. Present yourself for punishment." His voice was a low growl that managed to both scare her and arouse her.

She got to her feet, her muscles shaking. He was right. She would have to practice. After only a few minutes in slave pose, she was sore and a bit stiff. She was almost relieved to move back to the spanking bench. Leaning over, she made sure her backside was high in the air, her legs spread wide. This was what Tal wanted, and she was surprised to find herself sinking into the role. He needed this to take him away from the stresses of his life, but she was finding respite, too. Suddenly she wasn't worried about what might happen tomorrow or the day after. She simply felt, allowing herself to drift whichever way Talib took her.

"Do you know what happens to bad slaves?" Tal asked, his

hand on her cheek, cupping her softly.

"They get punished."

"No. They get tortured." His hand landed on her ass, but she was ready for it. She knew it would hurt at first before the pain sank in and throbbed its way to pleasure. She gripped the plush leather of the bench under her as Tal slapped her ass. Once, twice, three times he spanked, moving his hand all over her flesh, spreading out the pain and heat. Again and again until he'd reached twenty and tears pricked her eyes.

"Stay in position, Piper. What do you say to me now? Do you want to leave? Do you want to run to my brothers and their tender care? They will cosset you, treat you with the gentlest of touches while I will always want this. What do you say now?"

This was her test. He'd pushed her, thinking she would break, would run right back to Rafe and Kade, and then he would have exactly what he wanted. She wasn't stupid. He wanted her in a nice safe box where he could have sex with her, but he never had to really give anything of himself. She had no doubt he would come to her bed, but without this core piece of his soul, anything between them would be a simple, friendly exchange. Piper wanted—needed—more.

Rafe and Kade gave her acceptance and affection, taught her things about herself, about love and sex and intimacy. They were tender yet manly in their own ways. But she was rapidly discovering she wanted the sheer dominance only Talib could provide.

"I love you, Talib al Mussad. In this room, I belong only to you, my sheikh, my Master."

* * * *

Tal had to take a step back. He was damn glad she was obeying him because he couldn't look into her eyes.

I love you.

She wasn't fucking supposed to love him. His heart raced.

He knew that was wrong. He'd always known she would believe that she felt the emotion. Women needed such sentiments, but it was supposed to be an easy thing. I love you was something she was supposed to say because it was what a husband and wife said to one another over breakfast before going their separate ways.

But Piper meant it, and those words seared straight through his soul.

She held her position. It wasn't perfect. She hadn't spent hours training to make exceptional lines of her body. Unlike his other submissives, she hadn't been selected for her grace. So why did this woman move him in ways the others could not? Why did his heart ache the minute she walked in a room? Why did he get hard at the mere thought of her?

She stayed in place, though he could see her beginning to panic. She wasn't in a mental place where she could be serene yet. He hadn't gotten her there, hadn't truly earned the trust it would take. His silence was making her nervous. He could tell by the way her skin flushed. Her gorgeous ass was red from the spanking, but the rest of her fair flesh bore the mark of her fear. She'd said she loved him, and he was silent.

And brave because she didn't move a muscle, simply waited for him.

Tal didn't feel brave. His stomach tightened in knots. He couldn't love her. And he couldn't let her go. He knew he should walk away. He should order her to put her clothes back on, then show her the door. By this time tomorrow, he could have the whole dungeon dismantled and he would never rebuild it. He could shove this need down so deep it would never surface again.

But his feet didn't move for the door. They stayed in place as though his cock and his damn stupid heart had taken over, and his brain no longer functioned. To his horror, his hand moved right back to the globes of her ass, caressing them lovingly. He adored the pink sheen to her skin. "You are mine.

Here and now, no one exists but you and me."

Not his brothers. Not that fuck Khalil. Bezakistan didn't exist. No countries or people. No responsibility beyond her. He was just a man here. He wasn't a sheikh. He was simply her Master.

And he had some discipline to deliver. And a sweet little slave to fuck to his heart's content.

Piper relaxed. He hadn't said the words he knew she longed to hear, but she seemed satisfied that he hadn't run. Her spine was still straight, but the total rigor was gone. Her head released, dropping down as though simply waiting for his next command.

Tal caressed a hand down her spine, trailing along, tracing the marks he'd made. Perfectly pink, the imprint of his hand would be there for hours, if not days. He would see them and remember this private time with her even as he watched his brothers fuck her. A piece of him would still be with her.

"Stay in position, concubine. It's time to start your preparation. This isn't for discipline, though at times I might use it as such." He reached for the lube, parting her cheeks and getting his first real look at the beauty of her asshole.

She shivered a little, the sight going straight to his cock. He wasn't a pure sadist, but the fact that she was on the edge, apprehensive about what he would do to her, aroused him unbearably. One day he would delight in blindfolding her and leaving her on edge for hours, completely uncertain of what would happen next. Pleasure or pain? All roads would lead to ecstasy, but part of the journey would be in the suspense.

But for now, he had to prepare her for his cock. A slow shiver cascaded across her skin as he dribbled the lubricant between her cheeks.

"Tal," her voice was a breathy whisper. She knew what was going to happen now, and she seemed to want to protest.

Three sharp smacks to her ass silenced her. "Quiet. You will take the plug now or you'll get acquainted with the flogger and then take the plug." He fully intended to fuck her ass eventually. There would be no way around it for her, but he intended to make her love it as much as he would. Careful preparation was the key. "You took the small plug. Why are you so scared?"

"Because I saw that plug when I was looking at the clamps. It's not small, Sir. It's very big."

He chuckled a little as he lubed up the plug. "It's not as big as me, my darling girl. Not even close, and by the time we're done, you'll take me just fine."

His cock pulsed as though the fucking thing was jealous of the plug. Tal placed the plug against the rosette of her ass, just the tip. She clenched down.

Another smack. He wasn't going to be kept out. "Stop it, Piper. If you want to cease the play, you have only to say so, but my brothers and I won't take turns forever. We want to take you all at once. All three of your husbands fucking your every hole because you belong to us. If you keep clenching that little asshole to keep me out, I will introduce you to ginger oil and I doubt you will like the way it burns. But you will finally learn that this is mine and I want in."

Her head came up and she turned just a little, a fierce frown on her face. "You know we use ginger to cook in Texas. Y'all should try it sometime."

He loved her sass. Still, he smacked her cheek again, a low moan coming from her chest. "You would be surprised what else they do in Texas. I know quite a few people there who would shock you."

He pressed the plug in, satisfied when she breathed out and tried to accept it. Her back arched, and a deep shudder went through her body. She pushed back. Tal fucked the plug into her ass, gaining ground with each small foray. He gave himself completely to the task, the world narrowing to just her. Nothing mattered except preparing his concubine. Over and over, he circled the tight flesh with the plug until finally it sank deep, easing the way for his cock.

He leaned over, placing kisses along her spine. When he was finally balls deep inside her most forbidden place, would he feel like he'd come home?

Tal stood, brushing aside the thoughts that plagued him. He had other things to do. "Stand up. Arms behind your back. Feet spread wide."

He walked over to the small gold sink and washed his hands before picking up the lovely clover clamps he'd selected for her. The burnished gold would make her skin glow. He turned and had to catch his breath.

She might not be the most graceful submissive he'd ever kept, but damn she was the most beautiful. Her dark hair tumbled around her shoulders, the soft light picking up strands of red and amber, curling just below the curve of her shoulders. She'd followed his instructions to the letter, her fingers clasped behind her back. Her gloriously full breasts were thrust out, the nipples already peaked. Her legs were spread, and he could see the fine sheen of moisture on her pussy.

She wasn't shrinking from his darker desires. She wanted it. She wanted him to dominate and fuck her any way he pleased.

Fuck. She trusted him. A dangerous thing since he knew the man he was deep inside. A coward. Very nearly a traitor. He didn't deserve her, not for an instant. But he would still take her. She might never understand, but he'd decided. She was payment for his pain. She was his prize for surviving that day and every night since. Every ounce of hatred and torment he'd suffered would be paid for with her sweet flesh.

She would never know how he longed to love her, how he ached for something he'd lost and could never have again.

"Is this what you wanted, Sir?" Her eyes were wide, almost pleading with him to tell her she was good at this.

He couldn't turn her down. Her spine should be straighter, her fingers more tightly wound. Her feet weren't *en pointe* as they should be, her back too arched. He touched her cheek. "You're perfect. Absolutely perfect. Let me dress you up."

Her lips curled in a satisfied smile. He'd suspected she was submissive from their months of conversation, but the last few days had proven how ideal she was for him. She could hold her own, but preferred to please. If he treated her right, she would be his forever.

"Hold still." He got to his knees. She was petite, the perfect size for him. When he got to his knees, her nipples were right where he wanted them to be. He leaned forward and licked, a slow stroking of his tongue. Her scent and taste filled his every sense. Clean. Her skin always tasted so fresh, like a cool drink on a hot day. He'd grown addicted to the citrusy scent of her. He'd started getting a hard-on every time someone brought him a fucking orange.

He sucked her nipple into his mouth, reveling in her response. The musky smell of her arousal drowned out the citrus now. Every tug of his mouth brought forth a fresh coating. Her pussy was pulsing, begging for his attention, but he had a little torture in mind.

He pinched her nipple between his fingers, the nubbin elongating. He slipped the clamp on, tightening it just to the point that it dangled. The jewels pulled her nipple, angling it down. As she gasped and fought to absorb the sensations, he tongued the second nipple before slipping the clamp on. With nimble fingers, he adjusted it until they sat perfectly on her breasts.

She would look beautiful with rings pierced through her nipples and a gold chain hanging between them. He could pull on the chain while she rode his cock, every twist tightening the clamps until she screamed out her pleasure. He kissed his way down her torso.

Or he could let the chain dangle, running down the valley of her breasts toward her pussy, where it would connect to a gentle clamp he'd secure around the pearl of her clitoris. He breathed her in, her musk filling his world.

She was so responsive. Her little clit poked out of its hood, begging for his affection. This was what he needed. He'd denied himself for so long, never reentering this life he longed for. He didn't deserve to have a woman trust him so utterly, but now he realized how empty he'd been without it.

He let his tongue skim over the bud of her sex, delighting in the way she quivered. "Don't move or I'll stop."

"Yes, Sir." Her voice came out on a little squeak even as her hands twitched, as though she wanted to touch him.

But this was his time. There would be plenty of time later when he would let her explore to her heart's content, but not now. He rubbed his nose along her pussy, gathering her scent around him. He wanted to drown in it, in her spice and sweetness. His tongue delved in, the delicious essence of her arousal thrilling him.

Over and over, he licked her pussy, eating her up. She was more sweet than any dessert. He could make a meal of her every night and still be hungry for her in the morning. He was dangerously close to her—and not just physically. Alarm bells went off in the back of his head. He needed to retreat, to rethink this whole situation, but he speared up, fucking her with his tongue. He lost himself, in his role as Master, in Piper's sweet submission, in her giving heart.

"Come for me, concubine. Come all over my tongue." He pinched at her clit as his tongue surged up and Piper shook.

Low moans erupted from her chest as her pussy clenched, orgasm overtaking her. A fresh coat of sweet cream covered his tongue. He wanted to revel in it, but his cock had had enough. He had to fuck her.

Tal rose, well aware he was past all niceties. He'd never intended for Piper to see this side of him, but now that she had, there would be no hiding it again. "Present yourself to me. I want to fuck my slave."

She didn't hesitate. She turned and her ass was high in the

air, the pink plug he'd forced in her between her cheeks. She'd been a virgin just days before, but now Tal had trussed her up and manipulated her into things she couldn't be ready for, and he still couldn't stop. She looked wanton, his own sweet doll to fuck and punish and do with as he pleased.

"My way, Piper." He gripped her hips, lining up his unruly cock. He didn't bother with a condom because he would force this on her, too. He was nothing but an animal, taking what he wanted with no intentions of giving back because he was ruined on the inside. "You think you can handle me? You think you're ready for this? Because everything will be my way, my rules, my time. Tell me to stop or you'll open a door you can't close again. Please, Piper, let us just be friends."

He was begging her because he couldn't stop himself. He didn't want this. He didn't want to feel so much for her. His heart was already pounding, his dick on the edge, and he wasn't sure he could walk away if she said no.

Her head turned just enough for him to see the desperate desire on her face. "Take me, Sir. Please. Take me."

Nothing would stop him now. He shoved his cock in, forcing his way past any resistance in one long thrust. He let go of everything, becoming a beast in the moment. He was an animal, and she was his fucking mate. He mounted her, thrusting up again and again, paying no heed to anything but the silky feel of her, the tight heat of her pussy. Over and over he rammed inside, gripping her hips and slamming her down.

She felt so good, her heat surrounding him, pulling him in. He lost himself in the moment, glorying in all the sounds she made as he pushed her toward orgasm. Her skin heated beneath his hand as his heart thundered inside his chest. So close to heaven. He no longer cared about the reasons this wasn't a good idea. All that mattered was branding her, making her his.

Piper screamed as she came again, her pussy clenching down hard and forcing Tal to give up the game. His balls drew up, scalding heat pouring out of him in one long wave of pleasure. He came over and over, the orgasm rushing through his veins, binding him to her in ways he hadn't imagined.

She was everything he'd ever wanted.

Piper collapsed, taking Tal with her, his chest cradling her back as they spooned, only the soft leather of the bench keeping them from falling to the floor.

Sweet. It was so sweet to hold her, his cock still inside, still connected.

I love you, my Piper. The words were on his tongue, right there, a bomb waiting to be dropped.

He loved her, and if anyone ever knew just how close to his heart she was, they could use her against him. A vision of Lily screaming as the radicals cut her and raped her swam across his brain. He'd been forced to watch, unable to help her. He'd been weak. He'd been useless.

He hadn't loved her, and her death had nearly killed him. What would he do if they took Piper?

A cold chill crossed his spine. He couldn't, wouldn't, ever let her—or anyone else—know that he loved her.

Tal pulled himself out of her warmth and stood. His whole body shook, and he forced the emotion down with ruthless will. Since he refused to reveal his love to her, he needed to make sure she no longer loved him. "You can go now."

Piper stilled, her whole body going from languid to tense in a single second. With very deliberate movements, she turned. "What?"

Those eyes were going to kill him. He wanted to take her in his arms, but he couldn't. He had to let her go. "I'm through for the day. You can go."

Tears pooled in her eyes. She scrambled up, fumbling a bit as she stood. "I don't understand."

Tal sighed, covering his heartache. He'd learned to act over the years, to keep his every emotion hidden. It was a skill he'd learned from years of dealing with the press and politicians. He picked up her skirt, tossing it her way. "I no longer require your services." A thought struck him. Fuck. He was out of practice. "Aftercare. I forgot. Come here and I will take the clamps off and rub some salve on your nipples. Then you can go."

"Why are you acting so cold?" Piper asked, her lip trembling slightly. He was proud of her. She made no move to cover herself. She simply stood there, asking for information. She obviously wasn't going to run. But bloody hell, she was not making this easy on him.

So he had to make it hard on her. It was the only way to save her. Her heart should belong to his brothers. They were worthy of it. They had never broken, never cost a woman her life. They didn't wake up screaming some nights.

"I'm not acting cold, Piper. I am cold. And I'm done. I told you that you wouldn't like being my slave. I offered you a partnership, but you want to try to control me with sex. It can't work. I will not allow it. Now run along and see to my brothers. I'm sure they have need of your services, too."

Her eyes widened with obvious pain. "Wow. I did nothing to deserve that, Talib." She stood there for a moment, thinking. Damn, but he was worried about that brain of hers. "Why are you so scared of me?"

He wasn't going to play chess with her anytime soon. She would likely win. He forced himself to speak, keeping his voice even. He could not allow her to know she'd scored a direct hit. "I am not scared, Piper. Now I am merely bored."

"Bullshit." It was the first time he'd heard her curse. "Talib, I might have been a virgin, but I'm not dumb. What we just shared was something lovely and you're trying to make it ugly. Will you please sit down like the kind man I know you are and explain yourself to me? You're trying to make me run away. If you didn't care about me, you would simply explain it in a patient voice. But I mean something to you, and you can't stand it. You think you can say a few hateful words and get me to run, but I see you, Talib al Mussad. If there's one thing I've learned through all of this, it's that my love is stronger than you can imagine and a few little words aren't going to make me run. You'll have to be a man and ask me to leave."

She stood there, so beautiful and smart and proud, turning his every argument against him. He was the one who felt naked now. He shoved his legs into his pants. Cornered. She'd fucking cornered him. "I can't ask you to leave, Piper. I need this marriage to protect my crown."

She snorted, obviously unimpressed by his countermove. "Yes, you needed to marry a poor economist from Texas to protect your crown. I don't buy that, either. If you had to have a bride, you could have picked someone much more suitable. You *wanted* me."

Now at least he could give her some hard truths. "Yes, Piper, I wanted you because I knew I could never fall in love with you. You were perfect in that way."

A sad little smile crossed her face. "Poor Tal. You got caught in your own trap."

Would nothing work on her? Why could she see through him when no one else could? "I do not love you. I won't ever love you, but we're bound together. My god, woman, how can you stand there and say you love me? Don't you have any pride?"

"My love is worth more than my pride, Tal. And you wouldn't treat me this way if you didn't care about me. It's perverse, you know. Sometimes we hurt the ones we care about most because even the thought of loving them is too much. You're scared. I wish you would tell me why." It was said with an almost sympathetic tone as though she truly pitied him.

He couldn't stand it. "I tricked you into marriage. I've likely tricked you into a pregnancy. How do you feel about that?"

She held his eyes, hers clear and honest. "I can leave, Tal. I'm not some prisoner. Given the chance, I fully intended to sleep with your brothers, so you tricked me into nothing there. Oh, there won't be a pregnancy anytime soon. Just in case I decided to...expand my horizons, I went to the doctor the day before we left. He gave me a contraceptive shot. I'm good for another couple of months. Now, I should probably have insisted on condoms given where Kade's been, but he assured me he's healthy. As for the marriage, well, I have some time to deal with that, which is precisely why you should talk to me."

She didn't get it. And the thought that she'd blocked his play pissed him off. He didn't have to pretend anger now. "Get off the birth control, Piper. You are of no value to me if you can't fucking conceive. None of us is safe until you've spat out a couple of kids."

Finally she flushed, her whole body going red. "You don't mean that."

A weak spot. He could use that. He wasn't about to let her best him. "I mean it, Piper. I mean every word. I have no reason to fuck you if you cannot conceive. That shot lasts a few months? Well, I will see you then, my darling. Until that time, allow my brothers to service you."

She pleaded, her arms reaching for him. "Don't do this to us, Tal. It doesn't have to be this way."

But it did. He couldn't stand it a second longer. He turned and walked out the door.

Chapter Thirteen

Piper pulled the clamp off her breast, not quite able to stifle her scream. She really should have taken him up on the aftercare stuff. Her nipple had gone numb, but the minute she'd pulled the clamp off and her circulation returned, pain flooded her system.

Nothing like the hurt that had nearly broken her heart mere moments ago. She could handle the biting pain in her breasts, but the ache she felt in her gut was another matter entirely.

She felt stupid and right at the same time. Stupid because she'd thought she could get through to him. Right because despite his protestations, she knew he was scared. She'd made a study of the man. There wasn't a cruel bone in his body. He knew the names of every member of his staff, regularly asked about their kids. He was unfailingly polite. If he wanted a polite, friendly relationship, he would have sat down and talked it out logically with her.

But he'd plotted and schemed, and when he'd made love to her, he'd lost himself. There was nothing polite about the way he felt, but now she had to consider the possibility that Tal's past was more than a match for her love.

"Piper?"

She gasped, nearly diving for her clothes. She'd almost forgotten she was naked. The door to the dungeon opened and she reached for the skirt Tal had tossed toward her.

Rafe walked in, concern on his handsome face. "Piper? I just saw Tal walking down the hall. He looked angry. What the hell happened? You were only supposed to check the room out." He jogged across the room when he saw her. He pulled her into his arms before she could protest. "*Habibti*, what did he do to you?"

"He hurt her." Kade stood in the doorway, his mouth a flat line. "Motherfucker."

"Stop," Rafe said, sinking to his knees and cuddling her close. "She doesn't need more anger."

Rafe felt so good, solid. Piper knew she should get dressed. She needed to think, but she needed Rafe more. She let her arms drift around his neck. "Just hold me for a minute."

Rafe cradled her. "I need to get that clamp off you."

She shook her head. She was fine with the clamp. She didn't need that nipple. She would be all right with one. "It's fine."

Kade dropped down. "Bastard. He left her clamped. *Habibti*, this is going to sting."

She'd already figured that out. She braced herself, wincing as he took it off. He leaned over and gently sucked her nipple into his mouth, laving it with affection. Sure enough, that took the sting out.

Rafe smoothed back her hair. "This is what our bastard brother should have done. How is your backside?"

Plugged. Spanked. "I, uhm, have something to take out of that, too."

Rafe chuckled. "That can wait. You need to keep the plug in for a while, though Talib will not reap its benefits. Tell me what happened."

She'd tried. She'd failed. That was what had happened. "I

told him I loved him. He made crazy passionate love to me and then he ran away like a chicken. Help me up. I need to get dressed. We have dinner with the US ambassador in two hours." She gasped. "I can't do it. I can't sit with the ambassador while I have a pink piece of plastic up my backside."

Tears pooled in her eyes. She couldn't help it.

Kade looked helpless. "You don't have to. I'll cancel the dinner. Anything, Piper. Please don't cry."

She had to pull it together. No matter what Tal had done, she still had obligations to meet. She wasn't going to put off a huge state dinner because Tal had been an ass. "No. I can do it. I just need to shower and change."

Kade leaned over and pulled her into his arms. Without a pause, he stood, nestling her against his chest. "There's a shower in the back of the dungeon. We'll take care of you."

A long look passed between Kade and his brother. Piper didn't like that look. It was a secret look they shared when they were up to something. She'd grown accustomed to it, but she couldn't let them have their way this time. It wasn't a huge leap to figure out they were deciding which one of them would confront Talib. "Stop it. He needs time."

Rafe shook his head. "He needs a serious ass kicking, Piper. He cannot treat you like this. He will ruin everything!"

Kade eased her toward the back of the room, cuddling her close. "No. He simply won't be allowed in our bed. But Piper, we can't marry you on our own."

"We can if we abdicate the throne, brother." Rafe's pronouncement thudded through the dungeon, echoing off the walls.

Kade stopped and turned. "Would you really?"

She had to stop them. She couldn't let that happen. "No. No, he wouldn't."

Rafe stood back, his shoulders set. "I will if we must. I refuse to allow my brother to mistreat our wife. I also don't intend to separate from her because my brother cannot pull his head from his backside."

Misery swamped her. She'd pushed Tal. She'd known he was on the edge, and she'd deliberately sought out a piece of him he'd wanted to hide. "I don't want you to fight with Talib."

Rafe turned. "Take care of our wife, brother."

Kade led her back toward the shower. "Relax. Everything is going to be all right. I'll take care of you. We'll both get cleaned up, and I'll make sure you're ready for the ambassador. I'll have one of the servants bring you a robe. You'll look so beautiful."

"I don't want to look beautiful, Kadir. I want you to stop Rafe." She struggled against his hold.

Kade kicked open the door, and sure enough, there was a ridiculously opulent bathroom, complete with a hot tub in the middle. Kade set her on her feet. He crowded her, staring down. "I have no intention of stopping him. This is between brothers, Piper."

Stubborn. They were all so stubborn. "Am I not a member of this family?"

He didn't move, simply brushed her forehead with his lips. "You are the very best part of this family, but there will always be things that Rafiq, Talib, and I must work out."

"I shouldn't be one of those things."

His fingers sank into her hair, tugging back lightly. "I told you. You're the most important person in my life, in Rafe's life. If it's not the same with Tal, then perhaps it's time to move on. He still has a few months. He can find a cold bride to accept his bargain. He can have the kingdom. I want you."

But a cold bride and a stale bargain wasn't what Tal wanted. God, was she the only one who could see it? He could have had his bargain at any time, but he'd chosen her, a woman he'd spent months getting to know. Maybe he'd thought he could simply be friends with her at first, but it was so brutally obvious to her that he'd changed or he would still be the polite man she'd known online. Somewhere in that thick skull of his, he wanted more than a cool friendship.

Would time change Tal? Or was he too damaged for anyone to truly touch him? Could she remain married to a man who would only allow himself to view her as a state asset? How could she have children with him? Little babies who he would never allow himself to truly love.

"Hush." He kissed her again, this time on the tip of her nose. "I told you, it's going to be all right. I'm going to take care of you. But Piper, if Talib will not be swayed in this, you should know Rafe and I will leave the palace with nothing if we must." His voice got quiet. "We will have no money, but, *habibti*, you have to believe that we will take care of you."

Now she allowed the tears to flow because of all the things she'd believed she would find when she'd gotten on that plane and changed her life, this love was beyond them all. They would walk away from wealth, privilege, and fame for her? She let her hands find Kade's gorgeous face and silently thanked whatever being had blessed her. "I love you. I'll take care of you, too."

He shed his clothes after turning on the shower, leading her inside. As he gently washed her, she made a vow. She would take care of all her husbands. Even the stubborn one.

* * * *

"I have laid out your clothes for the evening, Your Highness." His butler nodded toward the bedrooms, then took his leave as Dane entered the room.

"You called."

He looked at his bodyguard and felt like shouting. "I thought someone was watching my concubine."

Bile rose in his throat. God, he'd treated her like a whore when she was the sweetest thing he'd ever known. Her sensuality had been generously given, and he'd tossed her aside. And he'd left her alone to take care of herself. He'd realized his mistake and had almost returned to Piper when he'd noticed his brothers coming down the hallway. They would treat her better than he could.

Dane's eyes were icy cold. "Cooper is on her."

Thank god he had a place to put his rage. "Cooper is fired. He has neglected his duties. The bastard let her get away from him and she found the dungeon."

Dane pulled his radio. "Coop, can I get an update on Her Highness?"

"The sweet one or the sour one?" Coop's voice cracked over the radio. "Sorry. Had to do it. Her Highness is in the dungeon with Kadir. Rafe just left, and let me tell you, his panties were in a big old wad. I think you might be looking at a throw down. Whatever happened to the sheikh to make him storm out of the dungeon seems to have gotten Rafe as well."

Dane pressed the talk button. "Thanks, buddy. Keep an eye out. The ambassador is bringing a whole crew in tonight, and Khalil is invited, naturally. I don't like it. Something feels wrong."

"Will do."

The radio went silent, and Dane turned back. "She was never out of his sight until she entered that room. It has one exit, no windows, and no one has been in there for over a year. I scarcely think someone laid in wait all that time. She's got to have privacy sometime."

And he'd fucked up again. God. He felt like his whole fucking life was spiraling out of control. "See that you keep my bride safe."

"Who should I protect her from? You?" Dane asked.

Tal turned.

Dane shrugged, a negligent gesture. "It was a good bet you would fuck up, Talib. You haven't fixed anything inside you, just like Alea. Those fuckers who hurt you can only win if you let them. But you're going to let them, aren't you?"

The last thing he needed was homilies provided by his

Southern guard. "You can go."

Dane stood there. "I could."

Dane needed to remember who was the boss here. "Goddamn it, Dane. Get the fuck out."

"That would be convenient, wouldn't it?" Dane's posture relaxed, his feet spreading out. "Everyone just does what you say. Does anyone actually fight with you? Do you have a single fucking ally who'll fight for you?"

He didn't have anyone but his brothers who would say a damn thing against him. Not to his face. Well, Piper. Piper had always bitched at him. In the months they had worked together, she'd often initiated arguments when she thought he was wrong. She hadn't known who he really was. He'd loved it. When they'd talked and she would throw down with him verbally, he would get such a thrill.

God, he'd been in love with her for months, and he hadn't been able to admit it.

"Get out."

Dane stood his ground. "I think not. I think you can fire my ass if you like, Sheikh, but I have a few things to say to you."

Heat flashed through him. "Get out now or I'll have you arrested."

Dane huffed. "That'll go over so well, Tal. Fine. Arrest me. It won't be the worst shit that happened to me. I'm going to say this once. Grow the fuck up and grow a goddamn pair of balls, man. I know it was bad. I know some shit happened to you that no one can understand, but that's the nature of your life. You're a leader, Talib. You got the fucking hard road. I'm not joking about that. I wouldn't trade for your gig, man. Everyone needs something from you, and not a single person will sacrifice for you. Except your brothers and that woman you married. And if you push her away, then everyone who has ever hurt you wins. And you lose."

A vicious pain had taken root in his gut. Dane was right about one thing. He couldn't possibly understand. "They won the minute they forced me to watch someone I cared about die. Do you fucking know what they did to me? Do you know what they made me do?"

Dane's face softened slightly. "I can imagine. They likely made you beg."

Beg. Plead. Abase himself. He'd done it all. He'd broken trying to spare Lily pain, and they had simply laughed and slit her throat anyway.

"Talib, you can't blame yourself for that, man. Everyone breaks."

Shame flushed through him. What would his brothers have thought of him if they knew he'd begged?

"Did you beg for your own life?" Dane asked. "I bet you didn't. Most men would. You begged for hers. You pleaded."

He'd been thrown to the ground and kicked and then forced to kiss the boot of the man who had done it. He'd wanted to fight, but Lily was his submissive. She had been in his care. He'd had to do anything he could to save her. Anything but betray his country. "I did everything they asked to try to spare her. They treated me like an animal. They beat me, starved me. They used a defibrillator to stop and start my heart once. I was dead, but they brought me back. I know what death is like. I was so angry when I realized I was alive again. I wanted that death."

"I can understand that. What didn't you do?" Dane asked. "Did they kill her for fun or would you not comply with some request?"

His hands were shaking. Fuck. He didn't want to talk about this. He wanted to forget it, but something forced him to speak. Years he'd spent with this brutal truth inside him. "They wanted me to make a video tape."

He'd barely been able to see the words they had wanted him to say. His eyes had been almost swollen shut from the beating he'd taken. Vile words meant to throw his country back into the dark ages. He'd been asked to renounce democracy.

He'd been told to spit on hundreds of years of his family's achievements.

Dane's calm voice echoed through the room. "I remember the time, sir. Had you made that tape, had the people seen it, there might have been real trouble. Something like that could have destabilized the country. The parliament wasn't in control. You were. There could have been riots, and the countries around you would have pounced. You did what you had to."

"Yes." Bitterness rose. "I had to choose my country over a woman who trusted me."

"You do not have easy choices, my brother."

Pure fear went through Tal as he realized Rafiq stood in the doorway. His brother had heard everything. His brother knew his shame. "Go away, Rafe. Go look after Piper."

"I came here to beat the crap out of you," Rafe admitted, his face flushed with emotion. "I planned to fight because you cannot treat our bride that way. She is not a piece of property, but that isn't why you rejected her, is it? I think she might be smarter than any of us. She told me you were afraid."

Everyone was backing him into a corner today. "I am not afraid. I simply don't want to be forced to deal with Piper's naïveté. This marriage is about protecting a kingdom, not falling in love."

Rafe walked in. His shoulders had relaxed, his fists unclenched. "It's about both. Tal, you did what you had to do in the worst of circumstances. But you survived. Our country survived. I am so sorry Lily did not, but you cannot spend the rest of your life punishing yourself. You did everything you could possibly do to save her. You made the right choice. One life for thousands. You had no other option."

And there was the heart of his problem. There was the precise reason he couldn't ever let himself love Piper. "And if I couldn't make that decision again? If I couldn't choose my country?"

Rafe's eyes flared, understanding dawning. "You're

worried if it happens again you would give everything up for Piper?"

He knew it deep in his gut. He could lie to her, but there was the truth. He was already over the edge. "I need to let her go. I can't make the choices I would need to. I can't protect my country and love my wife."

Rafe sighed. "That is untrue."

"Sir, your brother is right. You can't sacrifice everything. You have to take a risk at some point," Dane said.

But he didn't. He never had to risk another thing. Tal stood stiffly, his decision clear. "Rafe, you and Kade will abdicate your positions. You can take Piper and marry her. I'll make sure you have more money than you could ever need. I'll marry within the month. The throne will be secure, and if I never speak to her again, perhaps no one will think to hurt her in order to get to me."

Rafe's jaw hardened to a razor-sharp line. "That is the stupidest thing I have ever heard."

His brother was thinking with his heart and not his head. Tal knew one of them had to be rational. "It protects us all."

"Should Piper not have any say in whether she wants this?" Rafe asked. "You have not given her a real choice, Tal. If you care for her, then you should let her decide."

Let her decide if she wanted to risk her life? Not a chance. "I would think you would want her alive, Rafe. You're truly willing to risk her?"

Rafe groaned. "God, you should have been on the stage, Tal. Everything is a risk. Am I not going to get in a car because I could be in an accident? Not fly because I could crash? We have an amazing life, and it comes with risks. For every privilege we have, there is an ounce of pain and still, I would not take any of it back. I will not abdicate. Piper will not leave. You must learn that this is your family, and we will not abandon you, even when you do not deserve us. That is what family is. She is stronger than you can imagine, our concubine.

I know her. She is willing to take the risk."

"But I'm not." He couldn't do it. He just couldn't. He couldn't risk having to choose between her and his country. "I won't be moved, Rafe. Tell her to pack her things. You can go with her or not. I'll make sure she's financially cared for. She assures me there's no way she's carrying a child. Tell her she can choose to live anywhere she likes. Anywhere except here. I expect her to be gone by tomorrow." He pivoted away, his body moving on autopilot when all he wanted to do was fucking beat his head against the wall. He couldn't stand the thought of never seeing her again. She'd already wound her way around his heart. He would do his duty to his country, but he would go to his grave with the memory of her warmth in his heart. "I must attend the dinner tonight. I'll sleep in here. I'll meet with the press secretary in the morning. We'll need a good story. And have someone call the Dutch ambassador. I need to speak with him. They were eager to provide me with a bride."

"It won't work, brother." Rafe turned and walked out.

Dane simply turned away. Though he stood just outside the door, Tal was well aware he'd broken their friendship.

He was alone. It was the way he would spend the rest of his life.

Chapter Fourteen

"You're sure you want to do this, *habibti*?" Kade tucked a stray hair behind her head, his touch soft on her skin.

Piper was sure. She'd never been more sure of anything in her life. She didn't intend to take her walking papers with aplomb. Talib wanted to get rid of her? He would have a fight on his hands. After Rafe explained everything to her, all of Tal's fears and worries, she'd been more sure than ever that he needed her. She wasn't a masochist. She knew she could break, but she wasn't going to stop fighting until there was nothing left to fight for.

Tal wasn't cruel. He was just dumb. Very, very dumb. Lucky for him, she was awfully smart.

"She is sure, Kade." Rafe placed a hand on her hip, drawing her in. "And she's so damn beautiful. Have I told you how beautiful you are, *habibti*?"

"More than once, baby." She turned her face up, silently asking for a kiss. It was swiftly given. These two men were the best things that had ever happened to her. Not only had they told her she was beautiful, they made her believe it. The same way a man named Tal had managed to boost her confidence all those months ago. Now that she looked back at their odd relationship, she could see all the things he'd done for her. She would never have been strong enough to take this journey without him encouraging her. He'd been the one to tell her she was smart enough to take on this project. He'd been the one to give her ideas credit and real value.

She wasn't going to let a single one of her men go.

Kade turned her face up to his, and another sweet kiss fell on her lips. How the hell was a woman supposed to feel less than worthy when she'd spent hours in their arms? Tal had no idea what he was in for.

She took Kade's hand and let him lead her through the marbled entrance to the conservatory. Security was everywhere. Two big guards stood at the door to the conservatory, their khaki uniforms incongruous compared to the elegance around them.

"Your Highnesses." The men both bowed their heads in deference.

At least Talib hadn't barred her from the dinner. He likely thought she would be packing like the good girl he believed her to be. Maybe he hadn't studied her as thoroughly as he imagined. She hadn't managed to raise her sister and put herself through school without some serious willpower.

"Gentlemen." She nodded their way. It was odd, the deference she was shown, but she'd started to simply view it as courtesy.

A servant stood at the door, dressed in a resplendent uniform. She'd seen him around a bit, though she had trouble placing his face. He looked so familiar. She'd met so many. She needed to make it a priority to learn the members of her household by name and to be able to inquire about their families.

This young man frowned slightly before his face cleared and he smiled. "Your Highnesses. The Sheikh informed us just minutes ago that you would not be joining us this evening. Any of you. I'm afraid the cocktail hour has already begun. Dinner will be soon."

Kade studied the young man. "You are Hassem? How long have you been with us?"

Hassem stood a little straighter. "Just over a year, Your Highness. My father has been at the palace for twenty."

Rafe nodded. "He is Ahmed's youngest. The one who spent time in the army. I thank you, Hassem, but the sheikh was wrong. Her Highness decided to attend after all. Please open the door. We wouldn't want to miss dinner. I've heard chef came up with something amazing."

The servant flushed slightly, and his hand found the door. "Of course. If it is all right, I would provide refreshments for the guards. I have water bottles and some energy snacks for them. It will be a very long night, I can see."

Kade waved the young man away. "Do what you need to do. Thank you."

The double doors swung open. Soft harp music and elegant lighting made Piper think she was walking into a room from the last century. Everything was antique and beautifully crafted.

This was her world now. How odd to have come so far.

Twenty heads turned her way. She recognized many of the men in the room, including Khalil. He smiled her way, a predatory look.

"I'm going to kill him." Rafe's words whispered from a clenched jaw. "How dare he show his face in the palace."

Piper still wasn't sure Khalil had tried anything on her at all. She'd just been sick. It wasn't so surprising given she hadn't gotten used to her new country. She had to be careful about what she ate and drank until her body had adjusted. "He's here because he represents the western provinces. Until they choose to vote him out of office or you can find real evidence against him, you need to be careful."

She'd been studying everything she could about politics in the region. It had been easy to read between the lines. There was bad blood between the cousins. Khalil was an outspoken advocate of religious reform and wresting power from the sheikh, but his position in government meant he spent a lot of time at the palace. They had to deal carefully with him.

"I can very quietly kill him," Kade whispered.

She sent him a frown.

"Or not." Kade shrugged. "But don't be terribly surprised if he meets with a horrible accident. I've heard he is a terrible driver."

"Yes," Rafe's voice was filled with silky satisfaction. "There are many dangerous roads. Not that we would have anything to do with it."

She was going to give them a serious talking to about the evils of assassination, but Talib had finally seen her. His handsome face turned in her direction, then he flushed a deep scarlet. His eyes flared, and she realized just how much she'd challenged him.

He murmured something to the ambassador and began stalking across the room, his every move an example of predatory grace. He was so gorgeous in his perfectly cut tuxedo, but anger flashed in his eyes. He really didn't want her here. He might care about her, but what if she couldn't get through his pain to the emotions that might bind them together?

"Be brave," Rafe whispered.

"My brothers, would you like to explain yourselves?" He didn't even look at her. It was infuriating. She felt her anger start to rise.

"I was hungry. Did you intend to starve me before you ship me out?" She kept her voice low, a plastic smile on her face.

Tal's eyes finally caught hers, and she realized he thought this was all a plan of his brothers. He hadn't given her credit for knowing her own mind. "I will have food sent to you. Of course, I meant you no discomfort."

And now he was on the ropes, right where she wanted him. They had a very avid audience. She gave him a brilliant smile and leaned over to greet him with a kiss. So close, she could feel the heat coming off his body, see the way his lips firmed just before she pressed them with her own. She meant it to be a light kiss, a soft greeting, but his hands found her waist and pulled her close. He might not want her here, but his erection didn't have any such qualms. It was instantly hard against her belly.

"Don't think just because you win a single battle that you can claim victory in a war. I'll have you forcibly removed from the palace tomorrow morning. In fact, I can have you on a plane tonight. You can sit down and play the part one last time, but tomorrow you will be out of my life, Piper."

Tears threatened to blur her vision. "You don't care that I love you?"

His hands tightened, and his voice ground from his throat. "I want to do the right thing for you. For my country. Can't you see this is for the best?"

She let her eyes meet his again. "No. And I won't go away quietly. You think you can find some more biddable bride, but I'll make it hard on you. I'll fight for my family."

"So be it." He kissed her again, a hard meeting of lips. When he brought his head back up, he was perfectly calm again, the mask he wore slipping into place so easily. "Gentlemen, you will have to forgive me for the delay. My bride is looking exceptionally lovely tonight."

And by tomorrow, if Tal had his way, she would be gone. It was the hardest thing she'd ever done, but she plastered a smile on her face and joined the group, taking a glass of wine from one of the servants. She mingled, speaking to each politician, turning the conversation to the economy and politics when she could. She could feel Rafe's and Kade's warm eyes on her, giving her strength. And every time she looked up, Tal had to look away because she caught him staring.

She completed her circuit around the room, never allowing a moment when she wasn't smiling, wasn't charming. She found herself alone finally, on the far side of the room and away from the guests, staring out the big bay windows that overlooked the grounds. The sun had set, and silvery moonlight illuminated the gorgeous gardens. This land was foreign and beautiful and, in a few short days, had begun to feel like home.

Where would she be tomorrow? She'd spent so much of her life knowing exactly where she would be. She'd expected to live and die in a small Texas town, accepting her fate. At some point she'd discovered the strength to make her own way. Was she strong enough to keep her family together?

"You play the part well. I'll give that to you. You have the gracious queen act down."

She saw his reflection on the glass. Talib. Beautiful, remote, her sheikh. The thought of losing him hurt her heart. "I'm only doing it to please you."

"If you want to please me, you'll walk out and take my brothers with you," he shot back in a heated whisper. He stared out the windows, his face a polite blank, so unlike the man who'd spanked her and forced his cock deep in her body, binding them together just hours before. Now he was telling her to leave.

"If I really thought it would please you, I would leave, but I remember what it feels like with you inside me," she said softly. "I know how you make love, Tal."

There it was. Just a little twitch to let her know she'd scored a hit. If she hadn't been watching closely, she would have missed it. His face went blank again. "It was sex, Piper. You're too naïve to know. I fuck the same way every time."

She rolled her eyes. She couldn't help it. She turned, making sure to lean back so there was no way he could miss her breasts. Rafe had selected her gown, a gorgeous red designer item with a plunging V-neck. And there it was again, a little flare to his eyes and a tent in his slacks. Yes, he was utterly disinterested in her.

"Sure. Except you told me you haven't had a lover in your

dungeon in years. Me, Tal. I was in there," she murmured.

His eyes hardened. "You snuck in there."

"I was curious. If you really hadn't wanted me in there, you would have politely asked me to leave. I would have, you know. I would have left and never gone back, but that isn't what happened. What happened was you made love to me."

His jaw tightened, his eyes trailing to her breasts. "You overestimate your appeal."

Piper snorted. She couldn't help it. "Yes, I'm so good. So well-practiced. Tal, you can send me away, but I'll still love you."

"And I will forget you. Piper, I'll get married two weeks after you're gone and I will move on. You can wait all you like, but I'm done with you." He turned and walked away.

She stared at him. What the hell was she doing? If he'd really decided on this course, how could she change his mind? He would simply have his guards forcibly remove her from the country, and she wouldn't be allowed back in. If he didn't want to see her, he would never look on her face again.

"Your Highnesses, honored guests, please join us in the dining hall. Dinner is ready to be served." A turbaned servant in a black uniform smiled as he and his helper stood at the double doors that led to the dining hall. Piper stared as Tal walked toward the doors. He would put as much distance between them as possible. He would sit at one end of the long table, relegating her to the other. He would try not to speak to her again until he sent her away.

She could fight. But now she wasn't certain she would win.

The double doors opened, and Hassem stood there, two small metal objects in either hand. What was he doing? She got a glimpse of his face again and remembered where she'd seen him before. A brief memory flashed through her head. Hassem had been the one Khalil had called on for tea. She remembered his graceful hands as he'd placed the tray on the table and poured out the tea. He'd given her the slightest smile as he'd passed her the cup that she now suspected he'd placed a measure of poison in.

He had the same smile on his face as he threw the small canisters into the conservatory. Metal cylinders hit the floor and exploded, causing the whole world to flare. There was a horrible flash. Her vision fled, bleeding from fiery white to complete darkness in a second. A blast of sound hit her ears just before they stopped working. Piper stumbled, trying to find her balance, but she couldn't quite make her legs work.

Flash bang. She'd read about them. Stun grenades. She'd read an article about a terrorist attack that went into the use of flash bangs as a way to gain valuable seconds. They could incapacitate people for a few seconds, giving the bad guy time to do something really nasty. She let her body fall back. She needed to get to the floor. She couldn't stand. Falling back would save her arms, and she could turn to her belly and protect her head. Confusion threatened to swamp her, but she forced herself to stay calm. Five seconds. That was what she'd read. In five seconds her vision would start to clear. Her hearing would take longer, but she would be able to see. She had to get to Tal. They were coming for Tal.

But they weren't, she knew in just a second. A big hand reached down, and she was dragged across the floor, her body sagging as she was pulled from the room.

* * * *

Tal hit the floor, his ears ringing and his eyes black. He couldn't fucking see. What the hell had happened? One minute he'd been walking away from Piper, certain he was saving her, and the next, one of his household staff was tossing a goddamn grenade his way. It had hit his chest and bounced off before the flash bang had exploded and sent him into silent darkness. He forced himself to flip over. It didn't matter that he couldn't see. He had to get to Piper. Khalil was behind this. Khalil had paid off his staff to turn against him. It was the only explanation.

He felt the marble under his hands and at his knees. He tried to orient himself. He'd been facing away from Piper when the assault occurred. His vision swam in front of his eyes. He couldn't see a fucking thing. His ears felt like they were bleeding. Sound got through but it was muffled and distorted.

Piper. He had to reach her, protect her. He couldn't lose her. He could turn her away. He could live without her as long as he knew she was somewhere in the world, safe and sound. He didn't want to live in a world where Piper didn't exist. His heart pounded in his chest.

"Piper!" A muffled shout managed to get through his damaged ears. Rafe? Kade? They sounded so far away.

He stumbled to his feet. His eyes were beginning to clear, but the whole conservatory was chaos. Smoke filled the room. Where the hell were the guards? He'd made sure there were at least two at every door. Dane, Landon, and Cooper were patrolling. In his stubbornness, he had sent them as far away as he dared. Had they heard the noise?

Khalil couldn't expect to get out of the palace with Piper. He could have bribed one or two people without causing alarm, but more? He didn't believe it. His staff was loyal.

That meant Piper could already be dead. And then nothing would matter.

He nearly tripped over a body. The ambassador? He wasn't dead, but he was struggling to get up. Tal fell back to the floor. A strong hand lifted him up.

"You know my orders are to get you out of danger." Dane looked right at Tal. His eyes were perfectly clear. Dane had all his faculties because he hadn't been in the room when it exploded in light, smoke, and sound. Besides the flash bangs, the attacker seemed to have used some sort of smoke bomb. Tal coughed to try to clear his lungs.

"Piper." He could barely hear Dane, but he knew the gist of the words. Dane's chief mission was to protect the sheikh. If he didn't get away from Dane, he would find himself in protective custody while Khalil did god knew what to his bride. He tried to pull away. "I have to find Piper."

He couldn't let them waste time trying to get him somewhere secure. Piper, if she was still alive, had so little time.

"Stop. I know I'm supposed to protect you, but if that woman dies, you'll be worth nothing. Do you remember how to use a SIG, Your Highness?" Dane pressed a SIG Sauer into his palm. The cool metal felt substantial in his hand.

Fuck yeah, he remembered. He'd trained on the weapon religiously after escaping his captors. After tonight, he might simply carry one with him always. He flipped off the safety and forced his fucking legs to work.

Dane pointed to the hallway entrance to the conservatory. "I think they went out this way, Your Highness. The little fucker who threw the flash bangs hadn't counted on me and Landon to hang around. He tried to send us on a wild goose chase, but I know a traitor when he shows his face. Cooper went to check out the kid's story, but Landon and I stayed behind."

Thank god Dane's voice was loud. Tal was starting to get his presence of mind back. How did Khalil imagine he was going to get away with this? "Khalil has gone insane. Even if he had an escape path, someone would see him."

Where would he take her? Would he ransom her? Try to trade her for Talib? It didn't make sense.

"He's not crazy. He's got terminal cancer," Dane shouted back at him. "I found out a couple of days ago, but honestly I didn't want you to go soft on him. I'm also close to linking him to the radicals who took you and the slavers who grabbed Alea. It's all there in the financials, but I need some reports. I wanted all my ducks in a row so you could give me the go ahead to take him out." Dane's brow furrowed in a look of consternation. "He's only got six months to live. He's not trying to take the throne anymore. He just wants to hurt you. He's bitter. He hates you and the whole family."

Fear gripped Tal's stomach. Khalil really wanted to kill her. He wanted to make sure Tal suffered. He didn't care about getting away. There would be no negotiations. There would only be pain for his concubine, his Piper. Pain and death.

"Sarge, I think I've got something for you." Dane's radio squawked, Landon's voice coming over it as they made their way through the double doors. The two guards he'd placed there were both knocked out, bodies slumped to the floor. Water covered the marble. It looked like they had been drinking it when they fell. Tal hoped they weren't dead.

"Go, Lan."

"This little bastard, Hassem, says Khalil plans to rape and kill her on her husbands' bed. It should have been Khalil's, he claims. Then Khalil is going to kill himself. He's leaving a note stating that the royal family pushed him to it. He's trying to wreak all sorts of havoc."

Even before Dane spoke, they both started to jog toward the stairs. "How reliable is this intel? We don't have much time."

They couldn't afford to be led astray. Every moment they were delayed, Piper could be in unimaginable pain. The thought of her being hurt, raped, was almost too much for him to take.

"Well, Sarge, I have my pistol about halfway up his asshole, and I've threatened to pull the trigger. He seems real attached to his innards, if you know what I mean. I think I'll just keep it here until we're sure he's not lying."

Dane kept talking as he took the stairs two at a time. "Who's watching the brat?"

Alea. Khalil had really sold Alea into slavery. Khalil hated them so much, and all because they had a little more than he did. Khalil had money and a good life, but something deep inside of him was twisted and broken. Dane's face remained stony, but he'd flushed when he asked about Alea. The big guard really did care about her.

"Coop's on her. She's safe, Sarge. Coop will keep an eye on our girl and make sure she stays out of the line of fire. Even if she doesn't want to be safe. Check back and let me know if I need to blow this guy's ass away. Out."

Tal decided to never cross Landon Nix. He looked back, wishing his brothers were with him. He'd lost them in the throng, but he had no doubt they would be searching for Piper. His brothers. He'd never really been alone, he realized, because his brothers were always there. Even in that pisshole of a warehouse he'd been held in, when all felt like it was lost, he'd heard his brothers whispering to him, telling him to survive.

He should never have doubted them. He could have told them everything, and they would have taken their share of his burdens because that was what family did. They shared the hurt and pain, dividing it and making it bearable. They shared the joy and love, multiplying it into something more.

His brothers. His almost wife. He wasn't sure he could live without them. But if he saved her, he knew he would have to. Others would try. She would never be safe. Bile rose in his throat. What the hell could he do? Even if Khalil was dead, he would leave followers behind.

He pushed his panic down. Nothing mattered if she died. Nothing at all.

Dane put a fist up, stopping completely. His body went perfectly still. He could have been one of the many marble statues that decorated the grounds. His face was as hard as granite as he pointed to one of the corners.

A body. One of the servants. Even from here, Tal could see the blood beginning to pool around the body. A faithful employee, brought down by a monster. Guilt was starting to eat away at his panic. How many would die because Khalil was broken?

"Silencer." The word was a whisper from Dane's mouth. "He has to have one or I would have heard that."

Dane took a step forward, his big body making no sound.

He stepped on the balls of his feet, moving with natural grace. Tal matched his guard, clinging to the walls. Every step brought him closer to Piper, closer to finding out if she was still alive.

"Fucking bitch!" Khalil's scream echoed.

Dane put a hand out, stopping Tal from running forward. Tal calmed. His guard was right. Running screaming into the room wasn't the best way to save Piper. He could hear Khalil moan a little.

"I'm sorry. Did my heel hurt your balls?" Piper's voice was shaky, but there was a deep resolve in that Texas twang. "You try that again and I swear I'll take them off."

"Dumb bitch." Khalil's low growl echoed quietly through the room as Tal was allowed to move forward. It sounded like his cousin had managed to make his way to the bedroom. The outer sitting room was empty, but someone had put up a fight. A chair was knocked over and a table destroyed. Piper was fighting for her life, and she didn't seem to be doing it with courtesy.

A little thrill of pride in his bride lit his system. She was still alive, and she was giving Khalil hell.

A hand on his back had him turning. He bit back a yell.

Rafe and Kade were there, each with a gun in his hand.

Dane put a finger to his lips. *Silence.* It was the key word of the day.

Tal wasn't sure how his brothers had gotten here. More than likely they had followed Dane or been told by Landon where to go, but no matter how it had happened, Tal was deeply relieved his brothers were at his side. They fell in line behind him. He could feel their tension, but neither one would panic.

"It's not going to work," Piper said. Tal wished he could see her. "You can't hurt him through me. He doesn't really love me. All you're going to do is kill me, get yourself thrown in jail, and he'll have another bride by the end of the week. He has plenty of time to marry. He only needs a few weeks. He was shipping me out in the morning anyway."

Tal hated the way her voice trembled. He wondered if she really believed it. God, she couldn't die when she didn't believe he loved her. She was his whole world.

There was a pause. Dane inched toward the door, leading them all. Tal felt brutally inadequate. He couldn't just march in the room and start shooting. He had no idea where they were standing.

A horrible idea started to play at the back of his head. They needed an advantage. They needed the door open and a line of vision to the target. If Dane entered and Khalil had even a moment's advantage, Piper could be killed. Tal couldn't risk that. Khalil had nothing to lose. Tal had everything.

They needed a distraction.

Khalil's voice floated through the heavy doors. Tal could see Dane listening, trying to figure out where the jackal stood. The problem was the fact that sound tended to echo through the large room, making it impossible to really know where the target was without seeing it.

"I think my cousin cares more about you than you realize," Khalil snarled. "I've seen the way he looks at you. You must have seen it, too. Why else would you stay after I told you about all of your husbands' women, you stubborn American? Why else would you show up to this dinner tonight after your terrible argument earlier? Yes, I know all about it. We nearly called off the attack, you know. I intended to wait for another occasion when you would be present. But you waltzed into the room as if you had the Sheikh wrapped around your finger. Stupid whore. Now come here, and perhaps I will allow you to live. If you refuse, I can shoot you where you stand. Either way, I will bring Talib to his knees. You are the key."

A mountain of fury raged through Talib. And terror for Piper. That motherfucker. Khalil had just signed his own death warrant.

Dane's head shook slightly, as though he was trying to clear it so he could try again to place them in the room, but Tal couldn't be certain Khalil would speak first or shoot. Piper wasn't cooperating. He didn't have a minute to waste.

"Make certain he dies," he whispered to Dane. Then he laid the gun down on the table and walked to the door with his hands up in the air.

Dane cursed softly, his eyes flaring, but Tal knew he was too far away for the guard to catch him without making a lot of noise.

"Khalil, I'm alone and I'm coming in."

He could practically feel his brothers' tension. He sent them one long last look. His brothers. His closest friends. He'd been blessed to spend this lifetime with Rafe and Kade. They would watch after Piper. They would take care of the country.

I love you, my brothers. If he died, he wanted such good lives for them. Children. Happiness. Love.

"I swear to all that is holy, I'm going to kill you, Talib. I've tried for years. I was the one who aided the rebels. I was the one who gave them the codes to get onto the drill site so they could take you." His cousin's voice floated from the room.

Tal's gut churned. He'd known it deep down, but hearing the confession made it real. His own cousin had colluded to have him tortured. Yet, he had to stay unemotional. Piper's life was on the line. He had to calmly walk in and give Khalil a better target than Piper.

Once Khalil had taken his shot, Dane would know where he was. Piper could get down. Dane would rush in and everything precious in Tal's life would be saved.

He put a hand on the door, his heart racing. Would Khalil shoot right away or play with him for a while? He opened the door and immediately put his hands back in the air. "I love her. I've loved her for months. You were always smarter than I gave you credit for. I would trade myself for her. I'm the one you want. I'm the one who should pay."

Piper stood to his right, her face pale and her eyes wide. There was a scratch on her cheek and her dress was torn. All her elegance was gone, but nothing could make her less beautiful. "Tal."

"Don't you dare move, Piper." He spared her just a momentary glance. He needed to keep his eyes on Khalil.

A nasty grin split Khalil's face. Now that he knew, Tal could see the toll the cancer had taken on his cousin. Or perhaps it was just a life spent doing evil to the people around him that had sunken in his eyes, made his skin sallow. He could never feel an ounce of sympathy for Khalil. Whatever horrible death found him, it would be too easy.

"I told you he would come for you, dear," Khalil said. "And I will kill him, too, but not yet. He's just in time to watch you die."

Tal leapt just as Khalil lifted his gun. Time seemed to slow down, his vision centering on that gun. He had to save Piper, and there was only one way to do it. That bullet would have its victim. He simply had to make sure it wasn't her.

The sound was muffled by the long silencer on the end of the gun, but that shot shuddered through the room and a terrible lash of fire went through Tal's gut. It burned, cutting through his flesh.

Shot. He'd been shot.

He'd taken the bullet that would have likely ended Piper's life. Even as he hit the floor, he could feel the bullet lodging in his gut, safely away from Piper. His body crumpled, pain in his every cell.

"Damn you, Talib," Khalil cursed.

The door slammed open, kicked from the outside. In a second Dane was through, his big body moving faster than Tal could have imagined. The huge guard's face was a blank as he raised his weapon, firing three times in rapid succession without a hint of hesitation.

Tal looked up in time to see his cousin's body shudder with the impact of the bullets. Two in his chest and a neat shot that split his eyes. Khalil's face went blank, his body slumping to the floor, dead.

Relief swam through Talib. Now he could die in peace.

"Tal!" Piper's face came into view as she scrambled toward him, shoving the skirts of her destroyed gown aside. Tears coursed down her cheeks. She looked back up, seeming to find his brothers. "Someone call an ambulance. Kade, please tell them to hurry."

Blood. There was so much blood. He could feel his hands getting slippery with it. Was it his? The world seemed to have a soft glow about it. Piper put a hand to his face. She really was an angel. And she should be protected. She should never be shot at. How could he have ever thought for a minute she was plain?

He lifted a hand to her face. "So beautiful."

She leaned over and kissed his forehead. "Please stay with me. Please. Don't leave us. We need you."

But she needed something so much better than him. He tried to tell her, but the words wouldn't come. He just held on to the sight of her face now streaked with a small smear of blood. He could hear Dane barking orders through his radio.

"Forgive me," he managed to force out.

"Of course." Tears streaked down her face. "Always."

Rafe got to one knee, his hand on Piper's back, lending support. Kade was shouting for help. Everyone was moving around him, but all that mattered was Piper.

Darkness swallowed him whole, but not before one final thought consumed him.

I love you.

Chapter Fifteen

Three weeks later
Dallas, TX

Piper stared out at the night lights and tried to come up with a single enthusiastic thought. From the James family's penthouse suite, the views of Dallas were beyond spectacular, but all she could think about was how peaceful the gardens had been in Bezakistan. At night she would wander on to the balcony and watch the palms sway. Eventually one of her husbands would find her, slip an arm around her waist, and tell her how beautiful she was.

She'd had three amazing men. And now she was alone.

No longer a concubine. Never a queen.

"Hey, Jessa and I were wondering if you were going to come in and have a glass of wine before dinner? Come on. Someone has to drink for me." Hannah James stepped out onto the balcony, stroking her swollen belly. She started with a smile, but lost it when she looked at Piper. "Hon, you're crying again. I wish you would tell me what happened. All I know is you came home and needed a place to stay, and suddenly Cole and Burke were deeply interested in where you were twenty-four seven."

She sighed. Ever since her return, she'd been out of sorts. She felt homeless, aimless. The night she'd landed in Dallas, she'd wondered how she would get from the airport to a hotel. She'd been given a thousand US dollars and a credit card she vowed to never use, but as far as she'd known, no one had been advised that she was returning to Texas.

To her surprise, Burke and Cole Lennox had been waiting for her. Tal's big brooding guard, the one named Dane, had handed her over to them, and she'd found herself on her way to the James penthouse. She no longer had an apartment, thanks to Rafe and Kade. She'd cried because she didn't have a home. Oh, a real estate agent had contacted her the morning after her arrival in Dallas, a very nice woman who indicated that Piper could have any house of her choosing in the city, all paid for. She just had to select one. Piper hadn't returned the woman's calls. She wanted nothing more from the al Mussad brothers. So she'd been the James's very quiet houseguest for three weeks. And she'd been unwilling to share even a moment of her heartbreak. But maybe it was time.

Tomorrow, Piper would thank Hannah and her husbands for their hospitality, find her belongings in storage, then rebuild her life and try to move on.

"You know Tal was shot, right?" Piper said.

Hannah nodded. "I read it in the paper. He was shot by his cousin. I heard that's not the first time he tried to kill the sheikh."

No. It wasn't the first time Khalil had hurt the al Mussad family, and it wasn't really the last. His legacy of pain seemed to be destined to last a lifetime. "He's dead now, but Tal decided he didn't want to marry me."

"I don't understand that." Hannah put a hand on her arm. "I saw the pictures of the four of you together. You all looked so happy."

Piper couldn't stand to look at those pictures. "Tal is afraid that Khalil won't be the last person to try to hurt him by hurting me."

"He's scared of losing you," Hannah said, sympathy in her voice.

"But he's not scared of pushing me away." She looked back out over the dazzling lights of the city. "He wouldn't even let me say good-bye. I wasn't allowed into his hospital room. As soon as the doctors told us Tal would live and fully recover, he had his security detail take me away like some loose end he couldn't be bothered to deal with."

It had been horrible. One minute she'd been overjoyed, and the next she was being escorted away by two grim guards. She'd called out to Rafe and Kade, but they had disappeared into Tal's recovery room.

No one answered her calls. No one replied to her emails. She'd been so sure at least Rafe and Kade would stay with her, but they seemed to have decided that Tal was right.

After a few days, she'd realized what a fool she'd made of herself. Then last week, the news had come down that the Bezakistani Parliament had moved swiftly and decisively to strike down the law that the sheikh had to marry by age thirty-five. It seemed the incident at the palace had finally forced the government to allow the change, and they'd managed it without opening their constitution to unwanted influences. Hassem and the rest of Khalil's conspirators had been rounded up, arrested, found quilty, and sent to prison.

Tal, Rafe, and Kade were free…but they didn't want her anymore.

Piper knew the time had come to move on.

"Honey, do you think he might change his mind if you talk to him?" Hannah asked. "It just seems to me that he was in a bad place when he made that decision. Maybe he needs time."

Piper shook her head. Maybe Tal needed time, but Rafe and Kade's silence truly told the tale. "No. They're done. They don't need a wife anymore. They can keep their throne without me. I think now they realize I wasn't even close to their league."

"Or they had just witnessed their brother being shot and their bride almost dying, so they reacted poorly," Hannah replied. "Sometimes men do the dumbest things for the right reasons. You know I had a little trouble with Ashley's birth, right?"

Piper turned to her friend. She knew the story. Something had gone wrong in the delivery room, and Hannah had nearly bled out. "I know. You hemorrhaged."

Hannah took a long breath. "I almost died and so did Ashley. And my husbands were right there. They had three completely different reactions. I would have thought Gavin would be the one to really freak out, but he got closer. Slade became an expert on childbirth. I swear he read everything he could get his hands on trying to figure out what had gone wrong. And Dex." She sniffled a little, tears in her eyes. "Dex pulled away. He was so remote, so far from me. I thought I might lose him, but little by little he came out of it until one day I found him holding Ashley and crying his eyes out. He needed to process it. It was traumatic for all of us, but Dex especially. He grew up without a family. The thought of losing me devastated him. I think he's terrified about this baby, but he's here with me again."

Piper sighed, a deep, heartfelt breath because her story wouldn't end that way. "Weren't you mad at him for being distant?"

Hannah reached up, smoothing back Piper's hair. "Of course, but I wasn't willing to give up. He needed time. When he was ready to be brave again, I forgave him. Honey, I know they hurt you, but if you get a chance, think about forgiving them. Forgiveness heals and makes love possible. Even if they don't ever come back, think about forgiving them. Don't carry this hurt around. I couldn't stand the thought of this ruining your life. Fight for them if you still love them. And if that doesn't work, let it all go then move on, knowing you tried. Move on knowing you deserve a good life and as much love as you can handle."

A sob formed, but Piper held it in. "What if I can't love anyone else?"

"You will. There's too much love inside you. It's going to hurt for a long time, but you will live again and you will love again. I promise." She hugged Piper, pulling her close. "You need to get back to work. It's killing you, just sitting in your room day after day."

Hannah was right, and Piper had been thinking much the same. She needed to start moving forward. She needed to sink into a new project. "I have to find a new job."

"No." Hannah pulled back, her head shaking. "We want you with Black Oak, and that has nothing to do with how I feel about you. Gavin wants your brain. Look, hon, at some point in time we have to adapt, and you're the key to that. Please, listen to Gavin. He wants you to head a new green division for the company. We need you. It's a challenge and a huge promotion. It's also a big change. Don't make any decisions until you talk to him."

"All right." Piper wasn't sure what she wanted, but she would listen so she could think logically about her options. She couldn't just make a blanket decision. Leading a green division for a huge corporation would be a massive challenge. Of course, leading a green division at Black Oak would mean being forced to deal with representatives from Bezakistan, including members of the royal family like the sheikh and his brothers.

And this time, they would be forced to deal with her—on her terms.

It was a daunting prospect, but maybe she could still change the world.

She could have a full life, and she hoped someday to love again. She was stronger than she'd thought. Her heart would ache for the men she'd loved, but she would live on and find a way to give her love to someone who wanted it.

She stood a little taller and tried to smile at Hannah. "I'll think about it."

Black Oak Oil had offices all over the world. Her journey didn't have to be over because three men from Bezakistan couldn't love her.

Hannah took a step back. "You think hard because I don't think Gavin is going to let you go. He kind of cheered when you walked in the door again. He's missed you around the office. The new researcher is making him crazy. The kid struggles to work a calculator. So take a minute, then come in and join us for dinner. It's been fun to have everyone around again."

Piper frowned. "You know Burke and Cole are like my bodyguards, right?"

The big, hunky private investigators had been on her since the moment she'd stepped off the plane. Oh, they used their wife Jessa's sudden interest in business and marketing plans for her art business as a reason to stick close to her, but she wasn't an idiot. There was no doubt in her mind who was paying them.

Hannah grinned. "Yeah, I know. It's why I have hope. Oh, and your computer has been pinging for ten minutes. You better check it."

Piper sighed and followed her inside, hoping it was just her worrywart sister wanting to check in on her again and not another reporter offering to pay her an obscene amount of money for her story of danger, debauchery, and betrayal at the hands of three desert princes. She'd refused repeatedly, and still the press kept hounding her.

"I'll be there in a minute," Piper told her hostess. "And I promise to actually eat this time."

She'd lost some weight, but Hannah was right, it was time to start living again. And that meant answering her sister with something more than a terse note that she was fine. If she didn't talk to Mindy soon, her baby sister would likely show up on the

James's doorstep. Mindy had been worried ever since the news had come out that the sheikh's concubine had left the country, but Piper hadn't been willing to talk.

She closed the door to the guest bedroom and sat down at her computer, ready to tell her sister to call her, but Mindy's name wasn't the one that appeared.

It was Tal's.

Piper stared for a moment. It had to be a mistake, a nasty joke. She thought about closing the computer and ignoring it, but her phone signaled a text coming through.

Again, it was Tal.

After weeks of silence, he'd finally decided he needed something from her? She clicked on the text message.

Piper, my love, forgive a stupid man.

Piper sniffled, sudden tears pricking in her eyes. She took in a long breath. He wanted closure. By text? He was still a stupid man. And she wasn't sure she was ready to forgive any of them. Eventually, yes. But they wanted a clean slate now. They had used her for their own ends, and when they no longer needed a bride, they had simply disposed of her. At least that was how it looked.

But had they really? A little nagging voice kept at her. If they wanted to truly dispose of her, they wouldn't be paying two private detectives to watch her twenty-four seven. They wouldn't have carefully shipped back all her clothes. There wouldn't have been such a special gift in the packages.

A first edition of *Charlotte's Web* signed by E.B. White. Her favorite childhood book. The one she'd lost to the bank auction, now replaced by men who said they no longer cared about her.

Had they done it to assuage their guilt? Perhaps. Or maybe they'd needed a little closure of their own. Either way, the time had come to let them go in peace. She carefully texted back, tears clouding her eyes. *All is forgiven. I wish all three of you much love in your lives. And thank you for the book.*

There. Now their final communication to each other could be pleasant, polite.

Rafe, Kade, and I are getting married soon. We want you to be at the wedding.

She stared at his message for a minute, those words a stab in the heart. They couldn't be serious. After everything they had gone through to change the laws, they were turning right around and marrying someone? Had they been in love with this other woman all along? Piper couldn't help but wonder if they had used her to protect their new bride.

The phone trembled in her hands as she replied.

Think I'll pass. Don't contact me again.

So much for polite.

She tossed the phone onto the bed, her hands shaking with rage. She heard it ping once more, but she refused to answer him again. Ever. She would get rid of that phone. They were bastards, and for some reason they seemed to need to hurt her.

A knock came on her door. Piper wiped her eyes. "I'll be right there."

Another knock.

No one seemed to sense her need for space today. As frustration bubbled inside her, she crossed the floor and yanked the door open, ready to give whoever was on the other side a piece of her mind.

Tal, Rafe, and Kade stood in the hallway. Tal's hand was raised to knock again, but he lowered it slowly as he looked at her.

She felt her heart skip, her pulse jump. They were here, standing right in front of her. Why? Joy at seeing them again was completely crushed by penetrating rage. What game were they playing now?

"What do you want?"

"We want to come in, *habibti*." Kade's eyes took in every inch of her. "Please. We need to talk."

There was no way she was letting them near her again.

"You can talk from a phone. You seem to know my number."

She moved to slam the door in their ridiculously handsome faces, but Tal put a hand out, stopping it. He looked perfectly healthy, like he'd never taken a bullet for her. God, he'd nearly died saving her life. It was easy to forget that in the face of what had happened after, but he'd nearly sacrificed everything so she could live. She was sure now that he'd done it because of who he was, not because he loved her. Still, she owed him. She stopped trying to force the door closed.

"Piper, my love, I could call, but I doubt you would answer." Tal pressed his advantage, walking in past her, brushing his big body against hers. It reminded her of everything she'd had...and lost.

Why was he calling her 'his love?' What did he want? Her eyes narrowed as he stared at the phone she'd thrown.

"I suspect you intend to change your number."

She might owe him this one last confrontation, but she wasn't going to back down. "Yes, I think I will. We could all use a fresh start."

Rafe walked in next, his dark eyes flashing. "I agree." He reached down and lifted her into his arms, hauling her to his chest before she had a chance to protest. A smile split his face as he turned with her. "My Piper, you look good enough to eat."

"She does, brother," Kade said, his voice going low and sexy. He leaned in and brushed his nose against her hair. "She smells perfect, too. My brothers and I have talked about it. You have no idea what oranges do to us now, Piper. We can't eat breakfast with getting hard-ons."

What the hell were they doing? Saying? Why try to seduce her if they were marrying another woman? "Let go of me."

"Never again," Rafe replied, holding her tight. "I plan to hold you forever."

Tal chuckled even as she struggled in Rafe's arms. "They are impatient, my love. I told them we should sit down first and have a nice long talk, but I should have known they wouldn't do it." He sobered, his face grave in an instant. "Forgive me."

She could have sworn tears were in his eyes. He didn't shed them, but she felt a deep emotion coming from him. "I told you all is forgiven. Now please put me down. I wish you the best with your new bride. I'd appreciate it if you'd leave."

Tal's hand came out to touch her cheek. "I couldn't stand being parted from you. I thought it would be better if you were somewhere safe in the world, but these last weeks have proven to me how wrong I was."

"Piper, please understand, you were almost killed," Kade explained. "Tal barely pulled through. He came out of surgery, and all he asked was that we send you away."

Bitterness churned in her gut. He'd nearly died, and all he'd cared about was making sure she wasn't there when he woke up. "Well, you two took care of that. Please put me down."

All three men had a hand on her. Kade smoothed her hair back. "He was crazy with the thought that it could happen again. For nights afterward, he woke up screaming, thinking Khalil was back to rape and kill you. He tore his stitches three times before the nurses were smart enough to sedate him at night."

She went still. He'd been that worried? She couldn't compete with Tal's anxiety. She couldn't force him to see that it was worth the risk. "You don't have to worry about me anymore. I'm safe here. And I'll take care of myself."

Rafe shook his head. He couldn't seem to stop smiling even though, to Piper's mind, it was extremely inappropriate. "You don't have to take care of yourself. Not when you have three husbands dedicated to the job. Piper, we cannot live without you. Tal has finally come to his senses, and now we can move forward with our lives."

Rafe winked down at her as he turned and strode to the big bed. He tossed her lightly on it.

"Take off your clothes, *habibti* or I swear I will rip them off you." Kade was already working the buttons on his dress shirt, revealing gorgeous tanned skin.

Piper ignored the ribbon of need working through her and backed up, trying to get to her feet, but they blocked all three sides of the bed. "Wait. You told me you were getting married, and now you want me to sleep with you?"

But Rafe had also mentioned that she would have three husbands who couldn't live without her. Were they saying what she thought they were saying? Was she the bride?

Tal laughed outright, looking younger and lighter, as though some heavy weight had left him. "And you tell me you're so smart. Yes, my love, we're getting married. We have a lovely bride selected, though I managed to push the law through so she won't ever feel as if she was wed for any reason but love."

Tears started to pool. Hope bloomed, pushing out all thoughts of rage. Forgiveness really was a gift to them and herself. Forgiving them for being afraid meant she had a future. "And what happens to this bride if someone tries to hurt her? Will you lock her up in a gilded cage?"

Tal took a long breath. "Piper, I will cherish every moment I have with my bride. I will put aside my fear because she deserves a brave man. I will be the best husband possible and I will protect her with every cell in my body, but if the worst happens, I still want that time with you. I want a lifetime. Hell, I want forever, but I'll take what is given to me. I'll take every minute without an ounce of regret."

"I love you, Piper. I want children and a life, and I vow I will never leave you again," Rafe promised.

"I want you. I was lonely without you. I didn't know it before. I thought I was happy, but you showed me what real joy is," Kade said, his voice low and serious.

Now her tears fell without reluctance. Their words were everything she wanted, everything she'd waited a lifetime for. Her husbands. Her future. No amount of hurt was going to cost her a lifetime of joy. Still, she couldn't let their arrogance go unchallenged. She got to her knees, shoulders thrust back, the proud woman their love had molded her into. "I don't recall being asked to marry you."

Another one of those brilliant smiles lit Talib's face. "It's tradition in Bezakistan to steal a bride, my love. I think that's one tradition we intend to follow."

Kade tossed his shirt aside. "Once we have you in our clutches, don't think you can get away. Not for a moment."

"But you, our bride, are wearing a deplorable amount of clothing." Rafe shrugged out of his shirt and grabbed the bag he'd dropped on his way in the room. She could just guess what was inside. All sorts of toys to please and torture a newly stolen bride.

Her whole body heated up. She'd been so deeply alone since she'd been forced to leave them. She'd felt lonely before, but she'd never known the true meaning of the word until she'd contemplated a life without these men in it. "You have other traditions, but I think I'd like to make one of my own. That first night, you had your brothers present me to you, Tal. Now I think I would like to have all of my husbands present themselves to me."

Tal growled a little as he tossed off his jacket and dress shirt. "You want to see what belongs to you, my queen? Is that what you want? You want your men to show you everything they have to give you?"

A future and love was what they offered her. Years of joy and happiness. Children who would rule a country one day as wisely as their fathers. But yes, she definitely wanted to see them. "Show me."

Rafe shoved the slacks off his lean hips. "Such a bossy little queen."

Kade stood before her, his glorious body on full display. Kade, her playmate, the charmer. His broad shoulders were thrown back and his cock jutted up proudly. He stroked himself, winking at her, never far from being the naughty lover who stirred her senses. "For you, my wife, my queen. This is all for you."

Rafe stood beside his brother, slightly taller and every inch the elegant, sexy gentleman. He was the one she could sink into intellectual talks with, long hours spent in friendly discussions before he finally ended their debates by kissing her senseless. He ran a hand down his sculpted body. "Everything I have is yours."

Talib knelt on the bed, his cock seeming to know exactly what it wanted. He was already fully erect and pointing straight at her, a drop of pearly fluid seeping from the head. She eyed the fresh, puckered scar on his belly, grateful that he was alive to be here before her. "My kingdom, my body, my heart, my soul. They're yours, Piper. All you have to do is take us."

A Texas girl knew a good offer when she saw one. Piper tossed off her shirt. "Yes. Yes. Yes. I love you all so much. Please kiss me."

They descended on her, her clothes seeming to evaporate in their hands. Before she knew it, she was naked and right where she'd longed to be, skin to skin with them, enveloped in their warmth.

Kade pressed her down, laying her out on the bed. He kissed her mouth, his tongue tangling briefly before moving on to her neck. Rafe replaced him at her lips, touching their noses together before devouring her mouth. His tongue played against hers in a silky slide as hands rearranged her body, sensation flooding her.

She rode the wave. It didn't matter who touched her as long as they kept their hands on her. Someone, Talib she thought, pulled her ankles apart, spreading her legs and moving inside. Rafe finally gave up her mouth, and he and Kade moved like birds of prey toward her breasts, their heads sinking down in perfect time. She gasped as they tugged on her nipples, tongues curling before they each sucked a tip inside their mouths.

Tal's nose nuzzled her pussy. She felt his moan of

appreciation all along her skin. "I missed you so much. I missed everything about you. I missed your smile and the way you laugh. I missed how you fight with me, but god, Piper, I fucking missed this."

He licked at her pussy, a slow draw of his tongue that lit her up from the inside out. She was drowning in them. Tal suckled her clit, his teeth biting down so gently before he covered her whole pussy with his mouth. His tongue fucked up, deep inside her cunt, a naked promise of what he wanted to do with his cock.

"We need to get her ready, brothers." Rafe gave her nipple one last pull before rolling off the bed.

Kade offered her a slow smile. "Getting you ready will be a pleasure, my wife."

"I am ready," Piper promised. Her heart was pounding. She was already warm and wet for them. She needed them badly. "I'm so ready."

Tal's mouth abandoned her pussy just as she was on the edge of something wonderful. "You're not ready. But you will be. Who wants to make a feast of our lovely girl?"

Rafe tossed a blue jar at Tal and then got back on the bed. "You know she's my favorite meal. Come on, *habibti*. Sit on my face. Let me make you come. I want to taste it."

Kade pulled her up, turning her so she straddled Rafe, who groaned as he forced her upright, his big hands cupping her cheeks and drawing her down onto his mouth. His tongue fucked into her, taking up where Tal had left off.

Tal's hand pressed her down, forcing her to hold on to the headboard. She didn't care what he did to her as long as Rafe continued his slow exploration of every inch of her pussy. His tongue was bold, sucking and laving affection everywhere. He licked her thoroughly before settling to suckle her clit. Heat was building, pushing her toward the highest of highs.

"Spread her for me, Rafe," Tal commanded.

Rafe never stopped what he was doing, but his hands pulled

the cheeks of her ass apart, giving Tal what he wanted. She felt exposed, but oh so right. These were her husbands.

"God, she's so beautiful. I can't wait to fuck her ass," Kade said. "You're lovely everywhere, Piper. We're all going to want to shove our cocks deep."

"Oh, yes. I intend to claim her in every way," Tal replied.

Piper couldn't breathe, couldn't move. Rafe kept her right on the edge of orgasm, dangling it in front of her.

"Don't move, my love, or Rafe will have to stop. You have to be made ready for what we're going to do to you. We want to take you all at once and that means getting your pretty ass ready for a cock. You've taken a plug before. We just need to make sure you're properly prepared." Tal dripped cool lube between her cheeks.

They were going to do it. They were going to take her all at once, all three of her men loving her together. She would be so full of them. She struggled to hold herself still, not wanting to waste a minute of time. She needed this. After weeks of being alone, she needed to be surrounded by them.

A whimper started low in her throat as Tal worked the lube in. His fingers pressed in, tempting her to open for him. The odd jangly sensation warred with the pure pleasure of Rafe's tongue.

Kade was suddenly at her side, his hands on her breast. "You're so close, aren't you my darling? Rafe, you should give it to her good. I want her very satisfied and submissive when we finally, truly make her ours."

Tal's fingers broached the ring of her ass, slipping inside. He worked the lube all over, massaging her until she was moving against his fingers, swaying, pressing forward onto Rafe's tongue, then back against Tal's fingers.

"Yes," Tal said, spreading her gently. "That's what we want, wife. She's ready, Rafe."

Rafe sucked her clit hard. Pressure built and burst. Pleasure sent her straight over the edge. The orgasm swirled in her system, causing her to cry out.

Before she could come down, they were moving, Rafe pulling her down his body. "This sweet pussy is mine."

His cock thrust up, finding her wet and ready, then pressing home. Though she was slick from the orgasm, Rafe was still so big. He filled her, making her moan as she took him.

Kade knelt on the bed, his big cock in hand. "Suck me, my wife. I want to feel your mouth on me."

She wanted that, too. This was pure intimacy. This was true joining. She leaned forward and let the head of Kade's cock slip inside her mouth. She laved attention on him, loving the feel and taste of him.

"And now, this jewel is mine." Tal's dick pressed at her back entrance. He pushed at it, little thrusts that pressed in more and more with each pass.

"Hurry it up." Rafe was still under her, stroking into her slowly, but his voice was desperate. "I can't hold out forever. She feels so good."

Kade's hands tightened in her hair. "She feels like heaven."

He fucked her mouth in long thrusts. In and out. In and out. Every movement was as graceful as the man himself. His flavor tasted salty and fresh. She let her tongue run across his cock, reveling in his hardness and his groans.

They were everywhere. There wasn't an inch of skin that didn't seem to be pressed against one of her men. Tal worked behind her, pulling at her hips, trying to force his way inside.

"Relax, love. Let me in. I want to come inside you. I want to take you in every way a man can take a woman."

She did as he demanded, and Tal fucked into her, his cock finally foraging inside. Pressure built. It was almost too much, but she could handle it because this meant that they were hers. Finally.

She groaned around Kade's cock. Tal pushed in, gently fucking his way into her. Pain edged at her conscious, but somehow it mixed with pleasure and intimacy and created something completely new.

"Love, you're so hot and tight." Tal's hands smoothed down her back before settling on her waist. "You took every inch of me. This is for you."

He pulled back and nerves she'd never known existed lit up and practically sang out in pleasure.

Piper couldn't stay still a moment longer. She pressed back, unwilling to let the sensation go.

"She's ready." Rafe thrust up and all three men seemed to have been let off the leash.

Tal's hands tightened, pulling her back, his cock going deep before starting the long drag back out that made her want to howl. The minute Tal started to pull out, Rafe was pressing up. Every way she went she was filled with them.

She worked Kade's cock hard, sucking furiously, her tongue loving his flesh. With his fingers tangled in her hair, Kade fucked her mouth hard, his cock working its way to the back of her throat.

"Swallow me. Take it all." Kade's cock brushed the back of her throat. He shuddered as she swallowed, and his semen jetted across her tongue in long spurts.

Piper reveled in his essence, drinking him down, letting him coat her throat.

Kade fell back, his cock coming out of her mouth with a little pop. "That was perfect."

"So is this." Tal thrust in long rhythms, matching his strokes to Rafe's as they filled her in tandem. Every inch of them was a joy to her senses. Piper found her own rhythm, rolling her hips to follow them. Their golden skin surrounded her, enclosing her in warmth and love and pleasure. Kade got to his knees beside her, his hands cupping her breasts and tweaking her nipples.

"Give it to us," he ordered. "Don't hold back. We want to make you scream."

"I'm so close." Rafe picked up the pace. "She feels so

good. I can't wait much longer. Come with me, Piper."

"Come with us," Tal said, grinding into her. "Oh, love, you can't imagine how good you feel."

She couldn't, but she knew how amazing they felt. Kade pinched down hard on her nipples, and Piper couldn't wait another moment. The orgasm swallowed her, firing up her every nerve, and she rocked back and forth, milking every second of pleasure.

She felt the hot wash of Rafe's come coat her as he gave in. He shouted out her name as he bucked up.

Tal groaned behind her as he let go, his semen pouring from him and into her.

They filled her up. And then fell on her in a delightful heap.

Piper let a delicious languor invade her bones as she sank into the bed, arms and legs tangling together.

"I love you, my wife." Tal nestled close.

She reached out to all of them, caressing them each in turn. "I love you, my husbands."

They had shown her a new world, and she would give it back to them.

A new home, a new family, for them all.

* * * *

Read on for excerpts from Shayla Black and Lexi Blake.

Their Virgin Secretary
Masters of Ménage, Book 6
By Shayla Black and Lexi Blake
Now Available

Three determined bosses...

Tate Baxter, Eric Cohen, and Kellan Kent are partners for one of the most respected law practices in Chicago. But these three masters of the courtroom also share a partnership in the bedroom, fulfilling the darkest needs of their female submissives night after night. Everything was fine—until they hired Annabelle Wright as their administrative assistant.

One beautiful secretary...

Belle felt sure she'd hit the jackpot with her job, but in the last year, the three gorgeous attorneys have become far more than her bosses. They're her friends, her protectors, and in Belle's dreams, they're her lovers, too. But she's given her heart to them all, so how can she choose just one?

An unforgettable night...

When her bosses escort her to a wedding, drinks and dancing turn into foreplay and fantasy. Between heated kisses, Belle admits her innocence. Surprise becomes contention and tempers flare. Heartbroken and unwilling to drive them apart, Belle leaves the firm and flees to New Orleans.

That leads to danger.

Resolved to restore her late grandmother's home, she hopes she can move on without the men. Then Kellan, Tate, and Eric show up at her doorstep, seeking another chance. But something sinister is at work in the Crescent City and its sights are set on her. Before the trio can claim Annabelle for good, they just might have to save her life.

* * * *

Excerpt:

One year, two months, and four days. Four hundred thirty days all totaled, but Tate hated to calculate their time together that way. It depressed him. Ten thousand three hundred twenty hours wasn't much better, considering that was how long he'd gone without sex. Because that was how long it had been since he'd first laid eyes on Annabelle Wright. She'd walked into his office with her resume in hand, and he'd just stared, dumbstruck. He didn't believe in love at first sight, but he'd found lust in that single glance. Oh, yeah. He'd taken one look at the goddess applying for a job and known exactly why he'd gone to the gym five times a week since he'd turned seventeen.

But love? He'd taken a whole week of consideration before deciding that he had fallen in love with Belle. After all, he was a careful man. He liked to think things out.

"Indulgence leads to chaos. Dominic is going to rue the day he let his sub run wild." Kellan frowned at Kinley, then swiveled his gaze toward the dance floor. "Who is that?"

Tate followed Kellan's line of sight and scowled. Belle danced with some overgrown ape whose smile seemed way too friendly. She looked gorgeous in her emerald cocktail dress. Its V-neck and body-fitting lines showed off her every curve. She wasn't a tall woman, but those crazy-sexy black shoes she wore made her legs look deliciously long. Tate had no idea how women maintained their balance while walking on those high, thin heels. He was pretty sure, however, they would look great wrapped around his neck.

The only thing he didn't like about the way Belle looked was the animated expression she turned up at the lug hanging on her. Then she laughed—a sound that always did strange things to his insides.

Eric slapped a big hand across his back. "Chill, buddy. That's Cole Lennox. He's a PI here in Dallas. We've used his company before. He's happily married. I don't think he's trying to mack on our girl."

Tate still didn't like it. "Why isn't he dancing with his wife?"

He was rational enough to know that jealousy was a completely illogical response in this situation. Technically, Belle wasn't his. She'd never even gone on a real date with him. They'd had lunch exactly fifty-two times over the last year, but they'd mostly talked about work. He'd taken her to happy hour fifteen times, where she always ordered vodka tonics, Cîroc, or Grey Goose, with a half a twist of lime. They'd still talked about work. And the weather. None of that counted, though, because she'd treated him like a colleague, not a boyfriend. He hadn't kissed her yet or made his intentions clear, so he had no right to be jealous that Belle danced with another man. For once, he didn't care if he made less than perfect sense.

Kellan pointed to the other end of the floor. "He can't. His brother is dancing with her. They're twins and I've heard they share."

"Really?" Tate sat up and sent a challenging glance to Kell and Eric. "I'm seeing a picture here. The Lennox twins married the same girl. Those three oil tycoons over there have one wife, and we all saw the three royal princes walk in with their bride. Hell, the whole board of Anthony Anders decided to marry the same woman. But it can't work for us? Explain that."

That was the argument Tate had heard from Eric and especially Kellan for the past year, ever since the night they'd sat around the office and each admitted they were crazy about their new secretary. Administrative Assistant. Office Manager. Belle changed her title more than once. She took exception to the term secretary, but Tate thought it was kind of hot.

Kellan sighed, turning toward him. "Just because it works for some other people doesn't mean it would work for the two of you."

"The two of us? Really? You're still going to play it that way?" Eric challenged. "Tell me you don't want her, too."

Kellan's eyes hooded. Tate had made almost a scientific study of his friends in an attempt to really understand them. Kellan had four major expressions that he used like masks. This particular one Tate had named "stubborn asshole." Kellan used it a lot.

"Of course I want her. I've never denied that. She's a beautiful woman, not to mention lovely, kind, and very smart. If I was interested in getting married again, I would be all over her. But I'm not, and I doubt she's the type of woman to have no-strings-attached sex."

"I want strings." Tate needed to make that brutally clear because his partners seemed to constantly forget. They should take notes during their conversations the way he often did. But again, no one asked his opinion. "I want to be tangled up in all her strings. She's the one. I get that what we want is unusual, though it really doesn't seem that way today. I swear the two dogs are the only non-ménage relationship here. Belle might be surprised that we all want her, but she's not going to be shocked. She's fine with Kinley's marriage."

Eric sighed. "Maybe, but we need to be careful. She hasn't dated anyone since she started working with us."

Tate knew that very well since he'd been keeping an eye on her. Hopefully she never knew the extent of his observation because what he'd done was illegal. And possibly a little stalkerish.

"There's some reason for that," Eric went on.

Didn't they get it? "Because she's waiting for us to make a move."

"Or she's just working hard and isn't ready to settle down," Kellan pointed out. "She's young, man."

"It's not like we're old."

Tate didn't feel old. He was thirty-two. Given that the average life expectancy of an American male was seventy-six, that didn't sound old. Then he did the math and realized that he was forty-two percent of the way through his accepted life expectancy. Forty-two percent—closing in on half. When he looked at it that way, he did feel old. He refused to waste another second.

"That's it." Tate stood and straightened his tie. "I'm going in."

God, he hoped he looked halfway decent because he often got rumpled and didn't notice. He would probably still be wearing pocket protectors if he hadn't become good friends with Eric in tenth grade.

He'd tutored Eric through rudimentary algebra, and Eric had taught him that jeans weren't supposed to hit above the ankles. They'd been a weird duo, the jock and the nerd. But their relationship meant more to him than any other. His parents were cold intellectuals who told him he'd failed by not going into academic pursuits—because yeah, Harvard law had been a breeze. His brothers cared more about their experiments than their family. So Tate and Eric had stuck together like blood, and Kellan had joined them after college.

But Tate realized in that moment that he needed more. He needed Belle. So did they, but she had to come first. "I'm going to do it. I'm going to offer her my penis."

Eric's head hit the table and he groaned. "Dude, how do you ever get laid?"

So he wasn't smooth. At least he was honest. "She already has my heart. I would like for her to take my penis, too. Is that so much to ask?"

"If you ask her like that, she'll just smack you," Kellan pointed out.

Frustration welled. He sat back down. "Damn it, that's why we need to go after her as a pack. I'm not good at the smooth stuff."

"By smooth stuff, he means any type of actual communication with a woman." Eric rolled his eyes.

They were totally missing the point. "I communicate fine. She'll know what I want and how I want it."

"Which is precisely why she'll know where she wants to slap you next." Kellan shook his head. "This might be a bad idea, but it couldn't hurt for you to dance with her. Can you do that without asking her to take your penis in marriage?"

He wasn't completely sure. His cock had a mind of its own. "I think I can handle it."

"Good. Go on, then. I'll talk to Eric." Kell sighed. "I guess we really do need to figure out how to handle her. I can't stand the thought of another uncomfortable plane trip back. She didn't talk to me the whole flight down. Taking the hands-off approach isn't working. I get the feeling she's just about ready to throw in the towel and leave all of us." Kellan's eyes narrowed suddenly. "And that asshole isn't married. Go. Make sure he doesn't get his hands on Belle."

Tate's stare zipped to her. Sure enough, a guy was cutting in on Lennox. He leered down at Annabelle, then peered straight at her boobs.

Those boobs were his, damn it. At least he fully intended for those boobs to belong to him. Well, a third of them anyway. "You two work it out because I'm making a move by the end of the night…"

One Dom To Love
Doms of Her Life: Raine Falling, Book 1
by Shayla Black, Jenna Jacob, Isabella LaPearl
(available in eBook, print, and audio)

Want another ménage world full of passion and drama? Welcome to Doms of Her Life…

Two friends. One woman. Let the games begin…

Read ONE DOM TO LOVE, the first in the sexy Doms of Her Life: Raine Falling saga.

Raine Kendall has been in love with her boss, Macen Hammerman, for years. Determined to make the man notice that she's a grown woman with desires and needs, she pours out her heart and offers her body to him—only to be crushingly rejected. But when his friend, very single, very sexy Liam O'Neill watches the other Dom refuse to act on his obvious feelings for Raine, he resolves to step in and do whatever it takes to help Hammer find happiness again, even rousing his friend's possessive instincts by making the girl a proposition too tempting to refuse. But he never imagines that he'll end up falling for her himself.

Hammer has buried his lust for Raine for years. After rescuing the budding runaway from an alley behind his exclusive BDSM Dungeon, he has come to covet the pretty submissive. But tragedy has taught him that he can never be what she needs. So he watches over her while struggling to keep his distance. Liam's crafty plan blindsides Hammer, especially when he sees how determined his friend is to possess Raine for his own. Hammer isn't ready to give the lovely submissive over to any other Dom, but can he heal from his past and fight for her? Or will he lose Raine if she truly gives herself—heart, body, and soul—to Liam?

Discover Lexi Blake writing as Sophie Oak

Texas Sirens

Every girl dreams of her alpha cowboy, the one who sweeps her off her feet. In Texas Sirens, every girl gets two.

Set in both small Texas towns and cosmopolitan cities, Texas Sirens features beautifully broken heroes and heroines who discover that unconventional love is their best chance at happily ever after.

Small Town Siren
Siren in the City
Siren Enslaved
Siren Beloved
Siren in Waiting
Siren in Bloom
Siren Unleashed, Coming Spring 2019
More coming in 2019!

* * * *

Nights in Bliss

Bliss, Colorado, is home to nudists, squatchers, alien hunters, a bunch of ex-military men, and a surprising number of women on the run. Bliss is a place where cowboys hang out with vegan protestors, quirky is normal, and love is perfectly unconventional. So grab a chair and settle in. If you can forgive the oddly high per capita murder rate—and the occasional alien sighting—you'll find that life is better in Bliss.

Each Bliss story is a standalone, though found family is important so expect the characters to stick around, playing a part in each novel.

Three to Ride
Two to Love
One to Keep
Lost in Bliss
Found in Bliss
Pure Bliss, Coming March 5, 2019
More coming in 2019!

About Shayla Black

Shayla Black is the *New York Times* and *USA Today* bestselling author of more than sixty novels. For twenty years, she's written contemporary, erotic, paranormal, and historical romances via traditional, independent, foreign, and audio publishers. Her books have sold millions of copies and been published in a dozen languages.

Raised an only child, Shayla occupied herself with lots of daydreaming, much to the chagrin of her teachers. In college, she found her love for reading and realized that she could have a career publishing the stories spinning in her imagination. Though she graduated with a degree in Marketing/Advertising and embarked on a stint in corporate America to pay the bills, her heart has always been with her characters. She's thrilled that she's been living her dream as a full-time author for the past eight years.

Shayla currently lives in North Texas with her wonderfully supportive husband, her daughter, and two spoiled tabbies. In her "free" time, she enjoys reality TV, reading, and listening to an eclectic blend of music.

Connect with me online:
Website: http://shaylablack.com
VIP Reader Newsletter: http://shayla.link/nwsltr
Facebook Author Page:
    https://www.facebook.com/ShaylaBlackAuthor
Facebook Book Beauties Chat Group:
    http://shayla.link/FBChat
Instagram: https://instagram.com/ShaylaBlack/
Twitter: http://twitter.com/Shayla_Black
Amazon Author: http://shayla.link/AmazonFollow
BookBub: http://shayla.link/BookBub

Goodreads: http://shayla.link/goodreads
YouTube: http://shayla.link/youtube

If you enjoyed this book, please review it or recommend it to others.

Keep in touch by engaging with me through one of the links above. Subscribe to my VIP Readers newsletter for exclusive excerpts and hang out in my Facebook Book Beauties group for live weekly #WineWednesday video chats full of fun, community, book chatter, and prizes. I love talking to readers!

About Lexi Blake

Lexi Blake lives in North Texas with her husband, three kids, and the laziest rescue dog in the world. She began writing at a young age, concentrating on plays and journalism. It wasn't until she started writing romance that she found success. She likes to find humor in the strangest places. Lexi believes in happy endings no matter how odd the couple, threesome or foursome may seem. She also writes contemporary Western ménage as Sophie Oak.

Connect with Lexi online:

Facebook: https://www.facebook.com/lexi.blake.39
Twitter: twitter.com/authorlexiblake
Website: www.LexiBlake.net

Sign up for Lexi's free newsletter at www.lexiblake.net.

Also from Shayla Black and Lexi Blake

Masters of Ménage
Their Virgin Captive
Their Virgin's Secret
Their Virgin Concubine
Their Virgin Princess
Their Virgin Hostage
Their Virgin Secretary
Their Virgin Mistress

Series by Shayla Black

For more info about Shayla's books,
visit ShaylaBlack.com!

MORE THAN WORDS
Contemporary romances that depict a love so complete, it can't be expressed with mere words.

DEVOTED LOVERS
Steamy, character-driven romantic suspenses about heroes who will do anything to love and protect the women bold enough to be theirs. Begins where Wicked Lovers ended.

WICKED LOVERS
Dark, dangerous, beyond-sexy romantic suspenses about high-octane men and the daring women they risk all for, even their hearts.

PERFECT GENTLEMEN
Suspenseful contemporary romances about the "Perfect Gentlemen" of Creighton Academy. Privileged, wealthy, and powerful friends—with a wild side.

MASTERS OF MÉNAGE
Very sexy romances about men of power and danger who share a kink—and a special woman. Though she's inexperienced, she isn't afraid to embrace all she desires.

SEXY CAPERS
Sassy, sinful contemporary romances with a pinch of suspense that show both the fun and angst of falling in love while snaring bad guys.

DOMS OF HER LIFE: RAINE FALLING
Super-sexy serialized contemporary romances about one

tempestuous woman thoroughly in love with two friends and their battle to see who will ultimately win her heart.

DOMS OF HER LIFE: HEAVENLY RISING
Super-sexy serialized contemporary romances about one innocent and the two frenemies desperate to her touch, protect, and claim her as their own.

MISADVENTURES
Fun, sexy, rompy standalone contemporary romances with a fun premise, fast pace, and high heat.

STANDALONES
Romances published independent of a series, some sexy, some sweet, all with a happy ending that's finished and complete.

HISTORICALS
Sexy stories about the bold rakes and audacious beauties of lush eras gone by.

PARANORMAL
Set in contemporary London, magic, myth, and emotions blend in the passionate, good-versus-evil Doomsday Brethren series.

Also from Lexi Blake

ROMANTIC SUSPENSE

Masters And Mercenaries
The Dom Who Loved Me
The Men With The Golden Cuffs
A Dom is Forever
On Her Master's Secret Service
Sanctum: A Masters and Mercenaries Novella
Love and Let Die
Unconditional: A Masters and Mercenaries Novella
Dungeon Royale
Dungeon Games: A Masters and Mercenaries Novella
A View to a Thrill
Cherished: A Masters and Mercenaries Novella
You Only Love Twice
Luscious: Masters and Mercenaries~Topped
Adored: A Masters and Mercenaries Novella
Master No
Just One Taste: Masters and Mercenaries~Topped 2
From Sanctum with Love
Devoted: A Masters and Mercenaries Novella
Dominance Never Dies
Submission is Not Enough
Master Bits and Mercenary Bites~The Secret Recipes of Topped
Perfectly Paired: Masters and Mercenaries~Topped 3
For His Eyes Only
Arranged: A Masters and Mercenaries Novella
Love Another Day
At Your Service: Masters and Mercenaries~Topped 4
Master Bits and Mercenary Bites~Girls Night
Nobody Does It Better
Close Cover

Protected: A Masters and Mercenaries Novella
Enchanted: A Masters and Mercenaries Novella

Masters and Mercenaries: The Forgotten
Lost Hearts (Memento Mori)
Lost and Found, Coming February 26, 2019

Lawless
Ruthless
Satisfaction
Revenge

Courting Justice
Order of Protection
Evidence of Desire, Coming January 8, 2019

Masters Of Ménage (by Shayla Black and Lexi Blake)
Their Virgin Captive
Their Virgin's Secret
Their Virgin Concubine
Their Virgin Princess
Their Virgin Hostage
Their Virgin Secretary
Their Virgin Mistress

The Perfect Gentlemen (by Shayla Black and Lexi Blake)
Scandal Never Sleeps
Seduction in Session
Big Easy Temptation
Smoke and Sin
At the Pleasure of the President, Coming 2019

URBAN FANTASY

Thieves
Steal the Light
Steal the Day
Steal the Moon
Steal the Sun
Steal the Night
Ripper
Addict
Sleeper
Outcast

LEXI BLAKE WRITING AS SOPHIE OAK

Small Town Siren
Siren in the City
Away From Me
Three to Ride
Siren Enslaved
Two to Love
Siren Beloved
One to Keep
Siren in Waiting
Lost in Bliss
Found in Bliss
Siren in Bloom
Pure Bliss, Coming March 5, 2019
Siren Unleashed, Coming Spring 2019

Made in the
USA
Monee, IL